"What's wrong?" Jackson asked
as Cassie towed him out the front
door and around the corner
into the shadows.

"Did you remember more details about the robbery?"

"No. I want to make an important point." She pushed up on tiptoe, threw her arms around his broad shoulders and kissed him for all she was worth.

Didn't like men, he'd said. Indeed! *A woman's place was tending hearth and home,* he'd said. Ha!

She'd show him *hearth* when she burned his lips with a sizzling kiss! Were these the actions of a woman who didn't find men—this one in particular—physically attractive?

Suddenly he wrapped her in his arms and Cassie was shocked to realize that *she* was the one who caught flame....

* * *

Bandit Lawman, Texas Bride
Harlequin® Historical #995—June 2010

Praise for Carol Finch

"Carol Finch is known for her lightning-fast, roller-coaster-ride adventure romances that are brimming over with a large cast of characters and dozens of perilous escapades."
—*RT Book Reviews*

Texas Ranger, Runaway Heiress

"Finch offers another heartwarming western romance full of suspense, humor and strong characters…it's hard to put this one down."
—*RT Book Reviews*

McCavett's Bride

"For wild adventures, humor and Western atmosphere, Finch can't be beat. She fires off her quick-paced novels with the crack of a rifle and creates the atmosphere of the Wild West through laugh-out-loud dialogue and escapades that keep you smiling."
—*RT Book Reviews*

The Ranger's Woman

"Finch delivers her signature humor, along with a big dose of colorful Texas history, in a love and laughter romp."
—*RT Book Reviews*

Lone Wolf's Woman

"As always, Finch provides frying-pan-into-the-fire action that keeps the pages flying, then spices up her story with not one, but two romances, sensuality and strong emotions."
—*RT Book Reviews*

Bandit Lawman, Texas Bride

CAROL FINCH

HARLEQUIN®

TORONTO • NEW YORK • LONDON
AMSTERDAM • PARIS • SYDNEY • HAMBURG
STOCKHOLM • ATHENS • TOKYO • MILAN • MADRID
PRAGUE • WARSAW • BUDAPEST • AUCKLAND

Recycling programs
for this product may
not exist in your area.

ISBN-13: 978-0-373-29595-1

BANDIT LAWMAN, TEXAS BRIDE

Available from Harlequin® Historical and
CAROL FINCH

The Last Honest Outlaw #732
The Ranger's Woman #748
Lone Wolf's Woman #778
*The Ranger #805
*Fletcher's Woman #832
McCavett's Bride #852
Cooper's Woman #897
The Bounty Hunter and the Heiress #909
Texas Ranger, Runaway Heiress #927
Cowboy Christmas #963
"A Husband for Christmas"
The Kansas Lawman's Proposal #976
Bandit Lawman, Texas Bride #995

**The Hawk Brothers

Other works include:

Silhouette Special Edition

Not Just Another Cowboy #1242
Soul Mates #1320

Harlequin American Romance

Cupid and the Cowboy #1055

Harlequin Duets

The Family Feud #72
*Lonesome Ryder? #81
*Restaurant Romeo #81
*Fit To Be Frisked #105
*Mr. Cool Under Fire #105

**Bachelors of Hoot's Roost

Chapter One

Pepperville, Texas, Early 1880s

Cassandra Bixby paused from setting type for the newspaper to glance at the clock hanging over her desk. Pride and excitement bubbled inside her. In a few minutes, the bank would open its doors. She would be there to deposit her life savings into Aunt Louise's account.

Gerald Nash, owner and editor of the *Pepperville Times,* halted at the door of his private office. He was fortyish with hazel eyes and brown hair that was beginning to recede slightly. He was industrious and energetic, which accounted for his trim build. He had suffered a broken nose sometime in the past. Plus he had a slick red indentation above his left eyebrow and a half-moon scar on the underside of his jaw.

Cassie wondered how he'd come to have them but she'd never asked.

He glanced curiously at Cassie and frowned. "Is

something wrong? You've been watching the clock for a half hour."

"No." She pivoted to face him as she wiped the ink off her hands. "Everything is right today. I'm paying off my long-standing debt to Aunt Louise, soon as the bank opens. I've been pinching pennies for years. Since tomorrow is her birthday, it's going to be my gift to her."

"Very commendable," Gerald said approvingly. "But Louise doesn't seem the kind of woman who would expect compensation."

"She isn't, but she made all sorts of personal concessions and sacrifices to fetch me from an unpleasant situation after my parents died. She raised me as her own and paid for my schooling back East. I don't know why she decided to move from Hillsdale to set up another restaurant here, but that had to be another expense. I want to pay her what I owe."

Cassie glanced at the clock again. "I'll take my pouch to the bank but I shouldn't be gone but a few minutes."

"Save me a trip and take my deposits with you," he requested.

While Gerald strode back into his office to retrieve the collected money from newspaper sales, Cassie scooped up her bulging purse. The black cat that had adopted her when she moved to town bounded off the windowsill and hopped onto her desk. He rubbed himself against her arm until she petted him.

"Aunt Louise is definitely going to remember her thirty-seventh birthday," Cassie told Maxwell the tomcat. "Besides repaying my debt, we're having a city-wide surprise party at the restaurant. Not to mention the tribute recognizing her as the only female business owner in town."

Maxwell purred in reply. Cassie, who advocated women's rights and social reform, was proud of her aunt's assertiveness and accomplishments. In fact, Aunt Louise's modern philosophies and progressive thinking had molded Cassie into the woman she'd become.

"Here you go." Gerald dropped the hefty pouch in her hand then winked at her. "Thanks to your thought-provoking articles, our circulation has increased. So have profits. I'm glad Louise talked me into hiring you. Best decision I ever made."

Cassie beamed at the compliment as she rubbed Maxwell behind his half-bitten-off ear. She remembered arriving in town six weeks earlier to help Aunt Louise at Bixby Café. When she applied for this job, Gerald hadn't been particularly enthusiastic or receptive.

Cassie had returned to the café, discouraged by Gerald's reply: *Give me time to think it over. I'll be in touch when I decide.*

Louise Bixby—assertive, grab-the-bull-by-the-horns kind of woman that she was—had marched next door to the newspaper office to plead Cassie's case. She returned thirty minutes later to announce that Gerald had thought it over and decided a female assistant was exactly what he needed.

Cassie hadn't been privy to that conversation but she was thrilled with her new job. That was yet another example of Aunt Louise's dedication to seeing Cassie make a promising start in her chosen career.

Cassie shrugged into her coat to ward off the chill of the windy spring day, then headed for the door. Maxwell trailed along behind her. "I'll finish setting type when I return," she promised Gerald.

"Better your nimble fingers than mine." Gerald propped

his shoulder against the office door then wiggled the two stiff fingers on his right hand—she hadn't asked how he'd come by that injury, either. "You're twice as fast as I am. Another reason why I should have hired you without a moment's hesitation." He smiled guiltily. "But I made the mistake of thinking that as young and attractive as you are, you couldn't possibly..."

When his voice trailed off Cassie arched a blond brow. "Couldn't possibly have a brain in my head? I swear, that is the very attitude my kindred spirits are trying to dispel while crusading for the right to vote so we can have a voice in the legislature."

Gerald chuckled as he flung up both hands in supplication. "No need to lecture me. I've seen the error of my ways. Now I support women's suffrage wholeheartedly. Your aunt would pound me over the head with a rolling pin if I didn't."

"I suspect you're right." She frowned pensively as she studied her distinguished-looking but battle-scarred boss. He and Aunt Louise seemed to be friends, besides owning businesses that stood side-by-side. She wondered...

Gerald flicked his wrist dismissively. "When you look at me like that, it makes me nervous. You're making a monumental trip to the bank. Remember? Get to it, Cassie."

Cassie snapped to attention and discarded her thoughts of a budding romance between her boss and her aunt. She buttoned her coat and strode outside to cross town square. Which was, in actuality, a circle. An octagonal-shaped courthouse sat in the middle of the surrounding lawn. Nearby, steam rose from the hot mineral spring that gurgled from the rocky hillside, one of the many springs found in the area.

Local businesses encircled the park. Streets jutted off like spokes on a wagon wheel. Cassie wasn't sure why the founding family of Pepperville had laid out the town lots in peculiar shapes, but it made the town unique.

Her thoughts trailed off as she passed a whiskered old man—Wilbur Knox was his name. He sat on a bench beside the steaming springs, soaking both feet in a small tub.

"Mornin', Mizz Bixby," he mumbled as he readjusted his tattered clothing.

"Good morning to you, sir. Your gout and arthritis must be bothering you today," she replied. "Sorry to see that."

"Read your newspaper article about that Morris woman stirring up trouble in Wyoming—"

"She wasn't making trouble—" Cassie tried to interrupt but Wilbur talked over her.

"—by giving women the right to vote. Don't sound like a good idea to me," he said candidly.

Cassie watched Wilbur limp over to the steamy spring to heat up his basin of mineral water. "If you were a woman you might think it was a grand idea."

"Well, the legislature voted it down in '76 so that's that. Besides, you're too darn pretty to bother with suffrage campaigns. You need a man to support you instead of working at the newspaper office. Don't know what Gerald was thinking when he hired a woman."

Cassie gnashed her teeth and reminded herself that scads of small-minded males from the older generation resisted the thought of women gaining equality. In Cassie's opinion, the Western frontier was fertile ground for modern thinking and social reform. Here, women could hold jobs that were frowned upon and considered men's work in the East. The frontier lifestyle demanded men and women work together to establish farms, ranches and businesses.

Single women and widows could own property but married women were denied ownership in many states. Because of Spanish influence, women in Texas retained more rights than in the East where English tradition reigned supreme. But Texas had yet to grant women voting privileges that allowed them a voice to improve their lives and establish social reform.

Cassie frowned thoughtfully, wondering if Aunt Louise had settled in Texas so she could acquire the property for her two-year-old restaurant and the café she'd opened in Hillsdale before starting her business in Pepperville.

As for Cassie, she'd had difficulty getting her foot in the journalistic door after she'd finished her education in Boston. If her boss at the magazine office hadn't taken ill with influenza—he had required a month of bed rest to recuperate—she might not have had a chance to step into his shoes and subsequently be recognized as a serious journalist.

When Cassie discarded her wandering thoughts, she heard Wilbur make another comment about women staying in their proper places at home. She considered telling the hidebound old coot to soak his head instead of his feet in the mineral springs, but she clamped down on her tongue. She refused to let Wilbur spoil her grand mood. Starting today, she was free of the burden of obligation she felt to her aunt. Louise would have a tidy nest egg and Cassie could begin saving to purchase her own home rather than living at the boardinghouse.

With Maxwell beside her, she hiked across the park

encircle by a hotel, butcher shop, general store, opera house, bakery, the Bixby Café and several other thriving businesses. Excitement built inside her as she approached the bank. Forcing Max to wait outside, she took her place in line behind two men who were dressed like the trail drovers who passed through in the spring and fall, delivering cattle herds to the railhead in Dodge City.

Pepperville was close enough to the Chisholm Trail to accommodate drovers and cowboys who restocked supplies and wet their whistles at the local saloons on the northwest side of town—away from the more respectable businesses that lined the circular park. The cowboys also paid visits to the red-light district that Cassie would like to close down.

She'd wanted to write several scathing editorials about the brothels, but the city council was in favor of keeping them open. Gerald had suggested that she pick her battles and begin with the enlightenment of women. He insisted that trying to shut down the saloons and brothels would be as bad as stirring up a nest of angry wasps. That, he said, would be bad for *her* health and for *his* business and livelihood.

"What do you mean I can't withdraw cash?" the drover at the front of the line demanded, jostling Cassie from her pensive musings. "This is a bank, isn't it? I put money in here last fall when I brought my herd through. Now I need to restock supplies."

The scrawny teller in his late thirties, whose pointy nose and shifty eyes always reminded Cassie of a rodent, stared at the man through his thick wire-rimmed glasses. "I'm sorry, sir, but withdrawals that size take at least a day. If you could return tomorrow—"

"I plan to stock the wagons and be on the trail tomorrow," the drover interrupted gruffly. He shook his finger in Millard Stewart's face. "The money better be here bright and early in the morning. Otherwise, the bank owner and I are going to butt heads!"

The agitated customer lurched around and stamped off.

The second trail drover heard the same story from the teller and he issued a few threats of his own before he stalked out. A cold draft swept through the bank before he slammed the door with enough force to rattle the pane-glass windows.

Cassie waited impatiently while Gladys Truman, a plump elderly widow with a face like a wrinkled peach, deposited a small amount of money into her account. Cassie knew the white-haired woman had difficulty making ends meet and took in mending for extra money. Cassie and Aunt Louise took their clothing to Gladys, even if they could have tended the tasks themselves. Other kindhearted citizens did the same.

"You keep up those editorials to encourage women to speak out for their rights," Gladys said as she turned away from the teller's window. "My husband, God save his close-minded soul, considered me his servant and his property. You wouldn't believe how many times I was tempted to stitch his mouth shut so I could tell him, without interruption, what I thought of his backward ideas. This state has given black males the right to vote. Why not women, too?"

"I couldn't agree more," Cassie replied with a smile.

She liked Gladys Truman. A lot. She seemed to be enjoying her independence and widowhood more than her confining marriage. According to Aunt Louise, there had been no love lost between the Trumans. Their families had arranged the union and the couple simply tolerated each other.

In Cassie's opinion, marriage benefited men more than women and love rarely entered into the equation. Her parents were the exception. They had cared for and respected each other. Unlike the bickering that went on while Cassie lived with her mother's sister and her family for five endless years after her parents' tragic death in a carriage accident.

Five years of hell and the loss of her inheritance, Cassie mused bitterly. There was no telling what would have become of her if Aunt Louise—her father's younger sister—hadn't stormed in to retrieve her, despite the personal risk of traveling north during the war between the states. She had whisked Cassie off to Texas to care and provide for her.

"May I help you, Mizz Bixby?" the teller asked, drawing her from her wandering thoughts.

Cassie retrieved her pouch from her purse and set it on the counter. "I want to deposit these banknotes in Louise Bixby's account." She set Gerald's leather poke beside the heaping pouch. "This money goes in the newspaper account—"

Her voice dried up when a gust of cold air blasted through the bank. The door crashed against the wall and a collective gasp of alarm erupted behind her. Cassie glanced over her shoulder to see two men, dressed in long canvas dusters and sombreros, toting double-barrel shotguns.

They had covered their heads with black hoods. Cheesecloth inserts concealed the color of their eyes and shapes of their mouths. Both men towered over the customers like burly giants. They must have weighed at least three hundred pounds each. The *chink* of the large rowels on their silver spurs sounded like a death knell in the grim silence.

They motioned with the barrels of their shotguns, forcing customers to line up against the wall and raise their hands over their heads.

"That goes for you, too, señorita," the nearest bank robber said in a muffled voice.

Everything inside Cassie rebelled against the terse command delivered with the heavy Spanish accent. *No! No! No!* This was her big day. She was repaying her loan so she'd feel truly independent for the first time in her life! She had scrimped and sacrificed to collect this money. Plus, she was responsible for the profits Gerald had asked her to deposit in his account.

"Señorita…" The hombre's gruff voice held dangerous warning. He loomed over her like a thundercloud. "Do not cross us. My compadre is trigger-happy."

To reinforce the comment the second bandit leveled the business end of his shotgun at her heaving chest. Outgunned, defenseless, Cassie could do little more than glare holes in the first thief's black hood. When he tried to snatch the pouches, she held them protectively against her chest. When she refused to let go, the bandit jerked her arm backward at a sharp angle. She was forced to release the pouches—or lose the use of her arm.

"Bastard," she growled loudly enough for him to hear her.

"*Sí*, I am. But money makes me forget my shame." He half turned to rattle off a command in Spanish to his cohort.

Outraged, Cassie watched the second outlaw dig into

each customer's pockets to retrieve their watches and coins. Then the first bandit ordered the teller to stuff money in the canvas bag tossed at him.

While the nervous teller did as he was told, the door to the private office at the back of the bank swung open. Floyd Pettigrew, the red-haired banker who was dressed in the finest fashion seen on the East and West Coasts, sauntered down the hall. He froze to the spot beside the staircase leading to the second story when the first bandit took his measure with the shotgun. The banker's face turned white as cornstarch.

"Ah, señor, you're just in time to donate to our worthy cause. We take from the rich. *You.* And give to the poor. *Us.*"

Floyd's pallid face flushed with fury. He glowered at the outlaws as he relinquished his pocket watch and wallet.

"The two flashy rings and diamond stick pin will look good on me," the first bandit insisted as he caught the other items in midair. "Hand them over, gringo—"

The urge to pounce nearly overwhelmed Cassie. If she could divert the first bandit's attention and cause a distraction, the other customers could overtake the second bandit—even if he was as big as a barn also. Five-against-one odds seemed acceptable to Cassie.

Her fierce sense of justice and fair play soon overrode her initial fear. Before Cassie had time to consider the personal danger, she burst into action. She rammed her arm against the bandit's elbow, causing his weapon to swerve toward the ceiling. The bank president dived to the floor then slithered down the hall to slam his office door behind him. Not only was he a coward, but so were the five male customers plastered against the wall. They gaped at her in amazement instead of taking advantage of her diversion tactic.

Cassie yelped in dismay when the first bandit grabbed her by the nape of her coat, lifted her clean off the floor then shoved her none too gently against the wall. She couldn't translate the scowled utterances that spewed from beneath his black hood. Didn't need to. She could tell that he was furious with her daring attempt to disarm him.

"You think this is a good day to die, señorita?" he snarled ferociously. "I can arrange that…if you insist."

"No," she tweeted, with what little breath she had left after he'd slammed her into the wall.

"Too daring for your own good," he snapped. "You are lucky I have decided to let you live."

He let her slide very slowly, very deliberately down the wall until she was standing on her own two feet. Then, without releasing his tight grasp on her, he half turned to rattle off another brusque order in Spanish to his cohort.

Cassie swallowed uneasily when the second bandit inclined his head toward her and made a comment that she wished she could translate. The first bandit chuckled wickedly.

"He thinks I should bring you along to teach you a lesson, among other things, *chica*. What do you think?"

Difficult though it was, Cassie kept her mouth shut instead of telling the taunting bandit where he could go and what he could do with himself once he got there. Unfortunately, the desperado was exceptionally good at reading her venomous expression.

"I do not like what you are thinking, wildcat. Believe me, *I* can do much more damage to *you* than you can do to me."

Frustrated anger overrode her fear once again. She stared into the mesh holes in the black hood where his eyes should have been. "A shame looks don't kill, señor."

She stared pointedly at the money he had clamped under his arm while he used his shoulder to keep her pinned to the wall. The realization of all she was about to lose to this thieving hombre bombarded her again. Before she realized what she was doing, she found herself reaching for the pouches.

His furious growl erupted as he spun her around then snaked his arm across her chest to hold her against him. Cassie's feet never touched the floor when he stormed from the bank, hauling her along with him. He swore angrily when he stumbled over Maxwell. The tomcat screeched then darted away.

All sorts of horrible scenarios leaped to mind while the outlaw whisked her through the breezeway between the hotel and the bank. She could hear the second bandit trotting to keep up with his cohort's hurried strides. The two thieves scurried past the freight office and lumberyard that butted up against the back of the bank and hotel.

Cassie's breath came out in fits and spurts—the first bandit had tightened his grasp to such extremes that it was difficult to breathe. When the second outlaw muttered in Spanish, the first outlaw responded sharply. Cassie feared the worst when her captor shoved her toward the second bandit, who hooked his arm around her waist and held her suspended in the air. To her surprise, he slung her into a nearby wagon bed stacked with lumber. Her head was still spinning when the desperadoes dashed off. She heard the clatter of hooves as the thieves made a fast getaway.

She hopped to the ground then braced herself against the wagon when her wobbly legs nearly folded up beneath her. The onrush of anger gave way to fear and shock.

Cassie dragged in a restorative breath, but her heart was pounding in double time and she couldn't stop shaking.

"Sweet mercy!" she chirped. "What was I thinking? I must've gone temporarily insane!" This was a fine time to discover she was an individual who didn't get scared; she got angry enough to retaliate against injustice.

That was not always a good thing, she realized.

Then it hit her again—like an emotional avalanche that destroyed her composure in one fell swoop. She had lost every last cent of savings. Gerald's money was gone, too. Those burly brutes had swooped in like vultures to rob her at gunpoint, as well as the other five customers.

It had taken years to save enough money to pay her debt. Cassie felt like screaming in frustration—and so she did. She cursed the bandits for all she was worth while she was at it.

Jackson Culpepper waited until his horse plunged into the thick underbrush near the river before he slowed his breakneck pace. Muttering sourly, he jerked the sombrero off his head then removed the black hood.

"Can you believe that woman's audacity?" Harrison Culpepper, who was four years Jack's junior, snorted incredulously as he yanked off his disguise. His auburn hair glistened in the sunlight as he focused his vivid blue eyes on Jack. "She tried to attack you, for heaven's sake!"

No kidding, thought Jack. Everyone else in the bank had been quiet and cooperative. But not Cassandra Bixby. She had taken him completely by surprise with her bold daring.

Jack reached instinctively for one of the pistols holstered on his hips when he heard the approach of another rider. He relaxed when Jefferson Culpepper, who was two years younger, appeared from the underbrush.

"How'd it go? As uneventful as the first time, I hope?"

"Nowhere close," Jack grumbled as he pulled off the knee-length canvas jacket. Then he unfastened the bulky padding over his shirt and breeches that made him look a hundred pounds heavier and broader. "There were complications."

Jefferson's pale green eyes widened in alarm as he took Jack's disguise and rolled it into a ball so he could cram it into the carpetbag tied behind his saddle. "What kind of complications?"

"Cassandra Bixby complications, that's what kind," Harrison mumbled in annoyance then handed his padded clothing to Jefferson. "She launched a direct attack on Jack when he took her pouches of money away from her."

Jeff's mouth dropped open. "You are kidding."

"I wish we were." Jack plunked down on a fallen log to pull off his spurs and high-heeled, silver-toed Spanish-style boots that made him appear even taller than his six feet two inches. "I haven't checked to see how much Cassandra had stashed in the leather pouch she was about to deposit in the bank. But she was worse than a mother grizzly defending her cub. Apparently, she values her money more than her own life."

"What did you expect from a prissy Yank?" Jeff smirked. "As the story goes, she was born, bred and educated in Boston, even if she spent the between years in Texas with her aunt. You can bet all this stolen money in your saddlebag that an eastern beauty like her bows to the gods of gold and silver currency. No doubt, she's set her cap for a wealthy gent who can meet her high expectations. Like the bank president, for instance."

"No doubt," Harrison inserted as he yanked off his boots

then tossed them to Jefferson. He nodded his thanks when Jefferson handed over his everyday pair of work boots. "The five men I held at gunpoint didn't give me the slightest bit of trouble. But that firebrand was another matter entirely, even after Jack threatened all sorts of torture."

Jefferson grinned, and his pale green eyes twinkled with amusement. "Wish I'd been there to see that."

"Next time we rob the bank it will be *your* turn again," Jack insisted as he handed over the rest of his disguise then retrieved the ivory-handled pistols he usually carried.

And damn it, Jack felt guilty enough about his role in this fiasco without manhandling the newest arrival in town. If he could have figured out a better way to solve the crisis, he would have taken a different approach. However, there was too damn much at risk and he'd had to resort to drastic measures—and drag his younger brothers along with him.

Jack glanced around. "Where did you stash our horses?"

Jefferson gestured a brawny arm toward a thicket of redbud trees to the west. "Ready and waiting. Don't forget to jot down what you stole from each victim. Don't want any mix-up, ya know."

"I'll leave that to Harry." Jack hiked toward the copse of redbuds.

"Holy hell!" Harrison crowed.

"Holy hell *what?*" Jack demanded of his youngest brother.

"There's at least five thousand dollars in one bag and three hundred in the other." Owl-eyed, he glanced at Jack.

"Damn, maybe *she* robbed a bank before *you* robbed her today." Jefferson said. "Someone held up the bank at Oakridge last month. Daring as that Bixby chit is, maybe she did it, then waited until now to make a deposit in Pepperville."

"Wouldn't surprise me a bit," Harrison replied. "When a five-foot-nothing female takes on an outlaw over six and a half feet tall in his high-heeled boots who looks as if he outweighs her by a couple hundred pounds, she wouldn't bat an eyelash at robbing a bank herself."

"And who'd think to suspect that shapely blonde with expressive, thick-lashed green eyes and lush pink lips of wrongdoing?" Jefferson remarked.

Jack arched an eyebrow. Apparently, his brother had done his share of fantasizing about Pepperville's newest resident. She was exceptionally pleasing to the eye, even if she had stirred up conflicting emotions when discussing women's suffrage in her newspaper articles.

"I really doubt she's had time to plan bank heists, in between rabble-rousing and trumpeting women's rights," Jack commented as he led the two fresh horses from the bushes.

"Never know. Maybe she's financing her crusade," Harrison speculated. "Her newspaper articles keep mentioning her kindred spirits in Texas. Gotta have money to unite a statewide cause."

Jack checked himself thoroughly to make certain he hadn't overlooked part of his disguise.

"You're fine," Jefferson said, reading his mind. "Except for this." He flipped Jack's silver badge end over end through the air.

Jack caught his city marshal's badge, pinned it on his leather vest, then he swung into the saddle. The badge caused guilt to take another nip at him, but he ignored his grumbling conscience.

"Make sure the evidence is stashed from sight," he cautioned his younger brothers. "I want to make damn certain that Floyd Pettigrew can't accuse any of us of robbery."

"Pettigrew." Jefferson spat out the haughty bank president's name, as if it left a bad taste in his mouth—which Jack was sure it did. Same as it did with him and Harrison. "When he gets his due I'll be jumping for joy."

"I want to make *double* damn certain he's the culprit," Jack insisted.

"I *want* him to be the one because I don't like the cocky, self-important bastard," Harrison remarked.

"Cover our tracks while I ride back to town," Jack requested as he reined southeast. "We'll make the rest of our arrangements when I'm off duty tonight."

"Whatever you say, big brother. You're the ringleader of this gang," Harrison teased as he and Jefferson brushed away the tracks then grabbed the spare horses. "Marshal and ringleader, all rolled into one."

Yes, he was, Jack mused disconcertedly. He was playing a dangerous game with his family's reputation. He was breaking the law one day and upholding it the next as Pepperville's city marshal. Even though he'd been forced to resort to these desperate measures to investigate the possibility of fraud and embezzlement at the bank, his conscience wasn't letting him hear the end of it. If this scheme backfired, Jack swore his father and his grandfather would come back to haunt him.

As unnerving as that thought was, Jack's shocking physical reaction to Cassandra Bixby was even more disturbing. He'd gotten right in her face when she'd defied his intimidation tactics—and the alluring scent of her perfume had filtered through his concealing hood to assail his senses. Then, when he'd slung his arm diagonally across her chest to haul her outside he'd felt the voluptuous curve of her breasts against his arm. The suggestive glide of her shapely rump against his upper thighs had sidetracked him to such extremes that he'd stumbled over her oversize black tomcat.

Now, the erotic thought made the sap rise in his unruly body again. Damn, that woman with the alert evergreen eyes and honey-gold hair was the worst kind of trouble—alluring and daring at once.

Jack made a mental note to avoid her every chance he got.

Chapter Two

When Cassie burst into the newspaper office with the black tomcat at her heels, Gerald stared at her in alarm. "Are you all right? There's sawdust and wood chips stuck in your hair. Why is your dress twisted sideways? There's no color in your face and you look as if you're about to faint. *What happened?*"

Cassie spared a quick glance in the mirror Gerald used when working with woodcuts for newspaper illustrations. He was right, she decided as she assessed her reflection. The side seams of her green dress were twisted around her as if she were a maypole. She did look a frazzled mess after the gigantic outlaws had carted her off, tossed her into the back of a lumber wagon and all but left her for dead.

Well, that was a bit dramatic, but she was lucky to be alive after she'd fought back. She shouldn't have risked life and limb to recover her money.

But damn it all, it was important!

In the aftermath of the robbery, Cassie wilted into her chair. She was still shaking all over.

Gerald rushed over to her. "Tell me what happened."

"Bank robbery."

"What? Another one?" he howled in outrage.

She blinked, bemused. "There were others? When?"

"There was one about two months ago," Gerald reported. "It was right before you came to town."

Gerald pivoted toward the steps then dashed up to his apartment to fetch a damp cloth. When he returned he blotted her splotchy face then draped the cold cloth around her neck.

"The culprits were never apprehended. There was also a robbery reported at Oakridge. Don't know if it was the same thieves or not. They're still at large, too."

Cassie inhaled a calming breath and willed herself to stop shaking. "Did the victims give a description at the first robbery?"

Gerald shrugged. "We were told there were two men and they were huge."

"These bandits were gigantic, too," she confirmed.

"They came storming into the bank. Then poof! They disappeared," Gerald went on to say. "We figured they rode off with a trail herd headed to Dodge City."

"Did the robbery occur in the morning, too?" she asked.

"No, it was just before closing time, as I recall." Gerald pulled out a nearby chair and sat down in front of her. "Why do you look as if you've been in a wrestling match? Did one of those hooligans make untoward advances during the robbery?" he asked in concern.

Cassie shook her head and her tangled hair spilled over her shoulders—sawdust, wood chips and all. "Not exactly. I attacked the outlaw who snatched our money from my hand. We got into a tug-of-war."

"What?" Gerald hooted and his hazel eyes nearly popped from their sockets. "Good Lord, woman!"

"Good Lord what?" Aunt Louise demanded as she burst into the office. She skidded to a halt when she noticed Cassie's disheveled appearance. "My God…" Her voice trailed off as she plucked the bark and sawdust from the tangled strands of her hair and Cassie's green dress. "What happened?"

At thirty-seven—as of tomorrow—Louise Bixby was the picture of energy, femininity and independence. She was five feet two inches with a trim figure and nearly flawless skin. Her golden hair was only a few shades darker than Cassie's and her brown eyes glittered with alarm and outrage. Aunt Louise had always been there for Cassie. Now was no different. Her defensive stance and the expression on her face testified that she was ready to do battle on her behalf, if necessary.

"I heard there was a bank robbery. You were a victim, weren't you?" She gave Cassie the once-over—thrice. "But that doesn't explain your ruffled appearance."

"We were just getting to that." Gerald offered his chair to Louise. "There was a tussle."

"You were *physically* attacked?" Aunt Louise's dark eyes widened in alarm and her voice rose to a high pitch that threatened to shatter glass. "My God, hon!"

"Actually, Louise, it seems that Cassie attacked one of the outlaws," Gerald inserted.

"What in heaven's name were you thinking?" Louise squawked, horrified.

Cassie shrugged and blew out a shaky breath. "Apparently, I wasn't thinking at all. I simply reacted irrationally to losing my money."

"No amount of money is worth your life," Aunt Louise lectured sternly.

"It was to me." Tears filled her eyes when the realization of what had happened to her life savings swamped her again. "I've been saving as much money as I could spare to repay you for raising me and sending me to school. I went to the bank this morning to deposit the money in your account as a birthday surprise. In addition, I had Gerald's cash with me. Now it's all gone," she wailed, near hysterics. "All because of those big, greedy galoots!"

Aunt Louise slumped back in her chair while Cassie blubbered in tears. Gerald stood behind her aunt's chair and stared sympathetically at her.

"How much money are we discussing?" Aunt Louise asked.

"Five thousand hard-earned dollars," Cassie burst out between sobs. "This was to be your best birthday ever."

"It wouldn't have been a good birthday if you had been shot." Aunt Louise clasped both of Cassie's hands in hers. "I'm just thankful you're alive and unharmed."

Cassie smiled through her tears then wormed one hand from her aunt's grasp to wipe her flushed cheeks. "I still can't believe I snapped like that. One moment I was trembling with fear and then I saw myself flying at the outlaw who stole my money while he trained his shotgun on Floyd Pettigrew. That lily-livered coward crawled back into his office and slammed the door, leaving the rest of us to our uncertain fate."

"Fine example he is," Aunt Louise sniffed in annoyance.

"I tried to create a distraction to inspire the other victims to pounce on the second bandit," Cassie said on a seesaw breath. "But they stood there and stared at me as if I'd lost my mind. Which apparently I had. But the moment was lost and the bandits recovered control of the situation."

Aunt Louise shook her index finger in Cassie's puffy face. "Now you listen to me. Admirable though it is in theory, no more heroics for you... Isn't that right, Gerald?"

"Quite right," he seconded without hesitation.

"But I lost your money, too," she reminded Gerald.

He flicked his wrist dismissively. "We'll sell dozens more newspapers after you write your firsthand account of the incident. We'll make up the monetary losses in a week."

Cassie perked up immediately, then dragged the wet cloth off her neck to mop her face. "Of course, an article! I'll make it my mission to track down those thieves and inspire citizen awareness by giving a detailed description of the culprits. I can interview the other victims as well, in case I've overlooked some details."

"You can begin your crusade tomorrow," Aunt Louise decreed. "You've had a harried morning and you should take off the rest of the day to recuperate.... Shouldn't she, Gerald? And with pay, of course."

He shifted uncomfortably when Louise twisted in her chair to pin him with a hard stare. "I suppose that would be best. Although we have several fliers to print for the land office and advertising to distribute for the Pepperville Hotel, Sampson's Bakery and the general store in preparation for the other cattle herds that will be descending into the valley the next few weeks."

Cassie surged from her chair. Although her knees wobbled and her head spun slightly she pasted on a determined expression. "I will take off the rest of the morning to collect myself, but I will return after lunch to set type for the fliers," she insisted.

Aunt Louise didn't look pleased with her decision, but Gerald seemed relieved not to have to tackle all the projects under tight deadlines by himself. He'd told Cassie several times that she was twice as fast at setting type and she knew he had taken on many more projects now that she worked with him.

"Come along, hon." Aunt Louise guided Cassie toward the door. She flashed the newspaper editor a dour glance because he hadn't backed her up completely. "Gerald will have to manage by himself without your valuable assistance. Indeed, I don't know how he managed before you showed up."

Cassie watched Aunt Louise and Gerald stare each other down from twenty paces. One minute they shared companionable affection, followed by friction. Then came the seeming acceptance of their differences of opinions and personalities.

"I think you and Gerald should see each other socially," Cassie blurted out when she had closed the door behind her.

Aunt Louise stopped short. "What on earth made you say that out of the blue?"

Cassie shrugged then remembered to adjust her skewed gown. "I don't know. Just a feeling that you two might get on well together if you gave each other half a chance."

"Hmm," was all Aunt Louise said as she escorted Cassie next door to the restaurant then ushered her up the steps to the furnished apartment.

"You stay here and rest a bit." Aunt Louise gestured

toward the bed. "I'll have Suzannah bring up a lunch tray. She'll want to see for herself that you're all right."

Suzannah Mitchell was an attractive, blue-eyed brunette with an engaging smile and winning personality. She waited tables at the restaurant and she was a year younger than Cassie, who had celebrated her twenty-fourth birthday before she'd had arrived in Pepperville. They had become close friends the past six weeks and they lived in the same boardinghouse on Jackson Street.

Aunt Louise halted beside the door and turned back to Cassie. "The money isn't important to me—you should know that," she insisted. "When I could finally get to you after your parents died and that horrible woman tried to keep you from me, I promised that I'd raise you as my own. It doesn't matter that there's only a thirteen-year age difference between us.

"Besides, your father and mother watched over *me* until I made the foolish mistake of following the man I believed to be the love of my life. I watched him charm another woman who had the kind of wealth and connections I lacked."

Cassie nodded mutely as she removed her shoes so she could stretch out on the bed.

"I needed you as much as you needed me, hon. Never doubt that for a minute."

Cassie had blamed herself for years because her aunt had disregarded her own needs and neglected her social life to raise her orphaned niece while operating her first restaurant. Cassie frowned, wondering if her aunt had bypassed marriage to avoid the ridiculous law about women not retaining complete control of their property without a husband having the last say in the matter.

Since Roland—the rat—soured her aunt on men that likely played a major part in why she'd never married.

"When Roland cast me aside for his wealthy pigeon I realized he was an opportunistic adventurer. I was his meal ticket and a temporary amusement to him. I was devastated," she confided. "Raising you became my salvation. So don't think that I'd trade five thousand dollars for the joy and companionship we shared. As for Gerald Nash—"

A pounding on the door interrupted her. Aunt Louise twisted the latch. Suzannah Mitchell stood there with a tray of food, anxious to check on Cassie. Without invitation, Suzannah swept into the room to set the bread, cheese and coffee on the end table.

"Sweet merciful heavens!" she gasped as she surveyed Cassie's disheveled appearance. "Are you sure you're all right? The word circulating around town is that you tried to thwart the bank robbery…twice! The bandits carried you off then discarded you. Is that true?"

"Good gad," Aunt Louise chirped. "You didn't mention that part."

Cassie flapped her arms dismissively as Suzannah plunked down on the edge of the bed. "I was relatively unharmed, despite that big baboon carting me out the door and tripping over Maxwell. All I suffered was a momentary lapse of sanity when I tried to defend myself and inspire the other victims to do the same."

"The women who have joined our movement for rights and reform have hailed you as a brave heroine," Suzannah reported, then shook her finger in Cassie's face. "But do not do anything so daring again. You might not survive the ordeal."

"You want me to be a coward?" Cassie challenged wryly.

"No, of course not. That doesn't fit your personality."

"You can say that again," Aunt Louise inserted.

"You shouldn't have tried to fight back when those five men didn't show the slightest gumption," Suzannah huffed.

Cassie's lips twitched as she raised her hand and pledged, "I solemnly swear to restrain myself the next time I'm robbed."

Suzannah blew out her breath then leaned over to give Cassie an affectionate hug. "I'm holding you to it. You're my best friend and I have no intention of losing you so quickly."

"Come along, dear," Aunt Louise insisted. "Cassie needs rest and we have customers waiting downstairs."

When her aunt and her friend exited, Cassie sprawled out on the bed to relax for a few minutes. Despite the well-meaning order to take the morning off, Cassie intended to contact the city marshal. She wanted to give him a description of the two bandits so he could hunt down those big goons and recover her stolen money.

Cassie gobbled up the snack then freshened up. Determined of purpose, she exited the apartment and avoided the anticipated objections from her aunt by using the private staircase that descended into the side alley between the newspaper office and the restaurant.

Jack Culpepper checked himself thoroughly one last time to make sure there was no telltale evidence to link him to the robbery. He'd been in law enforcement long enough to know what precautions to take to throw officers off track. He'd made sure that he and his brothers wore silver-toed, high-heeled caballero boots and spurs that made them look taller. The footwear, ordinarily worn by cowboys who needed to secure their feet in the stirrups during high-speed chases to round up contrary cattle, were ones they used at his family's ranch.

In addition, padded clothing and long canvas dusters altered their appearance, making them appear much broader and heavier—larger than life. Leather gloves and black hoods with cheesecloth covering the eyes and mouth made accurate facial descriptions impossible and obscured the scars on their hands.

Although Jack's sense of fairness and his conscience were at war over the unorthodox investigation of bank fraud that he and his younger brothers were conducting, he couldn't risk being caught. The first robbery had gone without a hitch. But when that rabble-rousing Yankee became involved, things had gone to hell in a hurry.

Speak of the devil. Jack sighed inwardly when he glanced down the boardwalk to see Cassandra Bixby, her fat black cat at her heels, marching toward him in purposeful strides.

"Here comes trouble," said Wilbur Knox, who was sprawled negligently on the bench outside the office. "Just what Pepperville needs, a female suffragist running loose. Why can't women leave well enough alone?"

Jack tried to veer into his office, but Cassandra flapped her arms in expansive gestures, making it impossible to pretend he hadn't noticed her. He'd noticed her around town too many times as it was. Resigned, he waited for her to stride determinedly toward him.

"Have you had any luck tracking down the thieves?" she asked without preamble. She glanced sideways to acknowledge Wilbur. "Are you feeling better after treating your feet and legs in the mineral springs?"

Jack bit back a grin when the older man, whose wrinkled features were partially concealed by a gray beard and mustache, squinted up at the shapely blonde and said, "*Was.* Not so much now, though."

Her attempt to be polite was wasted on Wilbur. He had no use whatsoever for women who refused to stay in their place and even less for ones who wrote inflammatory articles in the local newspaper to convince other women to rally and protest.

"What robbery?" Jack asked with a carefully blank stare.

She squared her shoulders and faced him directly. "The one that took place a little more than an hour ago. You're the marshal in this town. How can you not know that?"

"I just arrived in town," he defended reasonably.

Her lovely face puckered in irritation. She huffed out a breath then said, "I want to give my statement and offer my description of the outlaws." She glanced pensively at Wilbur. "You were sitting by the hot springs in town square—"

"*Circle,*" Wilbur corrected. "It's a town *circle.*"

Jack swallowed another amused grin when Cassie gnashed her teeth. "Fine. Town circle is more accurate," she accommodated him. "You had a perfect view of the bank. Have you told the marshal what you saw?"

Wilbur swiveled on the wooden bench to peer up at Jack. "I didn't see nothin', Marshal. Didn't hear nothin', either."

"That is not possible," Cassie protested. "You could easily see the bank. From what direction did the outlaws enter the bank?"

"What outlaws?" Wilbur—cantankerous old goat that he was—squinted as if he was half-blind.

"How many were there?" Jack asked, as if he didn't know.

"Two," Cassandra huffed. "Didn't anyone contact you?"

"As I said, I've been gone. For two days," he added, lying through his teeth. "I escorted a prisoner for trial. I just returned to town a few minutes ago."

She glanced up and down the street. "Surely you have a deputy on staff. Maybe he left a note before he gave chase."

Jack stared down at Wilbur. "Have you seen James Suggs this morning?"

"Nope. I think he must've spent too much time checking the saloons and brothels while making his rounds last night."

When Cassandra muttered something half under her breath—something about the lack of competent law-enforcement officials available in Nowhere, Texas—Jack gestured toward his office. "Come inside and give your statement. I can't begin a search until I know who and what I'm looking for."

"You keep pussyfooting around and the outlaws will be long gone," she mumbled sourly.

Summoning his patience, Jack ignored Cassandra's annoyed glance. She squared her shoulders and swept regally into his office. The oversize cat darted inside before Jack could shut him out. Damn cat, he mused irritably. He'd tripped over the black devil during the getaway. Now here he was again. Dealing with Cassandra and her cat should be lots of fun, he thought sardonically. Probably worse than the damn robbery itself.

"Have a seat, Mizz Bixby."

She plunked down, but she perched attentively on the edge of the chair, primed and ready to launch into a detailed account of the robbery and a description of the outlaws.

Jack was about to find out how observant and accurate this female journalist was. Plus, he'd dearly love to know what possessed this daredevil woman to pounce on an armed outlaw—namely him. He still hadn't recovered from the shock of her attempt to disarm him and retake possession of her money.

He retrieved the proper form then sank down in the chair behind the desk. When the black cat hopped on the desk, Jack scraped him off then stared into Cassandra's intelligent evergreen eyes and said, "Okay, fire away, Mizz Bixby."

"I was robbed at the bank by two oversize thieves wearing canvas dusters that smelled mildewy and musty."

"Mildewy and musty as if they'd been used as rain-coats then rolled up and stuffed into saddlebags before they dried out?" he supplied helpfully. Jack had purposely used the old, smelly dusters to counter other scents a robbery victim might notice. "Perhaps they were used and stored on a cattle drive?"

"That's possible," she agreed. "Also, they wore silver-toed boots and silver spurs that clinked when they walked."

"Could you describe their faces?" Jack requested, knowing damn well she couldn't.

"No, they wore black hoods and wide-brimmed sombreros," she said, disgruntled. "Both men were similar in size and stature. They were exceptionally tall and as broad as buf-faloes. They spoke with a heavy Spanish accent and com-municated with each other in Spanish during the holdup."

He scribbled notes then glanced over at her. "So you think they were Mexican banditos, not trail hands?"

"Perhaps. They wore silver conchas on the seams of their breeches and they carried double-barreled shotguns with curlicue engravings on the stocks."

"Got it." He jotted a note. "Anything else?"

"No. I was informed the bank was first robbed before I arrived in town and the thieves were also gigantic and dressed in a similar fashion."

He nodded somberly. "Yeah, it sounds like the same men. Now tell me what happened."

Cassandra inhaled a deep breath that drew his attention to the full swells of her breasts. He made an extra effort to stare into her beguiling eyes rather than at her chest.

"I was about to make my deposit with the teller when two bandits burst inside to hold me and five men at gunpoint. They demanded money and jewelry."

"What did you do?" he asked, knowing full well this spirited female had proceeded to shock the hell out of him.

"First I tried to cling to my money pouches, but I was hopelessly outmuscled. Then Floyd Pettigrew stepped from his office unexpectedly while Millard Stewart was cramming money into the canvas pouch, as ordered. I tried to cause a diversion so the five men lined up against the wall could overtake the other bandit."

"Are you out of your mind?" Jack questioned—which is exactly what he'd wanted to ask her earlier that morning. "You could have been killed."

She met his scornful gaze and said, "I lost a great deal of money, Marshal. I suppose that retrieving it was my motivation. That and the fact the five male victims took the injustice sitting down—so to speak. We had those two hooligans outnumbered but the men lacked the gumption to stand up for what was right. It made me boiling mad and I reacted irrationally."

"No kidding, lady," he mumbled under his breath then jotted some more notes to look like he was doing his job.

"So...the thieves took your money and left," he summed up.

"No, they took me with them."

Jack glanced up and frowned, striving for an expression of baffled confusion to convince her that he hadn't been there and he didn't have the slightest notion why the bandits abducted her. But he knew exactly why he'd carted her off. He'd tried to put the fear of God in her so she wouldn't make that daring but dangerous mistake ever again.

"Why would they do that if they had successfully robbed the bank and its patrons?" he asked with feigned curiosity.

She glanced the other way and fidgeted in the chair. He swallowed a chuckle when she muttered and scowled.

"I was in a tug-of-war, trying to recover the money, and I was angry. The big baboon threatened to teach me a lesson."

He didn't appreciate being referred to as a big baboon, but he couldn't protest without incriminating himself.

"I have no idea what that goon thought I could possibly learn from a heathen with his lack of scruples and conscience." Clearly, rehashing the incident upset her and it took a moment to gather her composure so she could continue. "He hauled me outside and tripped over my cat." She stared at the spit wad of a cat and said, "Maxwell could probably identify him."

Ironically, Maxwell hopped into Jack's lap. When he tried to toss the pest aside, it sank its claws in his crotch. Finally, he dislodged the cussed cat and set it on the floor.

"Then what happened?" Jack asked through clenched teeth.

"Eventually the big brutes tossed me into the back of a wagon in the lumberyard and fled from town on horseback."

"Were you injured?" he inquired, taking a few more notes.

"No. When I recovered from shock and outrage, I wobbled back to the newspaper office."

"Did anyone chase after the banditos?" As if he didn't know the answer to that already. However, he anticipated a newspaper reporter like Cassandra would expect that question.

She shook her head and sunlight glinted around her silky hair like a golden halo. Jack had the crazed urge to spear his hand into those curly strands, but he restrained himself. He wondered why he'd developed this sudden preoccupation with Cassandra. She was nowhere close to his usual type.

"I don't think anyone gave chase… And what the blazes is the matter with people in this town?" she erupted, bounding to her feet to pace from one side of the room to the other.

When she reached the wall, where he displayed Wanted posters, she spun on her heels to stamp in the opposite direction. Jack caught himself staring in masculine appreciation at her voluptuous profile, then he gave himself a mental slap. This was not the time or the place. This definitely wasn't the woman, either. The less contact he had with the victim he'd carted off during the robbery the better.

Jack did not want to be fascinated by or attracted to Cassandra Bixby. Although he had noticed her—and what man hadn't?—the first week she arrived in town, he had kept his distance. She had waited tables at her aunt's café for a time and he had been nothing more than respectful and polite—until they had hooked horns at the robbery scene this morning.

Appealing though she was, she was too independent minded, too intense, too caught up in women's causes, too…*everything.* Considering his profession in dealing with wild and daring criminals for a dozen years, he preferred mild-mannered, unassuming women. Cassandra Bixby didn't come close to fitting that description.

"Well? What is your explanation, Marshal?"

Jack blinked and stumbled his way back to the point in conversation where he'd become sidetracked by her shapely feminine body, that glorious blond hair and those vivid green eyes that made brother Jefferson's eyes seem pale in comparison.

Jack gave himself a mental pinch to get back on track. Oh, yes, now he remembered. She'd asked what was wrong with people in this town.

"Most folks tend to let law-enforcement officials, who are trained and experienced at confronting criminals, do the job they are paid to do," he said with a pointed glance.

She crossed her arms beneath her bosom and stared him down. "Then what did you do to track down the thieves after the first robbery?"

Her tone indicated she didn't think he was capable or competent. It annoyed him, even if he hadn't made any effort to hunt the outlaws. Hell, he knew who they were and where to find them.

"I followed standard procedure," he replied as he leaned back to prop his feet on the edge of his desk. "I checked for any evidence that might link someone to the robbery. I also followed two sets of tracks—"

"And where did those tracks lead?" she interrupted.

"Straight to the river." He linked his hands behind his

head and lounged in his chair, despite her glance that indicated she didn't approve of his casual air. "The men were clever enough to brush away their tracks. They swam through the river to make themselves difficult to follow. I checked with drovers with northbound cattle herds, but they claimed they didn't know or see the two men I described."

"And that was it?" she challenged.

"What was it?" he asked, feigning ignorance.

"That was the extent of your so-called investigation? Is that *all* you did to hunt down the bank robbers?"

He drew his feet from the edge of the desk and leaned forward. He wanted to surge up to tower over her because she was beginning to annoy him with her condescending tone. But he couldn't risk having her notice any similarities between him and the outlaw who carted her from the bank and had her tossed in a wagon.

"Look, Mizz Bixby, Pepperville sits beside the Chisholm Trail and we have a constant influx of people. It's difficult to know and to keep track of everyone who comes and goes through here. But I assure you that I intend to investigate this second robbery."

"I should certainly hope so," she sniffed. "After all, this is *your* town. At least that's what I've been told. Your family founded this community. It's your namesake. I live on the street named after you."

"Exactly," he said through gritted teeth, marveling at how easily this woman got under his skin. "I take my responsibility to this town seriously. These people are my friends and neighbors. They came here at my father and grandfather's urging to settle the area after the Comanches were moved to the reservation in Indian Territory. But I can't be everywhere at once and I can't stop a robbery if I'm not in town, now can I?"

She frowned pensively. "Were you in town when the last robbery took place?"

"No, I was testifying in a court case against a drunken cowhand who accidentally shot through the wall of a bordello, injuring a prostitute and her client."

"Speaking of that, I don't approve of Bordello Row. It's offensive to women. Your family shouldn't have sold property to madams and saloonkeepers."

"We didn't," Jack informed her. "The original buyers sold out at excessive prices and there wasn't much we could do about it."

She accepted his explanation then frowned ponderously. "If you were out of town when the first robbery took place, too, there might be a local informant at work. These men might not be desperadoes or trail hands passing through town."

Jack gave the pretense of nodding thoughtfully. Damn, this woman was astute. "Maybe you're right. Then again, it could be coincidence." He distracted her from her train of thought by adding, "How much money did you lose?"

Her bewitching face puckered in irritation and she went back to pacing, her cat at her side. "Five thousand dollars."

"*Five?*" he asked with just the right amount of surprise.

"I was about to repay my aunt for all the years of commitment and financial support involved in raising me and ensuring I received a formal education. It was to be her birthday surprise for tomorrow."

He inclined his head slightly. "Very admirable of you. I also heard that you've invited the whole town to the surprise party tomorrow evening."

"A shame you can't make it," she retorted caustically. "But I'm sure you'll be too busy investigating the robbery."

Obviously he was an unwanted guest, unless he arrived bearing five thousand dollars of recovered money. "I'll make a point to stop in," he said just to aggravate her. "Louise Bixby is a local favorite. I wouldn't miss the chance to wish her well on her birthday."

Cassie flung him a disgusted glance that indicated exactly how much use she had for him—none whatsoever. "I'm sure she'll manage to celebrate without you."

What did he care if the feisty female considered him incompetent? He didn't. He had his reasons for the robberies and she wasn't privy to them.

Annoyed with her, he walked over to the corner closet to grab a broom then smirked at her and said, "Here's your broom and there's your black cat. Have a nice flight across town."

She glared at him before she swept out. Jack watched the little witch and her cat disappear from sight and he was damn glad to have her gone. For a number of reasons.

The first was that he was physically attracted to this aggravating female with her hypnotic green eyes, honey-colored hair and body he itched to get his hands on.

The last reason was because she was pressuring him into investigating *himself,* and his conscience was bothering him enough as it was.

Chapter Three

Cassie exited the marshal's office in a huff. First off, Jackson Culpepper's witch insinuation annoyed her. Secondly, she didn't appreciate his casual acceptance of the bank robbery. Granted, murder and thieving were likely everyday occurrences to a man in his profession. However, she took the matter very personally. She had lost a lot of hard-earned money and the marshal behaved as if he would begin the investigation when he got around to it.

If her irritation toward his lack of interest in pursuing his investigation wasn't enough to infuriate her, the fact that she found that raven-haired, amber-eyed marshal physically appealing bewildered her beyond words. True, she'd noticed the ruggedly handsome marshal while she waited tables at the café and she'd seen him around town while working for the newspaper. But today she'd been forced to deal directly with her unexplained attraction to the six-feet-two-inch, two-hundred-pound virile male—who was also the irritating marshal.

Her conflicting feelings for him frustrated her.

First off, Jackson Culpepper was nothing like the proper gentlemen she'd met in Boston. There was nothing dandified about Jackson. She'd recently discovered that she preferred men who had as much brawn as brain, but she'd like to brain *him* over the head for not bounding up and racing off like a jackrabbit in an effort to overtake the fleeing outlaws who had stolen her money.

The thought prompted Cassie to check her watch. She scowled when she remembered her timepiece had been stolen during the robbery. She estimated that she had enough time to trail after the bandits herself before reporting to the newspaper office after lunch. How hard could tracking outlaws be? She knew which direction they'd taken when they hightailed it out of town. Jackson had mentioned the bandits had headed to the river during the first robbery. They could be there right now, counting her money and celebrating. If the marshal wouldn't assert himself then, by damned, she would.

Determinedly, Cassie hiked to the livery stable that sat next door to the saddle and boot shop. Within a few minutes, she had rented a horse and trotted off in the direction the bandits had taken.

"Jackson! Jack!"

Jack bounded to his feet when he heard a loud feminine voice summoning him from outside his office. He whipped open the door to see Louise Bixby wringing her hands and huffing and puffing to catch her breath.

"Thank God you're back," she wheezed. "I'm afraid something terrible has happened."

"I already heard about the bank robbery."

She waved him off impatiently. "Not that. It was bad

enough, but now my niece is missing. I settled her on my bed in the upstairs apartment. When I went back to check on her she was gone! I'm afraid those horrible men who roughed her up during the robbery returned to kidnap her!"

Jack could guarantee that hadn't happened. He almost never kidnapped people. Further, the fiery Cassandra Bixby was at the very bottom of his list of people to abduct.

"Your niece came by my office an hour ago to give her statement," he declared. "She was fine then. But I can't say where she went after she left here."

"You have to search for her," Louise insisted. "It's lunch hour and we have customers flocking in. Otherwise I'd do it myself."

"I'll find her," he said, concealing his reluctance.

Two encounters with that spirited female was enough for one day. Nevertheless, as a favor to Louise he set off to find Cassandra.

Ten minutes later, he learned that Cassandra had rented a horse. He predicted that she had taken it upon herself to track the bandits since he wasn't doing it fast enough to suit her. Heaving an exasperated sigh, Jack mounted his horse then trotted toward the river.

Cassie muttered under her breath when she snagged her petticoats on the thistles and stickers growing on the sandbank near the river. She had been tramping around for almost an hour, hoping to catch sight of the thieves or their horses. She hadn't spotted any footprints to follow. Curse it, this was more difficult than she'd anticipated—

"Find anything useful?"

Cassie nearly leaped out of her skin when a deep, resonant voice came from so close behind her. She lurched around to see Jackson, sporting the same five o'clock shadow she'd noticed earlier, leaning negligently against a tree and chewing on a blade of grass.

"Not yet," she muttered.

"Too bad. Now it's time for you to go home. Louise asked me to find you."

He behaved as if she was a runaway child, and she didn't appreciate his judgmental attitude. Then she reminded herself that she had judged him and found him lacking as a law enforcement officer, so who was she to complain? She decided to ignore him and see if he'd go away.

While she checked for broken tree limbs and hoof prints in the sand Jackson ambled behind her.

"You could help, you know. After all, I am doing *your* job for you, Marshal."

"I don't seem to be having much luck then, do I?" he taunted. "Maybe I should hire someone who actually knows how to scout."

She rounded on him. "Obviously you don't know how to do it. You must have failed scouting school during your marshal training."

"I do well enough," he defended himself. "I tracked renegade Comanches and white and Mexican outlaws for several years with the Rangers."

She blinked, surprised. "Oh, well, good for you." She hated to admit that she was impressed. Texas Rangers were well-respected lawmen who fought against difficult odds in difficult conditions on the frontier. Still, she wasn't prepared to give Marshal Jackson Culpepper too much credit because he agitated her beyond words. "Were you fired? Did you ultimately lack the ambition needed to track renegades?"

When she flashed him a goading smile and batted her eyes at him, he snarled at her. Then suddenly his face lost all expression and he stepped away from her.

While she speculated on his odd behavior he said, "We might as well get things square between us, here and now, Mizz Bixby. Why don't you come right and tell me why you don't like me."

"Because you aren't taking this robbery seriously enough to suit me," she told him point-blank. "I like a man of action. Clearly, you have to work yourself up to easing into an investigation. I can't imagine how *cold* this trail is going to be when the spirit finally moves you." She peered up at him, annoyed that she had to tilt her head back to accommodate their difference in height. "Why do you have so little use for me, Marshal Culpepper?"

"Because you're a Yankee who thinks she's better than Western folks. We don't have polished manner and old money."

She stared at him, astonished. "You think I'm a snob? Ha! You couldn't be more wrong. Living in the East didn't suit me at all. There are hundreds of men in the East who share Wilbur's opinion because they're entrenched in traditions."

His lips twitched, but she gave him high marks because he had the good sense to keep his mouth shut.

"Not everyone in the West is a hidebound old coot. Out here, women work alongside men and the division lines are not so rigidly defined. I want equality for my sisters so we can choose where we live and what professions appeal to us. That hardly makes me a snob. It makes me a progressive thinker who is interested in necessary change and social reform."

"Anything else you want to get off your chest?" he asked.

"Yes. It's time to raise the age of consent so young girls don't find themselves forced into prostitution, abused and unable to prosecute," she informed him. "Secondly, I'd like to build an orphanage to protect children from slave labor. Thirdly, I'd like to shut down bordellos and saloons. Or at least limit their operating hours. And do not get me started on alcoholism and the problems it causes."

Jackson flapped his arms dismissively. "You can get down off your soap box, buttercup. I've read all about your crusades to save the world and to unite your kindred spirits in the newspaper. I'm talking about your holier-than-thou attitude toward *me*."

"I don't think I'm better than you, you brainless ass!" she spouted off. "I just want you to find my money!"

"Shh-shh. Any experienced scout and lawman knows better than to yell his head off when there might be ruthless bandits nearby. You might be bushwhacked…by someone besides *me*."

Cassie reflexively clenched her fists, wishing she could smack him upside the head without fearing that he'd haul her to jail for assaulting an officer. The man was infuriating, antagonizing…

Her thoughts trailed off when he flashed a devastating smile that assured her that he was teasing her playfully. She settled her ruffled feathers and asked herself why she was trying so hard to dislike him. The answer was that she liked him a little too much, even though she took exception to his lackadaisical approach to the investigation and his remark about her being a broom-riding witch.

Her gaze drifted over his angular features then settled on his chiseled lips. Suddenly she found herself wondering what it would be like to kiss him instead of verbally sparring with him. When his golden gaze locked on her, she felt her body sizzle with unfamiliar sensations. He angled his head and she held her breath, half hoping he'd kiss her and end the suspense. And half hoping he wouldn't.

A split-second later he backed away. Disappointment flittered through her. Sweet mercy! She was having too much difficulty dealing with the riptide of feelings and sensations Jackson Culpepper set off inside her.

He stared at the air over her head then said, "Maybe we should join forces to scout the river for bandits." He handed her one of the ivory handled Colt .45s that hung in the double hostlers on his lean hips. "Do you know how to use this?"

"No, but how hard can it be? You cock the hammer and squeeze the trigger, right?"

He chuckled and shook his dark head. Then he grabbed her elbow to steady her while they tramped through the underbrush. Five minutes later, they were standing on the cliff overlooking the steep riverbank and the clear blue water gliding leisurely downstream.

"See any bandits?" he asked.

Her shoulders slumped in disappointment. She had the depressing feeling that she could kiss her five thousand dollars goodbye forever. No doubt, those unscrupulous desperadoes would spend it on ammunition, whiskey and harlots.

"Cheer up. I'll contact the county sheriff and other city marshals in the area to see if anyone has seen your two outlaws. But for now, you had better head back to town. Your disappearance visibly upset Louise. She thought the bandits returned to whisk you away."

Sighing in defeat, Cassie allowed Jackson to guide her

back to the waiting horses. If she wasn't a strong, independent woman, she might have thrown herself in his brawny arms and bawled her head off, lamenting her lost money.

Damn those bandits! If Jackson ever captured them, she would be tempted to shoot them herself for frightening and angering her—to the extreme.

"What are you thinking?" he asked as he scooped her up and set her on her rented horse.

"That I'd like to murder those thieves," she said vindictively.

"Can't say that I blame you," he murmured, then looked away without meeting her gaze. "I'll stay here to look for evidence while you return to your life of headlines and deadlines."

Taking the reins, Cassie rode off, thankful for the reprieve from the disturbing marshal whose touch could set off the most startling sensations imaginable. She tried to convince herself that the robbery caused all this emotional upheaval inside her, but she knew it was a lie.

Jackson Culpepper—*the man*—was getting to her.

The next evening at the surprise birthday party, Jack took a seat in one of the chairs that lined the walls. The center of the café was reserved for dancing and greeting the guest of honor. Jack nodded discreetly for Harrison to sit down beside him. Since the first robbery, the Culpepper brothers had been careful not to stand side-by-side for too long at a time. All three were over six feet tall and tended to tower above crowds. Jack was wary of anyone making a connection between the Culpeppers and the bandits.

"Looks like Cassandra is spreading her charming smile around the restaurant," Harrison murmured, then sipped his punch. "She hardly resembles the fiery wildcat we encountered during the robbery."

Jack nodded mutely, and then cursed himself for allowing his gaze to follow the shapely blonde while she and her friend, Suzannah, served slices of pie and cake to guests who attended the come-and-go event. He also chastised himself for allowing Cassandra to occupy so much of his thoughts the past two days. And even more bewildering was that he'd nearly buckled to the insane impulse of kissing her while they'd stood atop the cliff overlooking the river.

What the devil had come over him? A close association with Cassandra had disaster written all over it. She'd see him hang from the tallest tree in Texas if she discovered he had stolen her money.... And that reminded him...

"When are you and Jefferson making the rounds to return the money and jewelry to the other victims?" he whispered.

"Jeff is tending to the task as we speak. Except for Cassandra's nest egg. We weren't sure what to do about it."

"I don't know what to do about it, either," he murmured, then glanced around to ensure no one overheard him. "Being a journalist, she might decide to make it public knowledge that her money and watch mysteriously reappeared in the dark of night. Our friend Pettigrew might become suspicious, too."

Harrison glanced up to note that Floyd Pettigrew had put in an appearance. "I have to hand it to that bastard, he does know how to make a grand entrance, doesn't he? Always dresses fit to kill, too. As if I don't know where he acquires his funds." He snorted then stared quizzically at Jack. "Have you been able to track down any information on him yet?"

"No. It's a slow process. There's also the possibility that he's using an alias."

A few minutes later, Jefferson arrived. He halted beside Harrison and Jack to say, "The packages, plus a tidy bonus to compensate for the inconvenience, have been delivered. Like last time, I added a note to request the money not be deposited in the bank until next week."

"Any problems?" Jack asked.

"Not even one," Jefferson reported. "The Robin Hood of Pepperville has come and gone.... Uh-oh..."

Jack tensed when he saw Cassandra juggling two plates of apple pie in each hand. Although she came bearing sweets, she had the look of a woman on a mission.

"Gentlemen, glad you could join us for Aunt Louise's birthday celebration."

Jack noticed she passed her smile to Harrison and Jefferson—and ignored him. He, of course, was supposed to be burning candles at both ends to locate her stolen money.

While Harrison and Jefferson mumbled something appropriate and accepted the dessert, Jack sat there wondering why he'd developed this ill-fated fascination for sun-kissed curly hair, Cupid's bow lips, entrancing cedar green eyes—to name only three of her beguiling attributes. Damn, he must have some sort of death wish, he decided.

When Jefferson elbowed him in the ribs, Jack snapped to attention then took the plate she held out to him. "Thanks...I'm not sure you've been introduced to my brothers."

She smiled amicably at them. "No, we haven't had a formal introduction, but I've seen both of you at the café."

"This is Harrison," Jack said. "He's in charge of training our horse herds. Jefferson is developing a crossbreed of cattle suited for this area." He glanced back at his brothers. "In case you've forgotten—" which of course they hadn't "—Cassandra recently hired on with Gerald Nash at the newspaper office."

Jefferson raised his cup in toast. "Here's to the young lady who is opening our eyes to women's rights and reform."

She smiled good-naturedly. "I do what I can to educate men to the changing times and to unite my kindred spirits."

When the band struck up a tune, Harrison stood up and Jefferson sat down. Two tall Culpeppers standing together in front of an observant robbery victim was a bad idea.

"Now that the formal introductions are out of the way, let's dance, Mizz Bixby," Harrison requested.

"It's Cassie. And thank you for the offer, but I was about to ask Marshal Cul—"

"It's Jack," he corrected her.

Harrison flung out his arm in an exaggerated gesture. "That marshalling business can wait, Cassie. It's Louise's party," he insisted with a quicksilver grin.

Jack knew exactly why Harrison had swept Cassie away. He was keeping the robbery victim distracted. Cassie was exceptionally astute and observant. The less she saw of the Culpeppers, collectively, the better.

"There you are, Jackson. I'm giving you the chance to ask me to dance before someone beats you to it."

Jack inwardly groaned when he dragged his gaze off Cassie to see Doreen Rowe batting her baby blues at him. Attractive though the pale-haired blonde was, she was a melodramatic social climber. At twenty-two, the butcher's daughter had made herself available to Jack and Jefferson every chance she got.

"Maybe Jefferson can accommodate you," Jack suggested.

"No, sorry. I twisted my knee this morning while we were branding cattle. Can't walk without a limp."

To prove his point, Jefferson hobbled off to refill his punch glass.

"Well, Jackson, I guess that leaves us." Doreen flashed another dimpled smile and held out her arms, leaving Jack no choice but to lead her onto the dance floor.

Resigned, Jack danced.

Doreen glanced over at Harrison and Cassie. Her face puckered in a disapproving frown. "I don't know why your youngest brother would want to twirl around that troublemaker. She's getting several women all stirred up with her silly notions that women are equal to men." Doreen tossed Jack another of her I'm-just-a-helpless-female expressions she wore so well. "Everybody knows men are supposed to take care of women and make all the important decisions. Don't you agree?"

Jack made a neutral sound. He wasn't about to be dragged into that heated debate. Besides, the graceful way Cassie moved in Harrison's arms reminded him of how he'd felt when he clamped her curvaceous body against his during the robbery getaway. The memory made his unruly body throb.

"Jackson?" Doreen prompted.

"Yes?" He dragged his attention back to Doreen.

"Tell me you haven't become bewitched by that outspoken suffragist." She pouted prettily. "Why, I have heard it whispered that she doesn't care all that much about men…if you know what I mean."

Jack blinked, startled, and missed a step. "Where did you hear that?"

She shrugged noncommittally. "I'm not at liberty to say, but it's rumored that Cassandra lost her job back East because she's a man-hater…to the extreme…"

Jack stopped dead still in the middle of the dance floor, shocked by the insinuation Doreen boldly suggested.

Doreen patted his shoulder and said, "But you don't have to worry about that with me. I am exceptionally fond of men. You in particular."

Ten minutes later, while Cassie was serving dessert to newly arrived guests, someone tapped her on the shoulder. She glanced back to see a fetching blonde, who looked to be a year or two younger, decked out in a lacy pink party gown.

"Would you like dessert?" Cassie asked cordially.

The pale-skinned blonde struck a sophisticated pose. "No, thank you. I rarely eat pastries unless I prepare them myself. They never quite measure up."

The woman's haughty pose and snide tone made Cassie grind her teeth. "Punch perhaps?" She'd like to offer the chit the kind of punch that wasn't served in a glass.

The woman frowned distastefully. "Did you make it? I tasted it already. One sip was more than plenty. I only came by to offer you my condolences about being robbed yesterday. I heard that you made the foolish mistake of fighting back."

"Who *are* you?" Cassie demanded, tired of the woman's needling games.

"Doreen Rowe." She flashed a sticky-sweet smile that dripped like maple syrup. "My father owns the butcher shop."

"And what do *you* do?" She allowed just the slightest bit of snide to infuse her voice.

"Why, nothing outside our home, of course. That's a woman's place, despite your newspaper articles to the contrary. Jackson was just saying the same thing to me when he asked me to dance a few minutes ago."

Cassie didn't know why that bit of information aggravated her, but it did. She glanced across the café to see Jackson chatting with another young woman—his fourth of the evening. But who was counting? Not her, of course. She didn't care what he did or whom he did it with, as long as he investigated the robbery and found her missing money.

"I was shocked when Jackson told me he'd heard rumors that you are a frigid man-hater who prefers female companionship."

Cassie's nearly dropped the plates of apple pie she held in her hands. "He told you that?"

"Didn't I just say so? Jefferson seconded the report. Not that I would pass judgment," she added quickly.

Doreen twirled around then tossed another of her pretentious smiles. "I won't keep you from your waitress duties. I'll pay my respects to your aunt and be on my way. So nice to have met you."

"Of all the…" Cassie broke off into muffled oaths as the spiteful blonde sauntered off. She found herself comparing Doreen to a rattlesnake. They each had their own nasty bites.

Her attention swung across the room to Jackson Culpepper. How dare he pass vicious rumors one minute and pretend to help her investigate the robbery the next.

Pretend, she contemplated. Marshal Culpepper was going through the motions of tracking down the bandits, but he wasn't giving the investigation much effort.

Cassie had half a mind to march herself over to him, drag the backstabber outside and kiss his lips right off his face to dispel the vicious rumor. It wasn't her fault that she had yet to meet a man who swept her off her feet, someone who tempted her to experiment with passion. Someone whose companionship inspired her to spend every spare minute in his company.

True, she had no use for men who were only interested in her body, and ignored the intelligence, character and personality that went along with it. But that didn't mean she didn't *like* men. It only meant that she was particular. Nothing wrong with that!

"Are you feeling all right?" Suzannah asked as she halted beside her. "Your face is flushed. It can't be problems with the birthday party. Things are going grandly."

"The party is progressing perfectly," Cassie agreed. "Thanks to your amazing organizational skills." She thrust the plates of pie at her friend. "Pass these around, please. I have an errand I need to tend. I'll be back in a few minutes."

She took only five steps before Aunt Louise rushed over to squeeze the stuffing out of her. "Thank you for putting together this celebration, hon. I'm thoroughly enjoying myself. Not like yesterday when you disappeared from my apartment and I was beside myself with worry."

"I'm sorry about that," Cassie murmured. "That was very inconsiderate of me. I've been taking care of myself for the past few years and I didn't stop to think that you might fear the worst."

Aunt Louise smiled radiantly. "All is forgiven and thanks again for the wonderful party."

When her aunt scurried away, Cassie squared her shoulders and made a beeline toward Jackson. She tossed the willowy brunette, who was hanging on his every word, an apologetic smile then grabbed his arm. "Sorry to tear the marshal away from you, but this is official police business."

"What's wrong?" Jackson asked as Cassie towed him out the front door and around the corner to the shadows in the side alley between the newspaper office and the restaurant. "Did you remember details about the robbery?"

"No. I want to make an important point." She pushed up on tiptoe, threw her arms around his broad shoulders and kissed him for all she was worth.

A frigid manhater, he'd said. Indeed! *A woman's place was tending the hearth and the home?* Ha!

She'd show him *hearth* when she burned off his lips with a sizzling kiss! She might not have excessive experience with men, but she was creative and she had watched other women entice men often enough to figure out how it was done.

When Jackson didn't move a muscle, just stood there, making her do all the work, she met the challenge. She arched against him and rubbed her body seductively against his muscled contours. There. Were these the actions of a woman who didn't find men—this one in particular—physically attractive?

Suddenly he wrapped her in his arms and plunged his tongue between her lips. Cassie was shocked to realize that she was the one who caught flame. The brawny marshal taught her a thing or two about kissing that she didn't know—and would never forget.

She couldn't breathe when she felt his hand glide over her rump to press her hips against the hard ridge between his legs. His familiar touch scorched her to the same extremes as his devouring kiss. Cassie forgot about teaching Jackson a lesson and trying to make her point. She couldn't think. Period. She could only respond to fervent need that exploded out of nowhere when his hands roamed over her sensitive body again—and again.

Her mind spun like a windmill while one fiery sensation after another bombarded her. Who would've thought this man—who aggravated her because he didn't take her demands for justice seriously and didn't approve of her causes—would be the one to ignite molten lust inside her. It wasn't fair…and she was going to launch herself from his sinewy arms and slap him silly for taking intimate privileges with her…any second now…

"Damn, you taste ten times better than apple pie." He trailed spine-tingling kisses down the column of her neck.

Cassie forced herself to lean back in the circle of his arms. She stared into those flame-colored eyes that reflected the flickering lamplight on the street. It took her a moment to formulate words—because her brain had melted into mush when he kissed and caressed her so familiarly.

"That should be answer enough," she said, her voice nowhere near as steady as she'd hoped.

"What was the question?" Jackson chirped. "Well, hell…"

She wheeled around and groaned in humiliation when she saw the younger Culpepper brothers lurking in the shadows. One stood in the alley. The other one stood up on the boardwalk. When they grinned in wicked amusement, embarrassment flooded over Cassie. Gathering what little dignity she could muster, she elevated her chin to a proud angle then wedged between the two men to return to the party.

On her way to the café, she asked herself what possessed her to prove anything to Marshal Culpepper. That was almost as outrageous and daring as attacking the oversize bandit during the robbery.

Cassie shook her head in dismay. She was seriously beginning to doubt her sanity.

Chapter Four

Jack's body was still vibrating like a tuning fork while he watched Cassie hurry off. He wasn't sure he could explain what had happened to him. One second he was trying his damnedest to resist the unexpected, lip-blistering kiss Cassie delivered. Then wham! He'd hauled her up against him as if he had been deprived of feminine attention for years on end.

What had become of the iron-willed self-control he'd spent thirty-two years nurturing and cultivating?

To make matters worse his brothers had witnessed the steamy embrace and were grinning like a couple of idiots.

Harrison arched a dark brow. "Mind telling us what *that* was all about?"

"Yeah, big brother, what *were* you doing? Interviewing one of the robbery victims?" Jefferson razzed him. "What did you find out?"

He'd discovered that he was dangerously susceptible to the alluring scent, addictive taste and luscious feel of the woman he'd robbed of her life's savings. Hell and damnation! Cassie had kissed him as if there were no tomorrow and she'd rubbed so sensuously against him that hungry need had come dangerously close to devouring him and his common sense.

"I thought we agreed that close encounters with victims wasn't a good idea," Harrison reminded him, still grinning in fiendish glee. "That encounter looked exceptionally close."

"Distance is best," Jefferson said. "Your words, I believe. You must've decided on a different strategy. Kiss her until her brain breaks down and she forgets everything she ever knew? Clever." He waggled his eyebrows and grinned scampishly.

"Go away," Jack muttered.

"No. I'm having too much fun," Jefferson said.

"Me, too," Harrison inserted. "But not as much fun as you seemed to be having."

"She started it," Jack burst out, annoyed that he sounded like a petulant child. Damn it, see what that woman had reduced him to!

"She might have started it, but you finished it," Jefferson pointed out.

Jack blew out his breath and glared at his smart-alecky brothers. "I need to make my rounds. Go pester someone else."

Harrison stepped aside to let Jack pass. "Okay, big brother, but you better watch out. You keep playing with fire and you'll get scorched."

Didn't he know it! If he'd had the slightest doubt about the rumor Doreen Rowe had passed along, Cassie's mind-boggling kiss had answered the question about her preferences. Jack's aroused body could attest to that.

* * *

The next morning Cassie ventured from the newspaper office with a stack of fliers ordered by the general store. After dropping them off, she spotted one of the robbery victims coming toward her on the boardwalk. She flashed a friendly smile and blocked the pot-bellied man's path.

"Excuse me, sir. I'm doing a newspaper article about the bank robbery. I was hoping you could give me your perspective and tell me what personal items were stolen."

"Nothing was stolen and I didn't see much," he said shortly.

Cassie blinked, baffled by his refusal to discuss the robbery. "I'm sure I saw you hand over a pocket watch."

He shook his dark head vigorously. "Don't be putting my name in your story, Mizz Bixby. I saw nothing and I heard nothing. I have work to do so I'll be on my way."

When he veered around her to hurry away, Cassie strode off to contact another of the men victimized at the bank. She knew Edgar Forrester was the blacksmith's assistant. Surely he wouldn't be as closemouthed about the incident.

"I'm writing an article about the robbery," she declared when she located Edgar, who was working the billows and making repairs on a damaged carriage.

Edgar bit down on the cigar sticking out the side of his mouth as he glanced over his thick shoulders at her. The muscles of his bare arms bulged as he stepped back to hammer the glowing metal into its proper shape. "Don't know what you're talking about, missy."

"Of course you do," she insisted. "You were right behind me in line at the bank. You were plastered up against the wall with the speaking end of a shotgun aimed at you. What did the second bandit take from you?"

"Nothin'. Nothin' at all." He emphasized his denial by clanking the hammer against the hot steel.

Cassie stared sternly at him. "What are you afraid of? Has someone threatened you if you mention the incident?"

"I'm not afraid of nothin'," he snapped brusquely.

His stubborn attitude inflamed her temper. "No? You looked afraid during the holdup. Plus, you didn't take action when I provided a distraction to overpower the bandits."

He paused long enough to look her up and down then scoffed. "That's because you shocked me with your crazed daring. And anyway, I don't hold with your views on givin' females more rights than they have already. Ain't no woman I know who can handle my job. But you got my wife thinkin' she deserves more and that I oughta listen to her advice and opinions more often." He brandished the hammer at her. "Now skedaddle. I got man's work to do and you're slowin' me down."

Cassie left the blacksmith's barn, feeling like a social pariah to the male gender. Clearly, her articles on women's rights didn't sit well with backward-thinking men in town. Even if the men didn't share her opinion that was no reason to behave as if the bank robbery never happened.

Disgruntled, she returned to the newspaper office to begin her account of the robbery. She didn't mention the male victims by name, but she was tempted to expose them for the small-minded cowards they had turned out to be.

"How is the story coming along?" Gerald asked as he came up beside her.

"Well enough, considering the other victims refuse to offer their account. I wonder if they were told not to speak out. If that's the case, why didn't the thieves pay *me* a threatening visit? It makes me think the thieves are familiar with locals and they have been sneaking around in the dark, putting the fear of God in their victims."

Gerald rubbed his chin thoughtfully. "Come to think of it, I received a similar response from the two men on hand at the first robbery. They didn't want to be named or interviewed. I considered it odd, but I suppose I became sidetracked and let it pass."

Cassie frowned pensively. "If these bandits turn out to be local rather than drifters, I should mention the names of all the victims and make our readers aware of the possibility of thieves among us. It might alarm the bandits and force them to make a mistake that could lead to an arrest."

Gerald shook his head grimly then directed her attention to his stiff fingers, the slick discoloration above his left eyebrow and the half-moon-shaped scar on the underside of his chin. "See these souvenirs? This is what can happen when an editor dares to print stories that anger certain individuals. I ran a newspaper office in Waco and I mentioned the members of an outlaw gang that frequented a local saloon without being arrested. They took offense and came after me. They ransacked my office and left me with two broken fingers."

"I'm sorry," she commiserated.

He directed her attention to the scars on his face and his broken nose. "I moved away to set up shop in Hillsdale—"

"Hillsdale? That's where Aunt Louise lived before moving farther west," Cassie interrupted. "Is that where you first met her?"

"Yes. That's also where I dared to complain about a corrupt politician who was sucking the town dry and taking all sorts of illegal privileges. He sent his thugs to work me over one night. They pounded on me until they knocked me out." He cast her a bleak glance. "I'm not the only Western editor who dared to speak the truth and suffered for it. I've heard of others who have been stuffed in jail, tarred, feathered and ridden out of town on a rail."

Cassie cringed, speculating on her own fate.

"I don't want you to come to harm over this, Cassie," Gerald said earnestly. "Your aunt would have a conniption fit if something bad happened to you. She was beyond upset the day she couldn't find you and presumed the thieves had sneaked into her apartment to abduct you and retaliate because you fought back during the robbery."

She expelled a frustrated breath. "Fine then, I won't mention anyone else's name. But it seems highly suspicious that citizens are clamming up and that both robberies occurred while the marshal was out of town, attending other duties. Someone around here is monitoring his activities."

She glanced at the clock. "I'm going to take an early lunch, tend a few errands and conduct a few more interviews before finishing this article."

"Just be careful who you rile up," he cautioned, then wheeled toward his office. "Save me a trip and drop off these new brochures at the opera house, will you? I have another print job I need to finish while you're gone."

Cassie thrust her arms into her coat then took the bulletins and brochures that announced the upcoming performance at the opera house. With Maxwell on her heels, she hiked off to make the delivery then headed for the marshal's office.

She slowed her pace and asked herself how she should act after her outrageous behavior the night of her aunt's town-wide party. She was annoyed with herself for allowing Doreen Rowe's comments to influence her. In most instances, she had learned to shrug off scorn and criticism because of her progressive views on social reform.

Yet, when Doreen told her that Jackson thought she didn't favor men, and that he disapproved of campaigning for women's rights, it set her off. As she recalled, he had sidestepped the issue of women's rights while they were searching for the bandit's tracks near the river.

Now, she had several important topics she wanted to discuss with the marshal. But those blazing kisses and bold caresses were right there between them and she was self-conscious to the very extreme.

Cassie halted outside the office and inhaled a fortifying breath. She thought it over and decided to pretend those mind-boggling kisses hadn't happened. She was here to discuss the possibility of the robbery being an inside job and to figure out why victims stubbornly refused to answer her questions.

When she entered the office, Jackson wasn't at his desk. Maxwell hopped on it and plopped down on a stack of papers, as if he owned the place.

Cassie heard someone rattling around behind the partially open door leading to the jail. "Marshal?" she called out.

"Just a minute."

She braced herself when his muscular body filled the doorway. A flash of memory bombarded her. There was something alarmingly familiar and equally tantalizing about the way he…

"What can I do for you, Cassandra?" he said in a no-nonsense tone that sent the burst of befuddling and conflicting memory flying right out of her head.

Clearly, he was as anxious to forget about the inappropriate encounter as she was. She gathered her composure and stared at the air over his left shoulder. "First off, I want to ask you if you've discovered any signs of the bandits."

"Yes and no." He walked over to ease a hip on his desk and stared at the black cat in annoyance. He picked up Max and dropped him on the floor. Then he focused his attention on the wall lined with Wanted posters instead of looking at her.

"Can't you do something with this annoying cat?"

"Yes and no," she said, tossing his words back at him. "Now which is it when it comes to locating the bandits? Did you find something useful or not?"

"I spotted two sets of hoof prints that disappeared into the shallows of the river," he reported matter-of-factly. "I searched upstream, but one of the cattle herds watered nearby and it was impossible to pick up a trail."

Jack hated lying, but he couldn't risk drawing Cassie into this complicated situation. She was better off not knowing what was going on and why.

"I'm writing the article about the robbery," she explained as she took a seat in front of him. "Unfortunately, when I interviewed two of the other victims they insisted nothing was taken from them and they saw nothing."

Of course not, thought Jack. Each had received a package with their returned belongings and money to compensate for the inconvenience. Plus, an attached note requesting they tell no one about the late-night visits and hold off making bank deposits. It was all the Culpeppers could say without drawing unwanted speculation or rousing suspicion about the undercover bank investigation.

"Huh," was all he could think to say in response.

"I find that very disturbing."

"Mmm," he said neutrally.

He noticed that Cassie had yet to make eye contact with him. She kept staring over his shoulder and her hands were clasped tightly in her lap. Obviously, she felt as awkward and uncomfortable about that fiery kiss as he did.

"The victims' odd behavior leads me to believe that someone has gotten to them and frightened them into keeping silent. It also suggests that the thieves are local or that they have someone here that is working with them in tandem."

"Huh," he said again.

She looked straight at him then. Her dark green eyes flashed with irritation. "All you have to say is *huh* and *mmm?* Law-abiding citizens in town are being terrorized and that doesn't infuriate you?"

He crossed his arms over his chest and met her challenging stare. "Did you stop to think that maybe the victims didn't want to be interviewed by you in particular? Maybe they are offended by your articles that inspire other women to speak out and don't want their names linked to yours in any manner."

"And *you* are one of those narrowed-minded men, aren't you?" she demanded sharply. "You are offended because I have a mind of my own and I know how to use it. Are you afraid of me, Marshal?"

Yes, he was. He was afraid that his unwanted attraction to this firebrand was going to complicate an already complicated situation that involved him as well as his brothers. He didn't want Cassie to know his part in the robbery and he sure as hell didn't want her caught in the middle of this fiasco.

"Well, Marshal?" she prodded relentlessly. "It's a simple, straightforward question that requires a simple answer. Yes or no?"

"You're trying to lure me into another debate," he protested, then flung out his arm in a dismissive gesture. "The point is that there are several possible explanations. The male victims might be angry with you because you put them at risk when you retaliated during the robbery. On the other hand, it might have nothing to do with being terrorized and more to do with differences of opinion about your cause of social reform. I can't speak for any of them because they haven't shared their thoughts with me, either."

She bolted to her feet to thrust her face into his. "You should be the one interviewing the victims. I should be receiving my information from you. But you're running the most lackadaisical investigation I've ever seen. I suspect you tramped around by the river for a few minutes, under the pretense of tracking those wily criminals, just to shut me up."

"I'm not sure that's possible, buttercup."

He knew the minute the sarcastic remark flew from his mouth that it was the wrong thing to say. Cassie was already puffed up with so much indignation that he wondered if she'd pop the delicate buttons on the bodice of her pale blue gown. Not that he would mind, but she looked furious with him.

"You are the most infuriating, uncooperative man I've ever met," she raged. "Furthermore, I intend to launch my own investigation."

"You do that," he suggested flippantly. "We'll see who gets the best results. Another thing—leave that pesky cat outside. He bothers me. Lastly, do *not* drag me outside in the dark to kiss me like that again. I still don't know what the hell that was all about."

He didn't think her bewitching face could turn a deeper shade of red than it was already. He was wrong.

"You know exactly what I was trying to prove. And don't you dare deny that you didn't kiss me back. Not that I'm surprised. I saw the parade of females you entertained at Aunt Louise's party." She cocked head and looked him up and down. "Do you threaten your women with jail time if they don't accommodate you when the mood strikes?"

Jack surged to his feet. "Now hold on, Cass," he protested hotly. "I'm not bribing anyone to shower me with attention. I am not that desperate."

"No? It certainly felt like it to me the other night."

On that parting shot, she exited his office like the whirling dervish she was. Jack lurched around then stalked off to finish freshening up the jail cells. In fact, he'd like to mop up the floor with that aggravating woman. She set off too many turbulent and contradicting emotions inside him. He was entirely too sensitive and reactionary when she was underfoot.

"What the hell does she expect?" he growled at the room at large. "She has me investigating myself and my brothers. How easy is that? Especially with that tormenting, maddening female breathing down my neck every step of the way!"

Cassie stormed from Jack's office and headed for the bank. No matter what, she was going to get some sort of information for her article on the bank holdup. Unfortunately, the moment she entered the bank, the customers stared at her in alarm. Millard Stewart, the bank teller, winced as he stepped back a pace. His rodentlike nose twitched and his narrow-spaced eyes shifted from her to the customer he tended.

Dear God, maybe Jack was right, she thought uneasily. Maybe she had offended too many people with her rousing editorials for reform and her rash reaction to being robbed. But that didn't matter, she rationalized. The pursuit of truth and justice was not an easy path and it wasn't for the faint of heart. Just look how her boss had suffered when he printed the truth in his newspaper.

"I would like to talk to the bank president," Cassie announced when it was her turn at the teller's window.

Millard hitched his thumb over his thin-bladed shoulder. "Mr. Pettigrew says he doesn't wish to be disturbed."

"I'll be back," she said, then turned on her heels.

"I was afraid you'd say that," Millard mumbled.

Squaring her shoulders, Cassie walked out to inhale a breath of fresh spring air. What was wrong with the people in this town? Did they believe those ridiculous rumors circulating about her? In addition to the gossip, she'd gained a reputation as a daredevil and agitator. Next thing she knew folks would be boycotting Bixby restaurant until Aunt Louise asked her to leave town before business dried up completely.

Fifteen minutes later, Cassie noticed a short, well-dressed man in a bowler hat scurrying between the bank and hotel. She presumed the man had conferred with Floyd Pettigrew or Millard—or both—before ducking into the hotel. Assuming the banker was available now, Cassie re-entered the building. She noted all the customers had concluded their business and left.

Millard winced uncomfortably at the sight of her, but

he hurried past the stairs and down the hall to rap on the banker's office door. "Mizz Bixby is here to see you."

"Which one?" Floyd asked.

"The younger one," Millard specified, then motioned for Cassie to veer around the teller's window.

While the mousy little man returned to his daily tasks, Cassie breezed into the private office to see Floyd puffing on his cigar and lounging at his oversize walnut desk. He looked to be a year or two older than Jackson Culpepper—though why she used that maddening marshal as comparison she didn't know.

Floyd's straight, thin hair was reddish-blond. His skin was pale and his eyes were brown. He was mildly handsome and dressed in the finest fashion money could buy. There was an arrogance about Floyd that reminded her of men she'd encountered in the East. But of course, she wasn't looking for a prospective suitor. She wanted to discuss the robberies.

"Are you here to ask for financial support for your progressive causes, my dear? If so, the robbery put a sizable dent in my charity funds."

Although Floyd didn't do her the courtesy of offering her a seat, Cassie sat down then retrieved a notepad from her purse. "I'm writing an article about the holdup. I was hoping you noticed details about the bandits that might aid in their arrest."

"I was more concerned with protecting myself when that big goon pointed his double-barreled shotgun at my chest," Floyd said, then blew lazy circles of smoke around his strawberry-colored head.

"I realize that," she replied. "You reversed direction rather quickly."

He thrust out his chin and squinted at her through a halo of smoke. "Are you implying that I'm a coward, Mizz Bixby?"

She lifted her shoulder in a nonchalant shrug. "I'm a journalist, sir. I try to accurately report what I see."

He regarded her for a long moment. "And if I offer you some facts about the incident, will you see your way clear to striking that comment from your editorial?"

She smiled wryly. "I see why you are the bank president. You are very astute…. Now then, how much money was stolen during the robbery?"

Floyd was suddenly forthcoming with his answers, Cassie noted as she continued the interview. When she glanced sideways, she noticed Millard was watching her closely from the end of the hall. He seemed to be paying particular attention to Floyd's responses. His behavior piqued Cassie's interest and she sought out the teller immediately after she wrapped up her interview with Floyd.

"I would like your input," she insisted as she came to stand beside the teller, who was only a few inches taller than her five-feet-four-inch frame.

Floyd appeared at the office door. "You're keeping Millard from the accounts." He shooed her on her way.

"I do apologize," she said. When Floyd turned to close the door, Cassie leaned over to speak confidentially to Millard. "Your observations about both robberies are important."

Millard glanced anxiously over his shoulder at Floyd's office door. "Now isn't a good time."

"When is?" she whispered.

"Later. I'll contact you later."

Nodding gratefully, Cassie left the empty bank. She

glanced through the pane-glass window to see Millard staring after her. He was as nervous as any man she ever recalled meeting. She had the intuitive feeling that he knew something. *What?* Unfortunately, she had no idea.

Left with no alternative but to wait until Millard sought her out, Cassie hiked off to grab a bite to eat at the café. Then she returned to the office to complete her article.

Chapter Five

Two days later Jack exited the overcrowded jail cells, heaved an exhausted sigh then ambled over to pour himself a steaming cup of coffee.

Jefferson entered the office and paused to take inventory of Jack's torn shirt. "Rough night?"

Jack nodded, then half collapsed in his chair behind his desk. "One of the trail herds camped north of town. Half of those love-starved, liquor-swigging yahoos descended on the town with a vengeance. My deputy and I had to round up several of them and corral them into the jail. They sang their drunken ditties until long after midnight. I didn't get much sleep, though I tried several times to catch a nap in my chair."

"That explains why you didn't make it to the ranch to snuggle up in your own comfy bed." Jefferson strode over to help himself to the coffee warming on the stove. "But this is guaranteed to wake you up."

Jack leaned forward when his brother tossed the morning edition of the *Pepperville Times* on his desk. His blood boiled when he read the front-page headline that leaped up to slap him in the face: Robbery Overlooked by Local Law Enforcement.

"Damn it to hell!" Jack growled after he read the first paragraph of Cassie's article.

"Keep reading. It gets even better," Jefferson said helpfully. "According to Cassie's interview with Floyd Pettigrew, the bandits stole fifteen thousand dollars from the bank, not counting her five thousand and the cash lifted from the other customers."

"That isn't right. We know it for a fact."

"Leave it to Pettigrew to take advantage of the situation." Jefferson scowled sourly then took a cautious sip of coffee.

"I'm sure that shyster is guilty of fraud, but I'm wondering if someone might be conspiring with him," Jack remarked. "I swear something else is going on. We just haven't been able to figure out what it is yet. I don't know what else to do besides keep the pressure on him and see what turns up."

"I agree, but I'd like to catch that redheaded weasel and whoever might be working with him."

"We've taken enough money now that he should have to replace what he's swindled from any accounts. Surely, he's concerned about a panic at the bank. He doesn't know we've been returning the money and valuables to the victims."

"I'm impatient. I'd like to catch that pretentious scoundrel at *something* without another robbery," Jefferson grumbled.

"We need to get inside the bank and take a look at the official ledger, not the one Pettigrew offers for audits."

Jack had first become suspicious when Nate Hudson,

his friend and fellow ex-Ranger turned cattle drover, complained that he couldn't withdraw the money he put in his account last fall to purchase supplies on his way north this spring. Something had to be going on.

Unfortunately, Jack couldn't conduct a straightforward investigation without alerting Pettigrew and sending him scrambling to conceal other fraudulent and unethical activities and destroy the necessary evidence needed to file formal charges. Neither did he want the banker to skip town and force a manhunt. In short, stealing from the shrewd banker was the only way to force his hand or make him replace the operating money. He had to wait and hope Pettigrew made a crucial mistake that left a paper trail.

"He's damn clever," Jefferson said begrudgingly. "I'll give him that."

"But if Pettigrew and his cohort, if there is one, don't slip up, we might have to resort to another robbery in a few weeks, damn it," Jack said, and scowled.

Breaking the law that Jack had sworn to uphold played hell with his conscience. He detested corrupted law enforcement officers, who used the power of their position to acquire wealth, privilege and favors. Although he wasn't out for money, he'd used drastic means to catch a cunning crook, and it needled him constantly.

"Still no report on Pettigrew's background?" Jefferson asked, drawing Jack from his pensive thoughts.

"No. Nothing in Texas. I've contacted authorities in Kansas and Nebraska to check on him. Hopefully I'll hear something by the end of the month."

"In the meantime, Mizz Social Reformer and Public Conscience is lambasting you on the front page of the newspaper," Jefferson teased. "She does have a way with words, even if half the population doesn't agree with her modern thinking. But this—" he tapped his finger on the article "—this might draw the kind of suspicion we don't need."

"Amen to that," Jack muttered, then read the next two paragraphs. His temper flared all over again.

Jefferson stared deliberately at Jack. "So…what are you going to do about Cassie? We don't need folks around here asking the wrong questions. Somehow, I don't think threats issued in the dark of night are going to intimidate her. Otherwise you wouldn't have clashed with her at the bank."

"You're right. Threats challenge her," Jack replied.

When he read the last damning paragraph, he exploded in an angry scowl.

"That's a great finish, isn't it?" Jefferson remarked.

Jack bolted to his feet. His chair rocked back on its hind legs then crashed into the wall.

"Going somewhere, big brother?" Jefferson snickered. "To a public thrashing perhaps? Can I come watch you clash with that gorgeous little hellion?"

"No," Jack snapped. "Stay here and mind the office." He waved his arm in an expansive gesture. "You're hereby deputized."

"Again?" Jefferson complained. "I thought I gave that up when we resigned our Ranger commissions."

"This is your town, too. It's your obligation to protect it while I'm occupied."

"Oh, yeah, how could I forget Dad's last words? 'Make our town a safe place to live, work and raise a family. Put the place on the map, boys. It's your legacy,'" he quoted.

Jack strode out the door with those words ringing in

his ears. *Our* town. *Our* friends and *our* neighbors. You must serve and protect.

After serving in the Civil War and watching Yankees burn towns and homes to the ground, his father, George Washington Culpepper, wanted to create a haven in these Texas hills. Now Jack and his brothers were obliged to defend the community with whatever means necessary.

It didn't help matters when that infuriating female made caustic comments about his lack of attention to the recent robberies. Folks around town didn't understand exactly what was going on, but they kept silent when money, bonuses and stolen items showed up on their doorsteps in the cloak of darkness.

Intent on his purpose, Jack didn't make his customary circle to greet shopkeepers each morning. He set off across town circle and passed the steamy spring where Wilbur Knox took his daily treatment of warm mineral water.

"Morning, Marshal," Wilbur greeted as he poured more hot water into his metal basin. "Saw the newspaper article, did you?"

"Yep." Jack kept right on walking.

"I'll bring the tar and feathers," Wilbur said helpfully.

"I'll let you know if I need 'em."

With a full head of steam, Jack burst into the newspaper office. He saw Cassie hunkered over her desk, holding her poison pen. Probably stabbing him in the back with another article, he predicted.

The moment their eyes locked and clashed, his ill-fated attraction for this maddening female crowded in on his roiling anger. He must be out of his mind to desire a woman who'd made it her mission in life to aggravate the living hell out of him.

Breaking the law to protect the town that bore his family's name was enough of a burden on him and his brothers. But, swear to God, this green-eyed, free-wheeling suffragist had pushed him right to the crumbling edge!

"Apparently, you can read," she smarted off as she nodded toward the newspaper crushed in his fist. "Good to know."

"I'll get to you later," he snarled on his way past her.

At a full boil, Jack stormed into Gerald's office to slam the crinkled newspaper down on his desk. He must have looked ferocious as he felt because Gerald recoiled in his chair.

"Damnation, Gerald!" he fumed. "Don't you have the slightest control over what your *hired help* prints in your newspaper?"

His voice ricocheted around the office like a blasting cannon. "Since when do you have the right to determine how I conduct an investigation and print this slanderous garbage?"

"Right to free speech," Cassie said from behind him.

"Right to free speech, my ass!" he boomed as he rounded on her. As usual, she didn't back down, just raised her chin to a defiant angle.

"You don't see me toting signs to protest your belief that women should have a voice and a vote."

"Of course not," she countered. "That would demand action on your part."

"Do not tell me how to do my job," he said slowly and deliberately.

"Then find my money," she blasted back at him. "Every time I remember how long and hard I worked to repay my debt to Aunt Louise, only to have my money stolen before I could deposit it in the bank, it makes me mad all over again."

Cassie watched Jack's thick black brows flatten over his glittering gold eyes and saw the scowl settle deeply in his bronzed features. She tried not to care that he looked exhausted, unshaven and roughed up.

She'd heard dozens of shots fired during the night and she suspected he'd had his hands full controlling the rowdy cowhands that blew into town like a bad spring storm. However, several days had passed since the robbery and she seemed to be the only one around town who demanded justice and answers. She wasn't going to let up now.

"If you write another derogatory article about me, you are going to have a very serious problem," Jack said through gritted teeth. "I've already heard whispers of tarring and feathering our local barnstorming reformer."

"Planning to look the other way when that happens, Marshal?" she sniped at him.

He took an ominous step toward her. Not to be outdone, she took a bold step toward him. They stood toe-to-toe and eye-to-eye until Gerald wedged his way between them.

"That's enough. Both of you need to calm down." Gerald pushed them an arm's length apart. "Now here's what we're going to do and I refuse to hear any argument from either of you."

He stared unblinkingly at Cassie. "You are going to write a human interest article about how this town came into existence. I should have done it when I first arrived in town, but I've been putting it off. It must have been fate that I procrastinated because you and Jack need to sit down together so he can give you the background and history of our founding fathers."

"You can write it," she said stubbornly, still giving Jack the evil eye—which he returned full force.

"I have nothing to say to this woman," Jack fired back.

"But you *are* going to say it, nonetheless," Gerald demanded sharply. "And Cassie is going to write it all down. Otherwise, I'm going to pen my own editorial about the friction between our do-nothing city marshal and our pushy social reformer who won't let other folks live and let live. I'll blast both of you out of the water." He stared stonily at one then the other. "Do you two understand me or shall I tell you again?"

Cassie nodded jerkily. "I understand you, boss. But I don't like the assignment."

"Same goes for me," Jack said curtly. "But this is *not* going to be an editorial or commentary. Otherwise, I'll refuse to cooperate. It has to be informational only. I'm not sure Mizz Barnstormer can stick to the rules."

"I can do my job, Mr. City Marshal," she sassed him. "You're the one whose competence is in question."

She was fairly certain Jack would have wrapped his lean fingers around her throat and given her a good shaking if Gerald hadn't been standing between them. Jack was tired and angry with her and it showed. But she wasn't happy with him, either. Feeling this unwanted, ridiculously illogical attraction to him didn't help her mood one whit. The most baffling part was that he looked dangerous and rough around the edges, but he *still* aroused and intrigued her.

"Now then, Cassie, get back to work at your desk," Gerald ordered brusquely. "And you, Jack, hightail it to your office. Word around town is that you spent a difficult night rounding up wild cowboys to protect the law-abiding citizens from possible injury. Thank you for that." His arm shot toward the door. "Now go."

Jack wheeled around like a soldier on parade to stalk out, then cursed when Maxwell shot off in front of him. "And keep that damn cat away from me!"

Cassie spun on her heels and marched back to her desk. It was difficult to inject civility into the article she was writing about a wedding that was to take place the upcoming weekend. Honestly, she didn't know what the bride was thinking to agree to marriage. She had enough trouble dealing with that bullheaded do-nothing marshal and they weren't even bound by law to live together.

Cassie huffed out her breath and wondered what it would be like to be married to a brawny, ruggedly handsome, hardheaded, infuriating man like Jackson Culpepper.

"It wouldn't be a question of how long we remained together under the same roof," she said to herself. "It would be a question of who killed each other first."

"Pardon?" Gerald called out to her.

"Nothing. Just thinking unpleasant thoughts out loud," she replied, then focused on her present assignment.

Jack plopped down on the sofa in the ranch house and expelled a weary sigh. After two days and nights of trying to keep a lid on the town, the cattle drovers had stocked supplies, celebrated their hearts out at the saloons and brothels, then moved north toward Dodge City.

"Here," Harrison said as he approached, bearing a tray of food. "The cook took one look at you this evening and decided you needed a hearty feast."

Jack accepted the heaping plate. He hadn't had much time to eat and the smell of food reminded him that he was as hungry as he was tired. At first bite, his taste buds went into full-scale riot.

"You're a lifesaver, Clara. Thank you," Jack called out loudly.

Clara Johnson poked her frizzy gray head around the corner and smiled as she wiped her hands on her apron. "Your mamma told me to take good care of you boys while she went off to tend her sister in Missouri. I'm taking my duties seriously. Now you eat every last bite and I'll bring your dessert."

Jack's mother had been away six months and he was reasonably certain that he and his brothers could have managed without the housekeeper. After all, they had practiced all manner of survival while patrolling the frontier with their Ranger battalion. Still, it was nice to be pampered.

Not that Cassandra, The Hellion Bixby, would cater to any man, he thought sourly. If they were married—God forbid—he might drag himself home, bleeding from gunshots wounds in both arms and legs and she would insist that he fix his own supper.

And warm up something for *her* while he was at it.

What frustrated him to no end was that while he had been having it out with Cassie in the newspaper office, he had actually admired the way she had stood up to him. Obviously, that was an integral part of her character and personality. She had held true to form during the robbery, too.

Secret admiration aside, he was still mad as hell at her for suggesting he was a mediocre law officer at best. Yet, when he compared her to the serene, ordinary women he had accompanied to social events before Cassie arrived, they seemed dull and uninteresting. Damn if he could figure out why. He *liked* calm and predictable. He dealt with plenty of action and excitement on the job.

Refusing to dwell on the maddening female, Jack gobbled up his food while Harrison started a fire in the hearth to ward off the evening chill.

"I hear you nearly came to blows with Cassie over the newspaper article," Harrison remarked.

"That rumor was grossly overexaggerated. We simply shouted at each other," he clarified. "That probably wasn't the smartest thing I could have done." He took another bite of tender steak. "But I was tired and cranky. The article set me off. And so did she when she sassed me."

Harrison sank down beside him then glanced toward the hall to make sure Clara couldn't overhear him. "What are we going to do about returning Cassie's money and timepiece? That would probably encourage her to back off."

"It might help, but if her money ended up on her doorstep in the dark of night she might ask too many questions. She has too many of them already. I've been contemplating *loaning* her the money."

Harrison nodded his dark head. "Better a loan than the Western version of Robin Hood returning her loot." He glanced cautiously over his shoulder again to ensure Clara wasn't stirring about. "How long before you think Pettigrew will be forced to make a move?"

"Soon, I hope. I'd rather not make another forced withdrawal if we don't have to. I sent a formal inquiry to the state legislature, but they move slower than turtles."

"If Pettigrew is embezzling money from accounts to pad his pockets, he will have to print more of his worthless banknotes eventually," Harrison predicted. "He could have them printed elsewhere and we wouldn't know it. There's only one place in town where he can do it." His intense blue eyes drilled into Jack. "Do you think Gerald Nash might be involved in this embezzling scheme, or whatever the hell's going on?"

"I'd like to think not." Jack frowned speculatively. "I doubt he can print banknotes with Cassie underfoot."

"Maybe we should include Cassie in our investigation—"

"Involve whom?" Jefferson questioned as he entered the room, carrying three tall glasses of whiskey.

"Thanks for the drink." Jack took a welcome sip. "We're discussing Cassandra Bixby."

"I vote to involve her. Maybe that will get her off your back, Jack."

"And put her in jeopardy," he reminded his brothers. "The more she knows the greater the threat she poses to Pettigrew." He glanced somberly at Harrison. "I don't have to tell you how daring she can be in the face of danger. There's not much difference between her and a cornered Comanche. Both will fight you to the death."

"No kidding." Harrison grimaced then sipped his drink. "I've known men who aren't as fearless as she is."

"One of us should court Cassie to calm her down. How about you, Jeff?" Jack suggested.

Someone should do it, Jack thought. Not *him*, of course.

"Me?" Jefferson hooted. *"You* were the one we saw sucking the breath out of her. Not to mention you had your hands—"

"That's enough," Jack barked sharply.

Jefferson grinned in wry amusement. "No need to bite

my head off, big brother. Harrison and I know what we saw…and we saw plenty."

"It's the only time I haven't seen her fight back," Harrison pointed out, then stared slyly at Jack. "It makes you wonder what that means, doesn't it?"

Jack muttered under his breath when thoughts of the disconcerting incident exploded in his mind. He downed the last swallow of whiskey, but it didn't diminish the remembered desire that had overwhelmed him the night his self-control abandoned him and he'd taken intimate liberties with Cassie.

"I'm going to get some shut-eye," he announced as he rose from the sofa.

"Sweet dreams," Harrison teased unmercifully—as only an ornery brother could.

There was nothing sweet about the hot, forbidden fantasy that accosted Jack when he fell asleep. He awakened at two o'clock in the morning, tormented and aroused. He cursed Cassie for having the starring role in his dream then he pounded his pillow and willed himself to go back to sleep.

He did…eventually.

Still restless and tormented by her conflicting feelings toward Jack, Cassie rapped on the door of her aunt's upstairs apartment. She needed to talk to someone. Aunt Louise was always the person she'd come to for comfort and support.

But tonight she knocked on the door and was met with silence. She knocked again, louder this time. "Aunt Louise? Are you all right?"

A few moments later Cassie heard her aunt scurrying

around on the other side of the door. "Whatever it is, hon, it has to wait until morning. I have a horrendous headache. Good night, dear. I'll see you tomorrow."

Disappointed, Cassie descended the outdoor exit that led into the side alley between the newspaper office and the restaurant. She wondered if it was her imagination, or if she hadn't heard the murmur of a man's voice coming from behind her aunt's door just now.

On the way to the boardinghouse, Cassie noticed the same unidentified gentleman she had seen at the back exit of the bank before she interviewed Floyd Pettigrew and the perpetually nervous teller. The stout, well-dressed gent appeared from the inky shadows in the side alley by the bank and walked briskly across town circle. He paused to dip his hand in the steaming water then disappeared into the trees on the rise of ground above the springs.

Frowning curiously, Cassie glanced back at the bank. She noticed a silhouette moving through the flickering lantern light glowing in the window. A moment later, the faint light appeared around the edges of the drawn curtain in the upstairs window. She would dearly love to know if Pettigrew—or Millard Stewart—had attended a clandestine meeting with the mysterious stranger.

The impulse to take a look around nearly overwhelmed her, but she forced herself to continue on her way. She contemplated her interview with Floyd Pettigrew and remembered the way the scrawny bank teller kept darting glances at her from the far end of the hall. Millard had insisted that he'd contact her later, but he hadn't sought her out. Facing a deadline, she'd had to finish the article and put it into print without his interview. She wondered if it had been a stall tactic or if he'd been threatened and feared lethal repercussions if he contacted her.

Instinct warned her that something peculiar was going on at the bank. She wished she knew if the teller was reluctant to speak out for fear of losing his job or fear of being beaten. Or maybe he was the outlaws' contact, she mused pensively. Was he the inside informant who knew when the bank was most vulnerable? Was Millard relaying messages to his cohorts so they'd know when Marshal Culpepper was out of town?

Her thoughts trailed off when she entered the boardinghouse and heard movement at the far end of the hall.

"There you are," Suzannah called softly as she moved into the light. "I was about to come looking for you." She motioned for Cassie to join her in her room.

"What's wrong?" Cassie asked in concern as Suzannah closed the door behind them.

"I wanted to talk to you about those outrageous rumors spreading around town," she said.

"Which ones?" Cassie sniffed distastefully as she plunked down in the chair beside the small round table in the corner. "The ones about how I hate men? Or the ones about how I've incited turmoil among women with my radical views?"

Oddly enough, those didn't bother her as much as the one *she'd* heard about Jack and Jefferson Culpepper pursuing Doreen Rowe. That tidbit of information upset her more than the personal attacks. Why? Cassie refused to delve too deeply to determine why the thought of Jack with that prissy, blue-eyed blonde annoyed her.

Just because Cassie had kissed Jack and felt her body go up in flames didn't imply that he meant something special to her or that he was interested in her. Heavens, they annoyed each other most of the time. It galled her to no end that she spent so much time dwelling on their love-hate relationship. Yet, despite everything, Jackson Culpepper could kiss a woman until every rational thought flew right out of her head. Even the potent memory of their explosive encounter in the dark alley made her body sizzle and burn.

"I want you to know that I am doing everything within my power to defend you when people speak ill of you and I will continue to do so," Suzannah said loyally.

"You are a good friend, Suz. Thank goodness I have you. Although dozens of women are eager to join the cause of equal rights and social reform, I seem to be making enemies of the men."

Suzannah chuckled as she walked over to the oak bureau to pour them both a drink of peach brandy. "That's to be suspected. Men cringe at the prospect of giving up their power. I've heard complaints from them while waiting tables at the café. Allowing women to have a voice in government and share equal partnerships in marriage or business ventures unsettles them. If that isn't a deciding factor against a woman marrying and giving up what few rights she does have, I don't know what is."

Cassie nodded in agreement then sipped her brandy. "Men don't seem to mind if a single *madam* owns and operates a bordello, as long as they get what they want and what they pay for. Yet, they expect to lord over their wives and have the final say without the slightest input or objection."

Suzannah bobbed her dark head. "Infuriating, isn't it?"

"It's the double standards that I dislike most."

"As for the nonsense about you hating men, I suggest you allow yourself to be escorted around town by a reputable man. That should put an end to the rumors."

Cassis smirked. "I'd have to *pay* someone to be my escort to compensate him for being ostracized for consorting with the enemy."

"How about Marshal Culpepper?" Suzannah suggested. "He commands considerable respect."

Cassie nearly choked on her drink. Suzannah hurried over to whack her between the shoulder blades until she could breathe normally.

"Jack dislikes me," Cassie wheezed. "I offended him with the article that hinted at his lack of attention to the robbery case."

"There is that." Suzannah winced as she sat down at the table. "But perhaps one of his brothers might be persuaded to help you bury the cruel rumor. They belong to the founding family, after all."

Cassie took the opening. "I heard Jack and Jefferson were pursuing Doreen Rowe."

"I wouldn't be surprised if that isn't wishful thinking on Doreen's part," Suzannah replied. "I went to school with that snippy girl who grew into a snippy woman. She's never been happy unless men bow and scrape over her. I would imagine that she considers any of the Culpeppers a prize catch. Who wouldn't? Jefferson is definitely the most attractive, but the other two run a close second."

Jefferson? Cassie stared speculatively at her friend. Apparently, Suz had a crush on the middle Culpepper. But as far as Cassie was concerned, Jackson was the one who inspired wild, feminine fantasies.

"I remember when the three of them returned to town

after they finished their service with the Rangers," Suz recalled with a smile. "Bigger than life. Handsome as the day is long."

Judging by the dreamy expression on Suz's attractive face, she was Jefferson's secret admirer. Cassie wasn't against doing some matchmaking for her friend. Might as well, she thought. Her quest to find the thieves that stole her money kept hitting a dead end.

"I better get to bed," Cassie said as she came to her feet. "Gerald is making me interview the marshal in the morning for an informative article about the town founders."

"That should be interesting. I've heard bits and pieces about how the town came into existence and the reason for its wagon-wheel-shaped layout. I'll be looking forward to reading your story."

Cassie studied her friend, then surveyed the room that looked much like her own. Suddenly, Suz looked lonely sitting there, surrounded by plain furnishings. There were no family photographs or interior decorations to make the room seem homey and welcoming. Come to think of it, Suz never mentioned her connection to this town.

"Where did you come from?" Cassie asked curiously.

Suz tried to hide her stricken expression, but not before Cassie noticed the flash of emotion in her eyes.

"I'm from a nameless town in the middle of nowhere. Past is past and I prefer to look ahead, not back."

In other words, Suz refused to resurrect the painful memories and emotions that prompted her to take refuge in Pepperville. She wondered if Suz had endured a difficult situation, much like Cassie had. Living with her mother's spiteful sister and family, who delighted in making her the brunt of their jokes and spent her inheritance as if it were their own, had been hellish for Cassie. It was an unjust practice she wanted to correct with social reform.

"I'm lucky Aunt Louise rescued me from my own misery," Cassie confided. "You need to know that when you're ready, I'll be here to lend a sympathetic ear, Suz. You are my friend and I'll do whatever necessary to see you happy."

Suzannah smiled. "Thank you, Cass. That's comforting to hear."

Cassie left the room, vowing to place Jefferson Culpepper in Suzannah's direct path—somehow. Whatever it was that tormented her friend, Cassie predicted that romantic encounters with Jefferson might satisfy her secret longings and make her forget her troubled past.

Chapter Six

Jack involuntarily cringed when he saw Cassie pass in front of the office window. His first reaction to seeing her alluring figure in the trim-fitting yellow gown was instant awareness of her as a woman. She reminded him of sunshine bursting through low-hanging clouds. His eager anticipation of seeing her quickly turned to unease. The woman incited too much conflict inside him.

When she swept into the office, sunlight glinted off her honey-gold hair and glowed on the creamy flesh exposed by her scoop-necked dress. To his bemusement, she walked over to place a silver dollar on his desk. His brows climbed higher when she graced him with a beaming smile.

"What the hell is going on?" he asked suspiciously.

"I'm bribing you."

"It's against the law," he reminded her.

She wrinkled her nose at him. "Well then, after our interview, I am inviting you out to lunch at my aunt's café and I will pay for your meal and your companionship."

He eased back to regard her warily. "What's the catch?"

She pushed the coin across his scarred desk with her forefinger then looked up at him from beneath long, thick lashes. "You have to be nice to me for a couple of hours."

"For one dollar?" he teased.

"I was robbed recently. I'm short of funds and this is all I can spare."

Jack smiled wryly. "Does your seeking my company have something to do with those rumors we both know couldn't be further from the truth? About hating men?"

Her face flushed slightly, but to her credit, she squared her shoulders and nodded her head. "Yes, so please join me, unless it upsets the rivalry between you and Jefferson in your romantic pursuit of Doreen Rowe. Wouldn't want to cause friction, you know."

Jack chuckled. "Really? I thought that was your middle name." He came to his feet then tucked the coin in his pocket. "I suppose we might as well dispel that rumor, too. Jefferson can have her. I'm bowing out."

She peered up at him when he took her arm to escort her from the office. "Jefferson is infatuated with Doreen? A pity, I had someone else in mind for him."

"Who?"

"Suzannah Mitchell."

"A matchmaking suffragist?" he teased. "Are you sure you have time for all your causes?"

His heart nearly melted down his ribs when she flashed him an impish grin and said, "Yes, I do. In fact, I'm a very complex individual, Marshal. I actually have a gentler side, believe it or not."

Jack couldn't help himself. He said, "You do?" Then he grinned rakishly and stared at the alluring curve of her derriere. "Ah, yes, there it is."

When he leaned around her to open the door, his arm brushed her shoulder inadvertently and he caught a whiff of her enticing scent. It saturated his senses in nothing flat. He hadn't realized how close his head was to hers until he found himself staring into her fathomless green eyes that sparkled like dew-covered evergreen trees. The urge to kiss her, right there and then, assailed him. He stared at her Cupid's bow lips and nearly groaned aloud when hungry desire hit him below the belt.

He was headed straight to hell—he was sure of it.

Cassie was being nice to him to redeem her reputation, which had been unjustly degraded by vicious rumors. She wanted to be seen with him and to call a temporary truce. And all Jack wanted was to find somewhere private to kiss and caress her until the tormenting desire she inspired in him ran its course and he regained his sanity.

It required every smidgen of self-discipline that he'd mastered to step away from forbidden temptation, but he managed the feat. He opened the door and noticed Wilbur Knox had parked himself on the wooden bench, as usual. Wilbur stared pointedly at him, then focused on Cassie. His expression indicated that he didn't approve of the company Jack was keeping.

"Do me a favor and mind the office until my deputy shows up," Jack requested.

Wilbur nodded jerkily. "Be glad to, Marshal. You oughta fire that deputy of yours. I don't think he could show up on time, even for his own funeral."

"Is your gout better today?" Cassie inquired.

The older man's gray brows shot up his forehead and his defensive demeanor toward her fizzled out when she flashed him a disarming smile. "Yep, as a matter of fact. Took my treatment at the spring this morning. Helps every time."

"I'm glad to hear it. Of course, when word gets around that the warm mineral water has curative qualities, people will flock here in droves. There are such places in Indian Territory and in Arkansas that have attracted notice."

"Don't want folks crowding my space," Wilbur mumbled.

"Neither do I," Jack agreed as he escorted Cassie down the boardwalk. "We'll be at the ranch then stop at the café for lunch if you need me, Wilbur."

When they were out of earshot, Cassie glanced curiously at him. "We're going to do the newspaper interview at your ranch?"

"Why not? That's where my grandfather and our family initially settled after the war."

"I'd like to see your ranch," she enthused.

"Have you noticed how much attention we're receiving?" he asked as they strolled across town circle to rent a buggy at the livery for their drive to the ranch.

She smiled. "That's the whole idea, Marshal."

"This is definitely going to cost you more than a dollar, buttercup," he teased. "You're getting a lot of mileage for your money."

Cassie perched on the buggy seat, marveling at the spacious stone-and-timber ranch house that sat on a rise of ground overlooking a spring-fed creek that meandered through a lush pasture. Cattle and horses grazed peacefully in the distance.

"I can see why your family chose this location. It's

spectacular. It looks as if these rolling hills and wooded creeks go on forever."

She watched Jack smile proudly as he scanned the property. "According to my parents, this land called to them. I understood what they meant when I returned from my tour of duty with the Rangers. I felt as if I were at peace for the first time in five years."

Cassie pointed to the pale wisp of smoke rising from the far side of the hill. "Is that a campfire?"

Jack shook his raven head. "That's steam, not smoke. Another warm spring trickles from the rocky hillside. There's another one where the tributary merges with a hot spring. The temperature is very nearly perfect for bathing, even in the dead of winter."

"May I see it?" she asked enthusiastically.

Ten minutes later, they were hiking uphill to the spring. A compact cabin sat on the hillside near a grove of trees. Cassie decided that if her crusade for reform provoked menfolk to run her out of town she would hide out in the secluded cabin. She could soak for hours in the spring.

"The tribes that roamed this area, before they were removed to Indian Territory, referred to this sacred spot as the Altar of the Moon. You'd know why if you saw starlight reflecting off the hollowed-out pool at midnight," Jack remarked.

Captivated, Cassie removed her shoes and hiked up her skirt to soak the lower half of her legs in the spacious pool. "Ah, this is the closest to heaven on earth I've ever come."

She glanced over her shoulder, wondering why Jack hadn't commented. Pleasure flooded through her when she realized he'd fixed his amber-eyed gaze on her bare legs. It was gratifying to know that he wasn't completely immune to her. For certain, she was entirely too aware of him.

When she caught him staring, he met her gaze. "I think you better start firing questions at me. You annoy the hell out of me at times, buttercup, but I'm still a man and you're too damn attractive for your own good."

She batted her eyes at him and drawled, "Why, Jackson Culpepper, I do declare. Are you saying that *you* find me desirable?"

His gaze swept from her bare feet to her knees then settled on the swells of her breasts. "You're an intelligent woman. What do you think?"

Heat that had nothing whatsoever to do with the warm water bubbling around her flashed through her body and caused her face to pulse with color. "Perhaps you do," she murmured.

"There's no perhaps about it."

"At least you're an honest man," she replied.

He looked away from her. "Ask your questions. I have to return to the office after our early lunch to fill out paperwork on horse thieving at a nearby ranch."

"For starters, tell me how the town came to have its unique shape."

"My father thought it would be clever to have the center of town as a hub for activities and the streets as spokes," he explained as he ambled over to park himself on a boulder overlooking the clear spring. "My mother thought it was a grand idea, too, and her opinion held equal importance."

"Equality." Cassie smiled as she paddled her feet in the water. "I think I'd like your mother."

"No doubt," he agreed. "She insisted on working

beside my father and grandfather to establish the ranch and create a community of upstanding citizens."

"Where is your mother?"

"Nursing Aunt Hilda back to health in Missouri. She's been away since last fall. When my aunt recovers enough for travel, after her bout with rheumatism, they are coming here together. Aunt Hilda is eager to try soaking in the mineral waters and anxious to be near her only family members."

"Tell me about establishing the community," Cassie requested as she reluctantly removed her feet from the invigorating water.

"My father, George Washington Culpepper—"

She burst out in a lighthearted giggle. "That explains you and your brothers' patriotic names."

Jack grinned as he ambled over to help her to her feet. "We are a patriotic clan. Our parents named us Andrew Jackson Culpepper, Thomas Jefferson Culpepper and William Harrison Culpepper. As for the town, my father advertised for settlers and shopkeepers who were interested in a civilized community. He offered reduced rates for town lots and interviewed newcomers to make sure they shared his values. That is, until some property owners sold out to bordellos and saloons then took their large profit and left town."

Jack scooped up her shoes and escorted her toward the cabin. "It was Mother's idea to lobby the legislature so we could become the county seat of the new area opened to settlement. The town won government jobs and we received contracts for cutting roads and construction projects."

"Smart woman, your mother."

"Very. With a county courthouse to house various

government agencies, we could provide dozens of jobs for citizens. The influx of trail herds came later. It increases sales, but it also brings cardsharps, drifters and rowdy cowboys."

"The price of progress," Cassie murmured as she padded barefoot alongside Jack. "I heard reports of the arrests you've made on the rowdy side of town. Busy week, not to mention heroic actions on your part."

Jack shrugged his broad shoulders. "For the most part this isn't as dangerous as battling renegade Indians and violent outlaws as a Ranger. Plus, my brothers are nearby for reinforcement. They are competent gunfighters and I've deputized them occasionally."

He opened the door to the three-room cabin and Cassie fell in love with the rustic handmade furniture, the braided rug that covered the planked floor and the grand views from the windows.

"I'll take it," she declared.

Jack studied her with an odd expression then said, "A citified Yankee like you would be satisfied in an isolated, unadorned cabin like this one?"

"I'll have you know I spent as many years in Texas as I did back East," she informed him crispy. "I like it here."

"It also suited my mother," he reported. "She lived here with my father and my grandfather until they could afford to construct the ranch house, barns and bunkhouse."

Cassie sank down in a chair to put on her shoes. "You don't have a very high opinion of me, do you, Jackson?"

He tossed her a lopsided smile. "You don't have a high opinion of me, do you, Cassandra? Preconception and misconceptions caused us to get off on the wrong foot."

An odd sensation trickled down Cassie's spine and

niggled her thoughts when Jack stood over her as she tied her shoelaces. There was something strangely familiar and unnerving about looking up at him. She'd experienced the odd feeling before. What was there about him that bothered her? She wished she could figure it out.

The thought flitted off when he pulled her to her feet and into his arms.

"I've wanted to do this all morning," he murmured huskily.

Then he kissed her with deliberate thoroughness and without the slightest warning. The unexpected embrace made it impossible for Cassie to do anything except respond instinctively to the feel of his powerful arms gathering her up and drawing her against the muscular planes and contours of his body. His mouth came down on hers again with hungry impatience and she opened her lips to him. She became dizzy and lightheaded when he practically stole the breath from her lungs. Then he offered it back with such amazing tenderness that she practically melted into a gooey puddle on the planked floor.

She didn't voice the slightest objection when he hooked his hand beneath her knee and guided her leg around his hip. She felt his throbbing length against her inner thigh, felt his hand drift beneath her skirt to skim her hip and lower abdomen. Raw, disturbing and powerful sensations riddled her body as he caressed her familiarly.

"Tell me to stop." His warm breath hovered over the side of her neck, leaving hot chills in its wake.

"In a minute," she whispered, brazenly sketching the hard length of his arousal through the fabric of his breeches.

"One or the other of us needs to be arrested," he said as he pulled the pins from her hair, letting the tangle of curls cascade over her shoulders. "I think it should be *you* since *I'm* the one wearing the badge."

Heat pooled in the core of her being when he nimbly unfastened the buttons on her bodice then caressed her nipple with thumb and forefinger of his right hand. His left hand continued on its scintillating course to trace the burning ache he'd ignited between her thighs.

Cassie's senses reeled and her inhibitions darted away from the bonfire that billowed inside her. Forbidden pleasure scorched her each place he touched, and aching need burgeoned until she was throbbing with the want of him.

She couldn't recall precisely how and when they came to be in the bedroom, rolling across the bed that was covered with a buffalo skin blanket. But they were there, clutching desperately at each other. His hands were all over her and his lips seared a burning path across her bare breasts. Her skirts rode high on her thighs while her hand tunneled beneath his shirt to explore his hair-roughened chest and the washboard muscles of his belly.

She boldly dipped her hand beneath the band of his breeches—and found herself flat on her back. Jack's lean, hard body covered hers and she squirmed restlessly beneath him, needing more than the teasing caresses he'd offered.

He propped himself on his elbows and stared down at her with blazing amber eyes. "You're driving me loco," he rasped as he ground his erection against her.

"You started this and I can't find the will to stop it."

Cassie couldn't remember wanting anyone or anything as much as she wanted Jack. He had set off so many emotions and sensations inside her that he left her breathless and impatient. She wasn't sure how to appease this ravenous need burning inside her. But the one thing she did know was that the intensity of pleasure radiating through every part of her being was impossible to fight.

Panting for breath, burning with the kind of desire she'd never realized existed, she stared into Jack's ruggedly handsome face and focused on his sensuous lips. He lowered his tousled head and kissed her with amazing tenderness. A carefully guarded corner of her heart crumbled in her chest.

Jackson Culpepper—part-time antagonist, part-time forbidden fantasy—made her feel the most indescribable sensations she'd ever experienced. Cassie linked her hands behind his neck and arched against him as he gyrated suggestively against her. She resented the layers of clothing that separated them, wondered how it would feel to be heart to heart and flesh to flesh with him.

It was what she wanted. Worse, it became the *only* thing she needed. She kissed him desperately as her hands drifted from his broad shoulders to his muscled back then down to his hips. She arched reflexively against him, savoring the scent, taste and feel of him as he glided his fingertips over her sensitive flesh…

"Yoo-hoo! Is somebody in there? Hey, you with the horse and buggy sitting by the springs! You're on private property!"

Jack leaped off the bed as if he'd suffered a snakebite. The sound of Harrison's voice rolling through the cabin snapped him out of the mindless haze of desire so fast that he staggered to keep his balance. He stared down at Cassie's honey-gold hair splayed across the pillow in disarray. Then his devouring gaze settled on her bare breasts, which spilled from the bodice of her yellow gown thanks to his obsessive need to touch her familiarly. Her silky thighs were exposed—because he'd dared to explore the secrets of her curvaceous body and he hadn't been satisfied until he felt her warm heat against his questing fingertips.

"Hey, you in there! You're trespassing. Come out with your hands up," Harrison shouted gruffly.

Scowling at being caught in a compromising situation with Cassie, who looked so damn tempting and vulnerable that it was killing him to back away, Jack managed to lurch around. He dragged in a steadying breath and tried to pull himself together. He had to intercept his youngest brother before he embarrassed Cassie.

"It's me, Harry!" Jack called out as he scrambled to tuck in his shirt. In afterthought, he whirled around to yank Cassie's skirt down to her ankles and tug at her gaping bodice—in case Harrison barged in unexpectedly.

Cassie was still lying there with a bewildered look on her flushed face. Cursing himself up one side and down the other, Jack headed for the parlor and partially closed the bedroom door behind him.

"Jack? What the hell are you doing up here? Why are you driving a buggy?" Harrison stuffed both pearl-handled pistols into his holsters as he strode into the parlor.

"I brought Cassie up here to see the cabin while she's interviewing me for the newspaper article about the town's origin and history."

A slow, wicked smile settled on Harrison's face as he assessed Jack's mussed hair and twisted clothing. "And which view from our homestead cabin did she enjoy most?"

Jack wanted to choke his little brother—all six feet two inches of him—when he waggled his dark brows and winked. Damn his ornery hide.

"I should've let you drown in the river when you were nine," he muttered spitefully.

"Yeah, well, it's too late now. You missed your chance," Harrison teased, his blue eyes twinkling devilishly. "Thank you for that, by the way. You'll always be my hero."

Jack plunked down in the nearest chair when he caught sight of Cassie at the bedroom door. He was always cautious about standing beside either of his brothers after the bank robberies. You just couldn't be too careful when a smart, observant female like Cassie was underfoot. God help all of them if she ever figured out who had robbed her.

When she entered the room, Jack gave her high marks for the regal way she carried herself. She held her head in a dignified manner and she was buttoned up in a respectable fashion. Except for her hair. He'd pulled out the pins in his eagerness to sink his fingers into those silky strands and there was no telling where those pins had landed.

"Good morning, Harrison," she greeted politely. "I'm very impressed with this cabin and the spectacular scenery. The story of how the Culpepper family established this ranch and the town is truly fascinating. How does it feel to be a part of the founding family?"

Harrison shrugged nonchalantly and moved a little farther away from Jack—just in case.

"It's like Jack says, founding this town makes us feel responsible for the safety and prosperity of its citizens. The town was once a part of Wagon Wheel Ranch. We campaigned long and hard to get a stagecoach line to deliver service from our community to Fort Worth. It's rewarding to be a part of history."

"Does it outrage you when bandits descend upon your

town to steal hard-earned money from your friends and neighbors?"

"Definitely." Harrison didn't miss a beat. "I don't know who is responsible or why Pepperville has been targeted. Perhaps they are random strikes. Perhaps it's premeditated. But I'm sure Jack will puzzle it out and the bandits will receive just punishment."

Cassie elevated a perfectly arched brow. "Would you join your brother's posse to help him track the outlaws?"

Harrison turned his head to stare at Jack. "I would in a minute. We defended each other's back during firefights as Rangers. He was my extra pair of eyes and Jeff was my extra set of ears while we were on patrol. We stand together."

Before Cassie fired more questions at Harrison, Jack surged off the chair and shoveled her toward the door. "We better get back to town."

"It was a pleasure to see you again, Harrison," Cassie said. "Thank you for answering a few questions."

Harrison flashed her one of the charming smiles he was famous for with the young women—from here to the Pecos. "Anything to help," he declared. "Also, I hope I didn't alarm you when I showed up. I protect our family property from trespassers whenever necessary."

When Cassie pried her arm from his grasp, Jack glanced back to see her take a bold step toward Harrison. Although her face flushed slightly, she stared him squarely in the eye.

"Are you going to hold this incident, and the one outside the café the night of my aunt's party, over me?"

Harrison chuckled unrepentantly. "If I need to I will."

They stared at each other for a long moment before Jack said, "He's kidding. Tell her you're kidding, Harry."

"I'm kidding," Harrison said very dutifully.

Her eyes glittered with undaunted spirit, her lips twitched in amusement as she glanced back at Jack. "You really should have drowned him when you had the chance."

"I won't make the mistake again," Jack said, teasing his brother. "Care to join us in town for lunch, Harry?"

"Some other time perhaps. We're branding weaning calves to send up the trail to Dodge next week."

"Did you contract with the Hudson Cattle Company again?"

"Yep. Reputable and reliable as always."

"Nate Hudson was in our Ranger battalion," Jack explained to Cassie as they hiked downhill to the buggy. "Nate lost the lower half of his left arm in a fiery gun battle, but it hasn't slowed him down. He can still rope and ride with the best of them."

"You've led an adventurous life. I envy that," she commented as he assisted her into the buggy.

"Nothing quite as adventurous as this morning," he mumbled as he stared back at Harrison who lounged on the stoop. "Damn brothers. You can't turn around without bumping into one of them."

"Even though they have seen me at my weakest moments, I still like both of your brothers."

"Good. I'll give them to you free of charge." Jack snapped the reins over the horse and sent the buggy bouncing along the rough road that led to town.

Chapter Seven

Cassie was pleased to see all eyes zero in on her and Jack when they entered Bixby Café. By then she had regained her composure—after the embarrassing incident at the cabin. It was glaringly apparent she couldn't trust herself alone with the brawny marshal.

For reasons beyond her comprehension, Jack had unleashed her inhibitions the instant he kissed her, causing her to lose the self-control she valued so highly. Indeed, she barely recognized herself when she was in his arms, matching him kiss for desperate kiss and caress for bold caress.

"Good afternoon," Suzannah greeted as she approached their table. She nodded politely to Jack, then leaned down to wink confidentially at Cassie.

"We'll take Aunt Louise's special," Cassie requested without preamble. "The marshal has to return to his office shortly and I'm behind in my duties at the newspaper office."

"By all means, go ahead and order for me," Jack teased.

"I'm sorry. That was presumptuous," she mumbled.

Suzannah waited expectantly but Jack shooed her on her way. "The special is fine. Everything Louise cooks is delicious and I'll eat whatever you bring me."

Aunt Louise passed Suzannah on the way to their table. "Good afternoon, Marshal, Cassie. Lunch is on the house." Louise cast Jack a wide smile. "Thank you for keeping those boisterous cowboys out of my café. I heard that wild bunch kept you busy several nights with their carousing."

Jack nodded his raven head. "Thankfully, they headed north with their herd. Dodge City's marshal will have to deal with them now. There is another herd camped on our ranch, but ordinarily, they're an orderly bunch."

"I never mind the extra business," Aunt Louise remarked. "But I don't want my café ransacked." Tossing out one last smile, she spun toward the kitchen. "You two enjoy lunch."

Cassie scanned the café to see that she and Jack were still the main attraction. Her gaze landed on Doreen Rowe, who was dressed in a fluffy blue gown, trimmed with dozens of rows of ruffles and a diving neckline that advertised her full breasts to their best advantage. The attractive blonde glowered at Cassie while she abandoned her male companion at the corner table to make a beeline toward Jack.

Fascinated, Cassie studied Doreen's drumroll walk and wondered how the woman could manage the feat without throwing out her hip. Doreen's glare transformed into a dazzling smile that displayed her dimples when Jack noticed her.

"Hello, Jack," Doreen gushed as she leaned down to buss his bronzed cheek. "Come by for supper this evening. I'll prepare a homemade feast for you."

"Thanks, but I'm on duty this evening."

"Then I'll deliver the meal to the jail. I can share your enjoyable companionship for a half hour."

You had to hand it to Doreen. If there was something—or someone—she wanted, she went after it. She would make a sensational advocate for social reform if she weren't so focused on hounding Jack or Jefferson until they gave in and offered her a much-wanted marriage proposal.

Doreen patted Cassie's shoulder with pretended civility then leaned close to her ear and hissed, "Don't think I don't know what you're doing, you devious witch. But I promise I'll make you pay dearly for trying to steal Jack away from me."

"Make a note, Marshal," Cassie commented. "If something happens to me, I want Doreen's name at the top of the suspect list."

Doreen's striking blue eyes flashed fire at Cassie before she struck a sophisticated pose and manufactured another charming smile for Jack. "I have no idea what she's talking about. But then, we all know Cassandra likes to stir trouble." She pressed another kiss to Jack's cheek. "I'll see you this evening," she insisted before she sauntered away.

"What did she say to you?" Jack asked when Doreen was out of earshot.

"She's going to make me sorry I'm beating her time with you. I didn't tell her that I paid for your escort services, because she might try the same tactic."

Jack smiled wryly. "Next time you ask for my company, the price will double. I might have to serve as your personal bodyguard to fend off your attackers."

"I think I can handle Doreen," she said confidently.

"Hers isn't the first threat I've received as a journalist or a reform activist."

Suzannah set two plates of steaming food in front of them and Cassie dug in like a field hand. Hiking around Culpepper Ranch and burning off another kind of energy at the homestead had left her famished.

Thirty minutes later she and Jack exited the café—with all eyes on them again. In Doreen's case, it was a vicious glare, but Cassie ignored her. Doreen was the type of woman who hated competition. She wasn't satisfied unless she conquered every male heart and added it to her collection.

"Be careful that Doreen doesn't poison your supper after you were seen in public with me," Cassie teased as she and Jack prepared to part company on the boardwalk. "I'd hate for her to take her anger for me out on you…."

Her voice trailed off when she spotted the same unidentified gent who had appeared from the alley to pass beside the mineral spring in town circle recently. "Do you know who he is?" Cassie asked as the stout, well-dressed man strode quickly down Culpepper Avenue.

Jack surveyed the stranger's retreating back. "He doesn't look familiar."

"I saw him sneaking around the bank after dark the other night. Then I noticed lantern light drifting past the teller's counter and up the steps. I also saw him scurrying from the back door of the bank the other day. He might be staying at the hotel or maybe meeting someone there. I'm curious what's going on."

Jack glanced up sharply and frowned. "What are you suggesting?"

"I'm wondering if someone in the bank is conspiring

with those two bandits," she explained. "The teller seemed tense and nervous while I interviewed Floyd about the robbery. Millard said he'd contact me later, but I never heard from him. I wonder if the well-dressed stranger is connected to the robberies."

"I'll check into it." Jack pivoted on his heels. "I don't want the stranger to know I'm keeping an eye on him, though. He won't incriminate himself if he thinks he's being watched."

"If you keep surveillance on him, maybe he'll lead you to the bandits and you can solve the case."

Jack nodded mutely then strode off to follow the unidentified stranger at a distance.

Cassie veered toward the general store to pick up a few supplies then literally bumped into Edgar Forrester, the assistant blacksmith and robbery victim. Edgar bit down on his stubby cigar and glowered at her as she backed up a step.

"I saw you playin' up to the marshal," he accused harshly. "What are you tryin' to do? Make him come around askin' questions about the robbery that I ain't gonna answer?"

"It's his job to investigate," she insisted. "You should have given the information to him voluntarily."

"Well, I still got nothin' to say about it. And I'm mad as hell at you for puttin' those independent ideas and that nonsense about equality in my wife's head. Mildred stamped off last night and didn't come back. That's *your* fault," he growled as he purposely collided with her shoulder, knocking her sideways as he lumbered off.

"Bullheaded bully," she mumbled as she strode into the general store to purchase her supplies.

A few minutes later, she exited the store to see

Maxwell darting from the alley. She wrinkled her nose at the cat's unpleasant order. "You've been crawling into garbage cans again, haven't you?" she muttered at the cat.

With the black cat at her heels, she hiked across town circle to return to the newspaper office.

Jack scowled when he strode down Culpepper Avenue and saw nothing of the mysterious stranger Cassie had pointed out. It was as if the man had vanished into thin air. Frowning, Jack glanced toward the public school and two churches. The opposite side of the street—which branched off town circle, like a spoke of a wheel—had yet to be cleared of trees that surrounded another warm spring bubbling from the hillside.

Jack checked his pocket watch then glanced over his shoulder. He needed to return to the jail to relieve his part-time deputy for lunch. He wished one of his brothers were in town so he could send him to track down the mysterious stranger. Unfortunately, they were gathering a herd of calves to send to the Kansas railhead with Nate Hudson's cattle company.

Locating the mysterious stranger would have to wait until later, Jack mused as he quickened his step.

While Jack was heading to the jail, Doreen flagged him down then flashed him a beaming smile. When they were within touching distance, she trailed her hand down his arm and batted her baby blues at him.

"I want you to know that I'm hurt beyond words that you had lunch with that rabble-rouser. Even though Papa pressured me into letting Sonny Burtram escort me to lunch, you know how I feel about you, Jack."

He made a noncommittal sound then backed away from her caress. Doreen was coming on strong—even for her.

"You know how I feel about you and you've discarded me in favor of that…freewheeling Yankee! She is not popular around here, you know. Your association with her will reflect badly on you, Jack."

Her smile turned upside down and Jack decided to heed Cassie's warning about testing any food that Doreen served him for poison.

"I don't recommend threatening me or Cassandra," he added with a steely glance.

"Is that what that lying suffragist told you?" Doreen scoffed. "I didn't threaten her. Obviously she is using deceitful tactics to turn you against me."

Jack gave her a no-nonsense stare. "Don't cause trouble or you will deal directly with me. Now, if you'll excuse me, I need to get to work."

"My father is going to hear about your heartless, insulting comments!" She stamped her foot, making her blond curls spring wildly around her delicate face.

"I'll take my chances." He tossed the words over his shoulder as he continued down the boardwalk.

Cassie arrived at the newspaper office just as Gerald was about to lock up for lunch.

"How did the interview work out?" Gerald asked as he held open the door for Cassie.

"We didn't come to blows, if that's what you expected." Instead, it came to ravishing kisses and intimate caresses that might have progressed even further if Harrison hadn't shown up.

"Glad to hear it." Gerald hitched his thumb over his

shoulder. "I'm going to grab lunch then make the rounds to collect weekly advertising fees from the shopkeepers. I should be back before time to lock up. If not, I'll see you in the morning."

As Gerald strode next door to the café, Cassie shooed the smelly cat outside then hurried to her desk to jot down notes for her article about the town's founding fathers. An hour later, she went in search of another writing tablet since she'd used up her supply. She halted beside the printing press to note that Gerald had left instructions for her to set type before she left for the day. Cassie glanced at the clock, calculating how long it would take to finish the job.

She strode into Gerald's office to restock paper. Considering all she had to do, it would be after dark before she walked home. Spending most of the morning at Culpepper Ranch had cost her extra hours. Not to mention the anxiety of inevitably having to deal with Harrison, who'd likely hold the embarrassing incident over her head for the rest of her life.

The image of Jack hovering above her while they tugged frantically at each other's clothing splashed across her mind for the umpteenth time. Cassie groaned in mortification. Until now, she'd spent her time fending off male advances rather than inviting or accepting them.

Then along came Andrew Jackson Culpepper—and she couldn't keep her hands off his muscular body.

Doreen Rowe would throw a tantrum if she knew that Jack and Cassie had done much more than share a meal. That jealous witch would probably boil Cassie in oil to retaliate.

Distracted, Cassie breezed into the small supply closet to rummage through crowded shelves to find the stockpile of paper. She gasped in shock when she stumbled upon recently printed banknotes.

"Dear God," she bleated as she studied the bills. "Not you, too, Gerald. What on earth is going on?"

The thought of her boss being involved in fraudulent activities—most likely with Pettigrew's bank—disappointed her beyond measure. Had Gerald printed counterfeit bills while she was out of the office this morning then hidden them in the supply closet? It would certainly seem so.

Clearly, he hadn't anticipated that Cassie would come looking to replace writing paper. But there were the paper bills, stacked beneath the writing tablets.

Her conspiracy theory kept expanding with each passing day. No wonder Jack hadn't been able to track down the thieves. There must be an entire ring of outlaws working to cover each other's tracks.

Hounded by disillusionment about her boss, Cassie retrieved the writing paper and gathered several banknotes to show to Jack. While she worked on her articles then set type, she tried to decide how to handle the discovery. Should she dash off to tell Jack about her findings? Or perhaps there was a logical explanation and she should give Gerald a chance to explain what was going on.

Difficult though it was, Cassie remained in the office and tried to keep her mind on writing the human-interest article that cast the Culpepper family in a favorable light. However, questions about Gerald Nash's integrity distracted her. Her thoughts also circled to the nervous bank teller who'd promised to meet with her—and never did. Something suspicious was going on. She was going to confront Millard Stewart instead of waiting until *he* got around to contacting *her.* He knew something and she was going to find out what it was.

Cassie was still hard at work when Gerald returned an hour after dark.

"Mercy, girl, didn't I mention that you don't get paid for extra hours?" Gerald teased as he breezed through the door.

"I'm dedicated to my career," she insisted. It was difficult for her to glance in his direction when suspicion about the freshly printed banknotes clouded her mind. "You were gone a long time."

She noticed Gerald shifting awkwardly from one foot to the other. She also noticed he wouldn't meet her intense gaze directly.

"I got tied up at various stores, chatting with people longer than I intended. Then I decided to have supper before I returned to stash my collected fees in the safe."

No doubt, he planned to cut out the forged banknotes and hide them in the safe, too, she mused disparagingly.

Cassie inhaled a fortifying breath as she came to her feet to face Gerald directly. "Is there something you want to tell me, Gerald? You know I am your friend and employee."

"What?" His hazel eyes widened noticeably and his rounded face surged with color. "I don't know what you mean."

If his wasn't an expression of discomfort and guilt, Cassie didn't know what was. "I think we should discuss this, Gerald," she said firmly. "I need to know what's going on."

He wheeled around and strode quickly to his office. "You are speaking to the wrong person, Cassie. I'm not in a position to say anything to anybody, so ask me no questions and I'll tell you no lies."

Gerald sounded like the robbery victims who were hesitant to offer their detailed account of the bank hold-up. *Him, too?* she thought to herself. Had someone threatened Gerald with bodily injury or death if he divulged information about printing the banknotes? And who the blazes was intimidating him? The mysterious stranger?

What had happened to Gerald's integrity? After all the battle scars he'd earned printing the truth in his newspapers, had he finally taken the path of least resistance?

"I will do whatever necessary to help—" Cassie offered, only to be interrupted in midsentence.

"We are *not* talking about it," he said authoritatively. "Finish up and go home for the night. We have to print the church bulletins in the morning. Plus typeset the newspaper tomorrow afternoon."

Grumbling at Gerald's refusal to confide in her, Cassie tidied up her desk. She had given Gerald the opportunity to proclaim his innocence, but he had refused. She had no recourse except to alert Jack to the recently printed banknotes Gerald had stashed in the supply closet.

Maybe Jack had the influence and authority to convince her boss to talk. Something complex and illegal seemed to be going on and Cassie was determined to get to the bottom of it.

She retrieved her jacket then strode outside to find Max waiting for her. She walked next door to grab a bite to eat. After a short visit with her aunt, Cassie returned to the street. She glanced up at the sky and scudding clouds.

"Bandit's moon," she murmured.

There was no more than a sliver of silver light that made it difficult to see who was lurking in the darkness, especially when the swift-moving clouds swallowed the stars and the wind whistled eerily around the buildings.

While Maxwell purred and curled affectionately around her legs, Cassie stared at the barred windows of the bank. She didn't see anyone scurrying through the inky shadows or tiptoeing through the building with a lantern to lead the way.

Cassie veered toward the marshal's office to share her findings of freshly printed currency with Jack. She thought she heard muffled footsteps in the side alley near the bakery. When Maxwell hissed and growled, she tried to wheel toward the street to escape whatever had alarmed her cat. Cassie gasped in alarm when someone hooked an arm around her neck and jerked her backward into the shadows of the alley.

She writhed for release and tried to scream for help, but her captor clamped a gloved hand over her mouth. She twisted her head to notice her attacker was wearing a long canvas duster, black hood and sombrero.

Sweet mercy! The vengeful bandit had returned to dispose of her! Determined to break free, Cassie threw a punch with her elbow. Her assailant snarled viciously then clubbed her on the back of the head. Stars exploded in front of her eyes. Pain pounded in the back of her skull. Her vision faded in and out as a wave of nausea splashed over her.

Despite her vow to remain on her feet and fight back, her knees folded up beneath her. The attacker was growling at her, but the buzzing in her ears made it difficult to fully comprehend what he said.

She thought she heard him say, "Serves you right for not minding your business." But she couldn't be certain. Her eyes rolled back in her head and she pitched forward on the ground. Powdery dirt filled her mouth as she tried unsuccessfully to cry out for help.

Then she passed out cold.

The next morning Jack ducked reflexively when a thunderclap boomed overhead. He quickened his step to reach the covered boardwalk before raindrops drenched him.

Although Jack had taken a second look around the empty property where the unidentified stranger had disappeared the previous afternoon, he hadn't located the elusive man. According to the hotel clerk, the mysterious Mr. Smythe had checked out of the hotel, paid in cash and left.

Jack wanted a better description of the stranger and he hoped Cassie could provide more details than the hotel clerk, who claimed the guest kept his head down and mumbled in response to questions.

Jack's thoughts scattered when lightning sizzled across the gloomy sky and thunder rumbled again. Rain came down in windblown sheets that turned the streets to mud instantly.

Jack was glad his brothers had taken the cattle and horse herds to join Nate Hudson's livestock before the spring storm descended. Hopefully, Nate was on the trail to Dodge City and far away from the path of the thunderstorm.

He knew from personal experience that lightning strikes and booming thunder could cause herds to stampede—sometimes trampling cowboys. Jack didn't miss those days of herding cattle to the railheads with his family or riding patrol with the Rangers when dangerous storms sent men scrambling for cover.

Brushing raindrops from his jacket, Jack stepped into the newspaper office to see Gerald setting type.

"About time you showed up… Oh, it's you, Marshal," Gerald said then nodded his head toward the pane-glass window. "Quite a toad strangler of a rainstorm going on out there." He scowled as he shook out his hand. "Confounded stiff joints. I guess I need to soak my hands in the warm mineral waters. I don't usually have to do this now that Cassie hired on. Her nimble fingers fly over the type and she works twice as fast as I do."

"Cassie doesn't strike me as the kind of person who shows up late," Jack remarked. "Is she working an assignment?"

Gerald glanced at the clock and frowned. "No, and you're right. She's usually on time. I've been struggling with the typesetting and I didn't realize how late it is. I can't imagine what's keeping her. Maybe Louise detained her at the café."

"I'll check on it." Jack pulled his hat low on his forehead then he jogged next door. He burst into the café, leaving puddles forming at his feet.

"Good morning, Marshal," Louise greeted cheerfully as she delivered a plate of food to one of her customers. "Have a seat. I'll bring you a cup of coffee to ward off the chill."

Jack followed Louise to see if Cassie might be helping in the kitchen. "I want to ask your niece a few questions. She hasn't shown up for work yet. I thought she might be here."

Louise frowned worriedly. "I haven't seen her since late afternoon yesterday. Did you check at the boardinghouse?" When Suzannah walked by with the coffeepot, Louise detained her. "Have you seen Cassie this morning?"

"No, I usually leave for work before she does," she reported. "What's wrong?"

Louise wrung her hands. "We don't know. Jack said she hasn't shown up for work yet."

Jack reversed direction and headed for the front door. He had to admit that Cassie's disappearance made him uneasy. She was nothing if not dependable and punctual. Something was definitely wrong. He could sense it.

By the time Jack reached the boardinghouse on Jackson Street, he was soaked to the bone. He rapped impatiently on Cassie's door, but he was met with silence. Another trickle of unease skittered down his spine, prompting him to track down Delbert Mathews, the landlord, to unlock Cassie's door.

When he and Delbert stepped into the room, he noted the bed was made. An empty bathtub stood beside the dressing screen and the room was tidy. Cassie was nowhere to be seen. Jack wasn't sure if she'd been here last night or if she had left the room neat and clean when she exited this morning.

Mumbling a thank-you to the barrel-chested landlord, Jack jogged down the street—and received another drenching. Despite the inclement weather, he refused to give up his search. He methodically peered into the window of each store he passed that faced town circle. He checked the side alleys and he called Cassie's name, but he heard no response over the pounding rain and howling wind.

Jack had nearly completed the circle when he stepped off the boardwalk between the general store and opera house. He heard the caterwauling of a cat and went to investigate. In the gloomy shadows and pouring rain he noticed a pair of women's shoes—which looked exactly like the ones Cassie had worn the previous day—sticking out from a tumbled stack of wooden crates.

Alarm slammed into him when he realized the shoes still had feet in them. He dashed off, splattering through the mud puddles in his haste to check on the sprawled body concealed by the fallen crates.

When Jack skidded to a halt, the black cat shot off in the rain. He stared down at Cassie's unmoving body. The shock of seeing Cassie rain-drenched and lifeless hit him like an unexpected fist in the underbelly. He forgot to breathe when he shoved aside two crates and noticed the pistol lying beside Cassie's fingertips.

"What the hell…?" Jack mumbled as he plowed his shoulder into the wooden crates to scatter them in all directions so he could obtain a better view of Cassie.

Crates tumbled helter-skelter, revealing Millard Stewart's sprawled form. The bank teller was lying face-down beside Cassie. A makeshift club lay in a mud puddle just beyond Millard's fingertips. Jack lifted Millard's shoulder to see a bullet hole in his chest and blood stains on his muddy shirt.

Disbelief hammered at Jack as he appraised the scene of what looked to be a double murder. "Cassie!" he yelled as he dropped to his knees beside her. He grasped her arm then felt for a pulse. He half collapsed in relief when he realized she was still breathing.

He couldn't say the same for Millard.

Frantic, he turned his attention back to Cassie. He eased her to her back to check for a bullet wound. Thankfully, she didn't have one.

"Cassie?" He gave her a jostling shake. "Can you hear me?"

Nothing. She didn't move or speak.

Jack swore colorfully when he brushed his hand over

the back of her head and felt the bloody knot at the base of her skull. He grabbed the discarded pistol, crammed it in the back waistband of his breeches then scooped Cassie's unresponsive body into his arms.

He cast one last glance at Millard before he rounded the corner of the building to carry Cassie to Bixby Café. Cassie might survive the blow to her head, but Millard was a different story. Jack knew *dead* when he saw it, and Millard Stewart was it.

Chapter Eight

"Oh, my God!" Louise howled in horror when Jack burst into the café with Cassie's limp body draped over his arms. She wheeled around to lead the way down the hall and up the steps to her upstairs apartment. "What happened?"

"Not sure yet." Jack refused to go into detail while the customers in the crowded café were hanging on his every word.

When he rounded the corner to the hall, he overheard several unflattering comments about Cassie, but he paid no heed in his haste to put her to bed and check her thoroughly for injuries.

Louise frowned pensively as she opened the door for Jack. "Do you think someone attacked her because she's stirred up other women to join the fight for her causes?"

Jack didn't take time to reply. Instead, he said, "Send someone to fetch Doc Hinton."

"I'll take care of it myself." Louise dashed from the apartment, leaving Jack holding Cassie and unsure what to do with her.

Cassie was wearing the same bright yellow dress she'd had on yesterday—only it was dripping wet and covered with mud. He couldn't put her on Louise's bed without undressing her first.

Jack had fantasized about undressing Cassie after their encounter in the homestead cabin, but the scene hadn't played out like this.

Well, hell, he thought. Louise would likely rake him over live coals for stripping Cassie from her clothes but he couldn't stand here all day. He propped her up on a chair beside the drop-leaf table to unbutton the bodice of her dress. He told himself not to enjoy the appealing sight of her satiny skin and lush body quite so much. But the damnable truth was this woman aroused him to the extreme and it was impossible to remain impersonal.

Jack did what he had to do—somebody had to undress her and he preferred it to be him. Then he gently tucked Cassie in bed and pulled the quilt over her naked body.

Hurriedly, he dipped a cloth in the basin of water to wipe her face and clean the wound on the back of her head. He scowled when he noticed the wound was deep and still bleeding.

"Damn it, what did you and Millard come to blows about?" he demanded in frustration.

Cassie didn't reply. She lay there like a rag doll, so pale and unmoving that it tormented Jack beyond words.

In afterthought, Jack bounded from the edge of the bed to do something—he wasn't sure what—with the muddy gown on the floor. That's when he noticed the wet banknotes tucked in her pocket. He swiveled his head around to glare accusingly at Cassie then tucked the money—as well as the pistol used to shoot Millard—out of sight.

Jack dropped the filthy gown in the hallway then turned back to the apartment. Relief washed over him when he saw Cassie shift slightly on the bed and heard her quiet groan.

"Cassie?" He sank down beside her to wipe away the last smudge of mud from her pallid face.

Her thick lashes fluttered up and she stared at him as if she didn't recognize him. Then she glanced around the apartment, as if viewing it for the first time. Her blank expression worried the hell out of him.

"Do you know what happened to you?" he asked urgently.

She frowned, bewildered. "Your voice sounds familiar, but you are a fuzzy blur. Who *are* you and where am I?"

Damn, talk about a brain-scrambling blow! "I'm Jack Culpepper, city marshal. You're in your aunt's apartment over the café. Do you know who you are?"

She blew out a breath then winced in pain. "It hurts to think. Maybe you could tell me who I am and end the suspense."

Hell and damnation, he mused. He had a murder and assault case to solve and the only witness was also a victim claiming she didn't know who she was. She also appeared to have been partially blinded by the blow to the back of her head. Worse, Jack had taken evidence from the scene of the crime and stashed it on his person.

Why not break a few more laws? he thought in exasperation as he blotted Cassie's waxen face with a clean cloth. Before long, he wouldn't be able to distinguish between himself and the outlaws he'd sworn to apprehend. His life was headed straight to hell and he wasn't sure how to stop it.

* * *

"Oh, thank God!" Louise erupted when she burst into her apartment to see that Cassie had regained consciousness.

Jack knew the instant Louise realized he had stripped Cassie naked and tucked her in bed. Louise's brown eyes zeroed in on him with blatant disapproval.

"I did what I had to do," he defended himself. However, he didn't add that he enjoyed the view a lot more than he should have.

Louise released him from her hard stare when Doc Hinton strode inside, but Jack knew he hadn't heard the last from her. She was fiercely protective of Cassie.

The young, curly-haired doctor who was Jack's age— more or less—sank down to check the dilation of Cassie's eyes. Then he inspected the knot on her head. The physician asked Cassie a few questions that she had difficulty answering.

"Concussion," he diagnosed, confirming Jack's suspicions. "She's going to need stitches."

"Then take care of it." Louise clutched Jack's hand and practically dragged him into the hall. Then she rounded on him with her dark eyes narrowed into hard slits. "I'd like to skin you alive for disrobing my niece, but first I want to know exactly what happened and I want to know now!"

"I found her unconscious in the alley," he reported grimly. "There was a pistol by her outstretched hand and Millard Stewart was beside her. He's been shot in the chest. An improvised club lying nearby explains the hard blow to Cassie's head."

Louise clutched her chest and gasped for breath as she staggered back to steady herself against the wall. "Sweet mercy! Is Millard dead?"

"Yes. Tell Doc to meet me in the side alley between the general store and opera house as soon as he's taken care of Cassie."

Nodding in numb disbelief, Louise wobbled into her apartment. Jack took the outside exit that descended into the side alley between the café and newspaper office to avoid questions from curious café patrons.

The rain tailed off to intermittent sprinkles as he slopped through the alley to reach the scene of the crime. Sure enough, Millard lay exactly where he'd been a quarter of an hour earlier.

Jack eased Millard to his back to check him thoroughly. While he waited for Doc Hinton to arrive to confirm his worst fears, Jack surveyed the area for signs of struggle, but there was nothing but mud and water puddles. The only visible footprints were the one's he'd left when he came upon the bodies then left for the café with Cassie in his arms.

"Oh, dear," the doctor mumbled when he saw the body.

Jack motioned the physician forward. "I already checked Millard's pulse. He doesn't have one."

"He's dead," Doc Hinton quickly confirmed. "Have you figured out what happened out here?"

"It looks as if Millard and Cassie had a volatile disagreement," Jack confided. "But that is privileged information until I have more details." He glanced curiously at the doctor. "How long before I can interrogate Cassie?"

Doc Hinton surged to his feet. "Hard to say. She needed two stitches and she's still complaining of blurred vision. However, she did recognize Louise by the time I left. I'm hoping Cassie will regain command of her senses in a few hours."

"Can she be moved?" Jack wanted to know.

Doc Hinton glanced at him, bemused. "Moved where? Why?"

"As you know, Cassie's campaign for women's rights and social reform has made as many female advocates as male enemies. Rumors are already flying."

The physician nodded his sandy-colored head. "I've heard a few of them."

"They are untrue, but they are fuel for fires," Jack said grimly. "When news of the bank teller's death gets out, I want Cassie where I can protect her from vigilantes. She is in no condition to protect herself. If she's at our ranch, she'll have ex-Texas Rangers as bodyguards."

Doc Hinton smiled wryly. "You think Louise will stand for that? Her niece in a house with three men?"

"She'll allow it if she wants to keep Cassie protected and alive long enough to gather her wits and give her statement about what happened in this alley." Jack rose to his feet. "I'll find someone to help us carry Millard from the alley."

"We'll be here," the physician said as he stared bleakly at Millard.

Cassie's stomach pitched and listed like a ship on a storm-tossed sea. Lightheaded, she tried to concentrate on the sequence of events that had left her dazed and in bed. Her vision was as blurry as her memory. Flashes of jumbled thoughts converged on her mind then flitted away before she could grasp their meaning.

After an hour, she remembered who she was. Her aunt remained by her side, spoon-feeding her breakfast and forcing her to take sips of water.

"Where's Jack?" Cassie squeaked, surprised that her voice sounded as if it had rusted. "I need to speak with him."

"He's on his way," her aunt replied. Then she stared anxiously at Cassie. "Do you remember what happened?"

Cassie nodded her head—carefully. The knot on her skull still pounded in rhythm with her pulse and the stitches pulled with each movement. "It's coming back to me gradually, but I want to give my official statement to Jack."

A few minutes later, she glanced up to see Jack approaching. His expression was grim. His wet clothes clung to him like a second skin, accentuating his appealing masculine form. Bad as she felt, she was still vividly aware of his effect on her.

He came to stand over her, causing another fuzzy memory to skitter through her aching head. "Are you up to moving?"

"I suppose so, but I seem to be without clothes and I can't remember why."

She glanced at her aunt who said, "Don't look at me. Ask Jack how you came to be naked in bed."

Cassie blushed profusely at the thought of Jack peeling off her clothing. Not that he hadn't managed half the feat at the isolated cabin. *That* tidbit of memory she recalled. But still…

"I sent Suz and Jefferson to the boardinghouse to pack your bag," Jack reported. "I haven't had any luck tracking down your cat after I saw him in the alley beside you."

Cassie frowned, even though it made her head hurt worse. "Why do I need a bag to get from here to there? I can borrow something from Aunt Louise for the short trip."

"You're headed to our ranch," Jack declared.

"There are too many rumors floating around already. That will add to them," she objected.

He waved his arms in expansive gestures to silence her protest. Cassie felt certain she wouldn't have tolerated his domineering attitude if her skull wasn't throbbing and her stomach rolling with nausea.

Two minutes later Suzannah and Jefferson appeared at the apartment door. Jack grabbed the carpetbag and shooed everyone but Suzannah from the room. "We'll wait outside if you need extra assistance dressing her."

Cassie levered herself upright then clutched the sagging quilt modestly to her breasts. "Well, this is one way to throw you and Jefferson together. Even if it was painful for me."

"I'm so sorry," Suzannah murmured as she handed over Cassie's clothing. "Although Jefferson realizes I'm alive now, I didn't want to make headway at your expense."

Cassie fumbled with her garments, but she managed to dress with a little assistance from her friend. When she tried to stand up the room careened around her and Suz reached over to steady her arm.

"Jack!" Suzannah called out hurriedly.

He was there in a flash to scoop Cassie up in his arms. She had to admit that after her ordeal she relished the comforting feel of snuggling against Jack's muscled chest and having his brawny arms holding her protectively.

"I'll come by this afternoon to see you during my break," Suzannah promised as Jack carried Cassie into the hall.

"So will I," Aunt Louise insisted. "You just rest now, hon. Everything is going to be just fine."

Cassie breathed a sigh of relief when she noticed the wagon—complete with padded bedding—waiting in the side alley. When Jack deposited her carefully on the pallet, she huddled beneath the quilt. Jack spoke not one word as he climbed onto the seat beside Jefferson.

The mile and a half ride to the ranch house was a bit bumpy, but Cassie endured. She doubted even a smooth ride would alleviate her hellish headache.

"I still can't fathom why you thought it was necessary to remove me from town," she said to Jack. "Unless you expect me to receive another unpleasant visit from the bandit who clobbered me last night."

Jack swiveled on the seat to gape at her.

Jefferson shot a quick glance over his shoulder while he guided the horses down the muddy road.

Then both men looked at each other with puzzled expressions on their faces.

"What the blazes are you talking about?" Jack asked.

"I'm talking about walking from the newspaper office last night and being accosted by one of those bank robbers."

"You must still be confused," Jack insisted. "You took a severe blow to the head, you know."

"I'm telling you that one of the bandits hit me last night," she reported.

Jefferson and Jack did double takes.

"Bandit," she prompted caustically. "Sombrero, black hood, canvas duster. This time he had a club and he used it on me when I gouged him in the belly with my elbow. I tried to make a run for it, but he pounded my head. The last thing I remember before I passed out was that he said it served me right for causing so much trouble."

"Did the bandit sound like a man or a woman?"

"I can't say for sure. I was dazed when I heard the hissing whisper. I just presumed it was a man."

Jefferson and Jack stared at her as if she were loco. "What about Millard Stewart?" Jack asked a moment later.

"What about him?" she asked blankly.

"Do you remember him?"

Apparently, Jack was testing her to see if she was recovering from her confusion and concussion. "Of course, I remember him. He's the scrawny bank teller with beady eyes and rodentlike nose. He told me days ago that he'd contact me to answer my questions about the robbery, but he never has."

"And he never will," Jack grumbled morosely.

Bemused, Cassie peered up at Jack. Again, there was something oddly familiar—yet alarming—about having Jefferson and Jack hovering above her. For the life of her, she couldn't figure out why. "What does that mean?" she asked.

Jack twisted on the seat to stare directly at her. "Millard is dead, Cassie."

"What? When?" she choked in disbelief.

Jefferson and Jack stared at her as if she ought to know.

"Millard was lying beside you in the mud in the alley," Jack reported. "He has a bullet hole in his chest."

"What?" she croaked.

Jack reached into the back waistband of his breeches to retrieve a pistol. "I found this weapon six inches from your outstretched hand."

"That's impossible," she gasped. "I don't own a gun."

"There was a club beside Millard's hand," he continued somberly. "I presume he used it on you during your confrontation."

"We did not have a confrontation!" she said sharply then grabbed her head when it reverberated with pain.

"If you're trying to milk my sympathy it isn't working," Jack told her. "I need straight answers. Now tell me why I found these in the pocket of your gown." He waved the stack of banknotes Cassie had swiped from Gerald's office at her.

"Oh, dear," she mumbled uneasily. "I can explain that."

He cocked a thick brow and regarded her skeptically. "You can explain this stack of money, but you can't explain the dead body that was lying beside you?"

Cassie felt nauseated again, and it had nothing whatsoever to do with the throbbing pain in her skull. Watching Jack stare accusingly at her stung her pride and upset her beyond measure.

"How could you possibly think I attacked Millard?"

"It's not hard, *daredevil,* given that you attacked a bank robber who held you at gunpoint," Jack pointed out.

Curse it, this was not going well. "No matter what you think, I didn't shoot Millard," she maintained. "I admit that I wanted to fire questions concerning the robbery at him. But I don't know what he was doing beside me in the alley, unless he and the bandit who attacked me were in cahoots. Maybe the bandit decided to silence Millard permanently, while setting me up for the crime."

Frustrated, Cassie watched Jack and Jefferson exchange glances again. "I am not the criminal here!" she snapped, despite the pain she inflicted on herself. "I'm the victim. Same as I was at the bank!"

"This case is becoming more complicated by the day," Jack muttered.

"You're telling me, big brother," said Jefferson.

Jack stared into Cassie's peaked face then looked back

at Jefferson. "Do you have the slightest idea what she's talking about?"

"How the hell should I know? I was at the ranch last night and so was Harry. That leaves *you* without an alibi."

"Well, *I* sure as hell didn't do it," Jack protested.

"Didn't do what?" Cassie demanded.

Jack blew out an exasperated breath. "I think someone posed as a bank robber then attacked you last night."

"Why would you think that…?" Her voice fizzled out when she frowned. Then she winced uncomfortably and touched the back of her head. "Wait a minute, you could be right. I don't recall the musty scent of the canvas duster when the bandit grabbed me. I don't recall the chink of spurs, only muffled steps in the dirt." She shrugged dismissively. "But then again, someone might have washed and dried the garments after the bank robbery. But whether it was one of the original outlaws or someone using the convenient disguise, the question is *why* was I targeted?"

"I wish I knew," Jack murmured pensively.

"How many enemies have you made since you arrived in town?" Jefferson asked as he steered the horse and wagon toward the front door of the spacious, two-story ranch house.

"More than I can count on both hands," she admitted. "Doreen threatened me if I didn't keep my distance from you and Jack. Plus, Edgar Forrester chewed on my ear recently," Cassie continued. "He claims it's my fault that his wife, Mildred, moved out and has joined the cause of women's rights and social reform."

"There's two possible suspects," Jack commented, then waved the banknotes at her again. "I also need to know why these bills were in your pocket. I'm hoping it's not because you stole them from Millard and that provoked your fight."

"For the last time," she railed in exasperation. "I didn't have a confrontation with Millard." She glanced at Jefferson then stared at Jack. "I'm not sure I should explain about the money in front of Jefferson."

"You can trust him," Jack insisted. "Right, Jeff?"

"I'm honest as the day is long," Jefferson declared at the prompt. "Now, who did you rob if not Millard? Who was carrying the banknotes you stole?"

"Stop tormenting me," she grumbled. "I already have a headache from hell and you're making it worse."

"Sorry. I suppose you do have more than your fair share of trouble at the moment," Jefferson agreed.

"Yes I do," she huffed. "It isn't every day I'm carted away from town and placed under house arrest for murder." Cassie propped herself up on her elbow to stare at Jack. "Are you anticipating a lynch mob?"

"The thought crossed my mind." Jack hopped to the ground the moment Jefferson drew the wagon to a halt. "My brothers can keep an eye on you here while you recuperate. No need to have your neck stretched past its limits before the gash on the back of your head heals."

He scooped Cassie into his arms then strode quickly toward the covered porch. The door opened without prompting and Harrison stared worriedly at him.

"Is she okay?"

"She'll live if a lynch mob doesn't get hold of her. However, Millard Stewart won't be standing his post at the teller's window. He's made his last withdrawal."

"He's dead?" Harrison blinked. "How'd that happen?"

Jefferson hitched his thumb toward Cassie. "He hit

her with a club. She shot him. So let that be a lesson to you. If you annoy her you'll be dreadfully sorry."

"Stop that," Jack ordered. "She's having a bad day without you two taunting her."

"A horrible day," Cassie corrected as she stared down Jack's brothers. "You two might be my next victims, so you better watch out if you know what's good for you."

Jack headed for the steps with Cassie cradled in his arms. He carried her upstairs to his spacious bedroom then put her on his bed. Here was yet another fantasy that hadn't played out the way he'd imagined. But he couldn't think about that right now.

Had she come to blows with the bank teller and refused to admit it? Or was she so confused after suffering a blow to the head that maybe her original conflict with a bank robber had somehow linked itself in her mind to the conflict that left Millard dead in the alley?

Sighing in frustration Jack turned around and left Cassie to rest. Maybe he wasn't *going* to hell, he thought dismally. Maybe he was already *there*.

Leaving Clara to check on Cassie periodically, Jack changed into dry clothes then motioned for his brothers to follow him outside.

He stared solemnly at Jefferson and then at Harrison. "I need to know the truth. Were either of you in town last night? Did you use your disguise to attack Cassie?"

His brothers puffed up with so much indignation they nearly popped the buttons on their shirts.

"Hell, no! We only rob banks as a last resort," Jefferson huffed.

"We don't go around pounding women on the head for the sport of it, either," Harrison added, insulted.

"I had to ask," Jack said. "Evidently someone knew about Cassie's reported tussle with a bandit during the bank holdup and used it as cover to stage his own attack."

Jefferson nodded his auburn head. "It was the perfect disguise, except that she didn't notice a musty scent or the chink of spurs as she did the first time."

"Do you suppose Cassie is telling the truth?" Harrison asked. "Maybe the killer attacked Millard while in disguise, and then put both victims in the same place to confuse the issue."

Jack wanted to believe Cassie's story, he really did. But there was still the issue of the money in her pocket and the pistol near her hand. She could have claimed self-defense and he would've been ready and willing to believe her. Damn, the incident was confusing as hell. Plus Jack hadn't checked to see if someone had clubbed Millard in the head, too. He needed to do that the first chance he got. Maybe both of them had been knocked unconscious and left for dead.

"I think we should tell her the truth," Jefferson blurted unexpectedly.

"Me, too," Harrison seconded.

"Not now," Jack refused. "One man is dead and Cassie's brain is scrambled. And I'm curious whether Floyd Pettigrew had a hand in this incident. According to Cassie, Millard Stewart was reluctant to talk to her at the bank while Pettigrew hovered around. Maybe he knew something and Pettigrew decided to silence him. Or perhaps Stewart didn't want Pettigrew to become suspicious. After all, Nate Hudson said Stewart was the one who refused to let him make a large withdrawal. Then, of course, there is the unidentified stranger Cassie spotted scurrying around the back door of the bank. She said Pettigrew's office door was closed when she first entered the bank. Whether the stranger met with Pettigrew or Stewart or both, we don't know for sure."

"This is going to blow up in our faces," Jefferson prophesied grimly. "I can feel it. The robberies have set off a chain reaction. No telling who'll end up dead next."

Guilt hammered at Jack. He could tell that it was eating away at his brothers, too. Damn it, Pettigrew had to be involved in this…didn't he? The bastard was as cagey as he was arrogant. Whatever he was doing would inevitably hurt his unsuspecting customers. Catching him and his cohorts was proving to be difficult. He needed evidence not speculation.

"Jackson!"

He glanced over his shoulder to see Clara poke her gray head out the door. "Your guest would like to speak with you."

"Coming." Jack pivoted away from his brothers.

"I still say we should tell her," Jefferson persisted. "I'd prefer to have her on our side."

"Same goes for me," Harrison put in.

"Not now," Jack muttered emphatically again. "We have too many facts to sort out."

Besides, he dreaded telling Cassie, especially now that her opinion of him mattered so much. He didn't want to see the look of disappointment and outrage on her face when he admitted that he was a marshal and bandit all rolled into one.

Chapter Nine

Cassie was sitting up in bed, waiting for Jack, when he breezed into the room. "First off, I want to thank you for trying to protect me," she said. "But it isn't necessary. I can take care of myself."

He chuckled. "Right. You were doing such a fine job of it when I found you sprawled in the muddy alley."

"Well, except for that," she had to admit. "But I'll go back to town this evening so I won't inconvenience your family more than I have already."

Jack loomed over her. "Don't you get it, buttercup? People are trying to kill you. Or you're trying to kill them. I'm still trying to figure out which. Either way, I want you off the streets."

He swooped down unexpectedly and kissed her right smack dab on the lips. "Damn, I've wanted to do that since I found you in the mud…dead…or at least I thought you were. Unfortunately, there have been dozens of people milling about. I haven't been able to get you alone *and* conscious at the same moment."

He was in an odd mood, she decided. He was half serious and half teasing, but the instant his sensuous lips slanted over hers, she forgot everything except the erotic pleasure drifting over her.

"Do that again," she murmured. "I think it's curing my concussion."

A slow, wicked smile slid across his lips as his golden eyes focused pointedly on her mouth. "If you think it helps, I'm at your service."

Cassie looped her arms around his broad shoulders and savored the warmth of desire that channeled through her body. She reminded herself that if the blow to her head had cracked open her skull she might be dead right now.

She would have missed this delicious pleasure. Jack might have reservations about her possible involvement in the bank teller's death, but he seemed to be as vulnerable to this explosive attraction between them as she was. She wondered if it was purely physical on his part. Most likely, she decided, but she wasn't asking for more than Jack could give.

When his hands drifted over her breasts, setting off sweet tormenting sensations, Cassie admitted to herself that she was slowly but steadily falling in love with Jack. It wasn't just physical. She *liked* him. She liked being with him, liked matching wits with him. True, he infuriated her at times, but he was a good, honest, caring and protective man.

She might even be willing to risk her heart if she knew that he actually enjoyed her company and respected her opinions. Sometimes she got the impression that he did like her for who she was and what she stood for. Then he'd get that carefully guarded expression on his face and retreat emotionally. For the life of her, she couldn't figure out what troubled him.

When his hands moved gently over her again, she decided she didn't care about anything except the pleasure of his touch. She was caressing him and he was caressing her. She would savor the moment for as long as it lasted and worry about getting her heart broken later.

"What the hell am I doing?" Jack reared back, putting an arm's length between them. "I swear, woman, we can be in the middle of turmoil—which we definitely are— and I still can't keep my hands off you. We have to get this case solved."

He blew out his breath, raked his fingers through his raven hair and said, "I can't explain what's going on in town, but I'm inclined to believe that you didn't shoot Millard Stewart."

She would have preferred to go on kissing him, but he was right. They had a case to solve. "Thank you for the vote of confidence. I honestly don't know how Millard ended up with me in the alley. The last thing I remember is battling the bandit."

He retrieved the banknotes from his pocket and waved them under her nose once again. "But where did these come from, buttercup? Rob a bank? Hmm?"

Cassie grimaced. She didn't want to point an accusing finger at Gerald. Furthermore, she didn't want to believe he was involved in a fraudulent scheme. Yet, there seemed to be no other explanation.

"Cassie," he prodded as he dropped the incriminating bills in her lap. "If you want my help in proving your innocence, you better start talking. Otherwise, your *un-*

known assailant and your *known* enemies are going to try to pin murder on you."

She stared him squarely in the eye. "If I tell you then you must promise not to arrest anyone until I find out exactly what is going on," she negotiated.

Jack frowned, befuddled. "Arrest whom?"

"Don't try to outsmart me, Marshal," she chided. "Just give me your word of honor."

He didn't have a word of honor these days. He'd given it away when he concocted this desperate scheme to flush out Floyd Pettigrew—or whoever was trying to swindle citizens out of their hard-earned money. Now Millard was dead and Cassie had been clobbered over the head and set up for murder. Not to mention she was carrying several thousand dollars worth of banknotes—after she claimed she'd lost her entire life savings during the bank robbery

"Okay, word of honor," he accommodated her, if only to get her talking. "Now what the hell is going on?"

She inhaled a deep breath that drew his attention to the full swells of her breasts. Then she burst out with, "I swiped them from Gerald's storage closet. The ink was barely dry on them and he had tucked them out of sight. I think he's printing counterfeit money."

Jack was afraid that might be the case, but he hated having his suspicions confirmed. "Gerald?"

"That's what *I* said, but there they were, hidden under some writing tablets. I grabbed a handful of them yesterday evening while Gerald was out of the office," she explained. "When he returned, I asked him if there was anything he needed to tell me."

"What did he say to that?" Jack asked intently.

"He wouldn't look me in the eye. All he said was that

it wasn't his place to say. He told me that he wasn't the one I should ask."

"What do you suppose that meant?"

Cassie shrugged. "I have no idea. Then he left the office and I closed up after I reworked the article I'm writing about your family. When I walked past the alley on my way home, I heard muffled footsteps. Maxwell hissed in warning, but I didn't react quickly enough when the bandit pounced. I fought back until I suffered the mind-numbing blow to the head. That's all I recall before I blacked out."

"So someone was using the bandit's disguise to implicate you in Millard's murder. The question is *why?*"

"I don't understand why you're so thoroughly convinced that it couldn't have been one of the bank robbers. I challenged him at the bank and he might have wanted revenge. It is, after all, a strong motivator. If he killed Millard and set me up for murder then he'd have the last laugh." She frowned then stared attentively at him. "Are you implying that you found evidence that suggests someone you know robbed the bank and couldn't have been involved last night? Who was it?"

Jack waved her off. "Let's get back to the freshly printed currency. Did your assailant know you were carrying money?"

"I don't know. If he did, why didn't he empty my pockets after he knocked me out? If one of the original thieves—"

Jack pressed his forefinger to her lips to shush her. "I'm sticking to the theory that someone used the disguise you described in your newspaper article about the robbery to throw us off track."

He kept hearing his brothers' voices echoing around his head, urging him to take Cassie into his confidence.

But he was still reluctant. Seeing the shock and disillusionment in her evergreen eyes would cut him to the core. And damn it, he *didn't* want Cassie to matter so much, but he'd become emotionally involved and he wasn't even sure he could pinpoint the time or the place it happened. His feelings for her had just sneaked up on him while he was trying so hard to resist her.

Seeing her lying in the mud, looking about as dead as a woman could get, had rattled him to the extreme and he hadn't recovered yet. In fact, she had provoked every protective and possessive instinct inside him.

"All right. For the sake of argument, we'll say that someone dressed up like the bandit I described in my news article," she accommodated him. "He clobbered me then left me in the side alley between the bakery and butcher shop—"

"That's not where I found you," Jack interrupted.

She blinked like a disturbed owl. "That's where I was when I was attacked. Where *did* you find me?"

"In the side alley between the opera house and general store," Jack informed her. "Maybe that was where Millard was shot and the killer carted you there afterward. It will be difficult to tell because the downpour washed away evidence and we are back to square one. Who wanted you dead…or at the very least, wanted to see you accused of murdering the bank teller?"

Cassie held her aching head. Curlicues of blond hair stuck out from her beguiling face—which was beginning to lose its color again.

"You should rest," Jack advised. "We'll sort through this later. Louise and Suzannah will be here to visit you and I'm going to check out a few things in town."

"Please don't arrest Gerald," she implored him. "Not yet anyway. Can't we keep this between you and me for a while?"

Jack flashed a relenting smile because she looked so adorable and yet so exhausted. He pressed a kiss to the tip of her nose then walked away, grateful that he had insisted on stashing Cassie at the ranch for safekeeping. Instinct warned him that she was still in danger, but damn if he could figure out why someone was after her or who it was. If he didn't figure it out soon, she might end up like Millard Stewart.

The gruesome thought hit Jack right where he lived. Things had changed since Cassie had arrived in Pepperville to liven up his world. The prospect of not having the spirited firebrand around left him with an empty feeling....

Hell! What was happening to him?

He decided not to delve too deeply into the dynamics of that question. Instead, he focused his effort on tracking down the murderer before Cassie became the next victim.

By nightfall, Cassie was feeling much better. Her headache had been reduced to a dull throb, thanks to the medication Dr. Hinton sent along with Louise and Suzannah. In addition, Cassie had feasted on Clara Johnson's evening meal. She had assured Clara that Louise would hire her in nothing flat if she decided to change jobs. Of course, the Culpeppers would be outraged if that happened and they'd be out for her blood.

They'd have to get in line, she thought with a grimace.

Anxious for a breath of fresh air, Cassie ventured outside to survey the star-studded sky and rolling hills. Once again, she found herself staring up at what she referred to as bandit's moon… She tensed when she heard footsteps that reminded her of her confrontation with the outlaw the previous night. Apprehensively, she whirled around, poised to defend herself at the first sign of danger.

She sagged in relief when Harrison materialized from the shadows of the veranda. Something about the way he moved niggled her, but she was at a loss to explain the odd feeling. Maybe he simply reminded her of Jack, she thought dismissively. After all, there was a strong family resemblance among the Culpepper brothers.

"You aren't supposed to be out here. Jack would have my head if he knew you were roaming around without a bodyguard." He came to stand beside her then looked out into the night. "You gave my big brother quite a scare this morning."

"It's nothing personal, you understand," she insisted. "He's only doing his job. Dead bodies don't look good on his spotless record."

Harrison snickered, but his amusement died quickly. He looked away from her to survey the sliver of moon and twinkling stars. He was silent for a long moment, seemingly lost in thought.

Then out of the blue he said, "Are you sweet on my big brother?"

Cassie felt an instant blush crawl up her neck to stain her cheeks and forehead. "You don't mince words, do you, Harrison?"

"Nope. Saves time. And you're avoiding the question."

She tilted her chin to a defiant angle. "And you're poking your nose into *my* business."

He flashed a teasing grin. "Well, you *are* sleeping in Jack's bed."

"But *he* is sleeping elsewhere," she pointed out.

"I want to make sure you aren't using him for your fiendish purposes, only to discard him heartlessly when you grow tired of him. And you will," Harrison added playfully. "I get tired of him all the time."

Cassie burst out laughing at the thought of anyone using Jack then casting him aside like a worn-out shirt. "Doreen Rowe would snatch him up in a flash. And I know for a fact that Jack is in great demand because I saw women flock around him at Aunt's Louise's birthday party. I doubt that Jack would lack for feminine attention."

Harrison lifted a dark brow and stared at her with those intense eyes that were so blue they appeared silver when they reflected light. "It might not be my business, but I still want to know where my brother stands with you."

His serious tone surprised her. Evidently, Harrison was as protective of his two brothers as they were of him. Nevertheless, her feelings for Jack were too private and personal, and she was too self-conscious to share them with Harrison, no matter how much he badgered her. "I am not using your big brother," she assured him. "Although I'm borrowing his bed, at *his* insistence, I might add, there is nothing going on that should concern you."

"Good." He tossed her a roguish smile. "Then you can use *me* for whatever purpose you dream up. You can share my room with me any time you please. All you have to do is ask."

"You are incorrigible," she said, shaking her head.

"Thank you." He waggled his brows and grinned wickedly.

"I have to question your common sense," she remarked as she strolled to the south side of the veranda. "You're flirting outrageously with me, even though I'm suspected of murder and thievery. I didn't know you enjoyed living quite so dangerously."

"You'd probably be shocked if you knew," he murmured before he turned away and headed for the front door.

Cassie watched him disappear into the shadowed doorway. She wondered what he meant by that enigmatic remark.

In town the next morning, Jack listened to his share of grumbling about Cassie's probable connection to the murder victim. Several citizens had asked him where he'd stashed the suspect, but he refused to discuss the case. He spent his spare time searching the side alley between the bakery and butcher shop then concentrated his efforts on the breezeway between the general store and the opera house.

To his exasperation, he didn't locate a single clue to explain how—or why—the assailant had planted Cassie in one alley after accosting her in another. Furthermore, he had no idea if Millard's killer had shot him elsewhere then toted or dragged him to the breezeway to stage the scene while Cassie was unconscious.

"Any luck?"

Jack glanced back to see Jefferson ambling toward him. "What are you doing in town? I asked you to stand watch over Cassie."

"Her commands take precedence," Jefferson teased as he ambled up beside Jack. "She wants me to contact Suzannah and ask her to tend the cat. We're supposed to fetch a few more articles of clothing that we overlooked in our haste yesterday. She asked me to bring her writing tablet so she can work on her editorials and news articles."

Jack bit back a grin. If he remembered correctly, Cassie had earmarked Jefferson for her friend Suzannah. Concussion or not, Cassie seemed perfectly capable of matchmaking.

Jack's smile faded as he paced back and forth in the side alley. "I find it odd that no one claimed to hear a gunshot."

"Might be difficult if Millard was shot during the thunderstorm," Jefferson pointed out.

"Doc Hinton confirmed Millard hadn't been dead too long before I discovered his body. Also there were rope burns on his wrists, but Doc couldn't tell if his ankles were tied because of the boots." Jack glanced at the buildings on either side of him. "The opera house was closed last night. So was the general store. Even so, the shot should have been heard at a distance."

"Maybe both bodies were delivered in a wagon," Jefferson speculated.

"Or the back of a horse," Jack suggested. "Yet, Millard could've been dragged by his heels. I can't say for sure because the storm destroyed all the tracks."

"So the question still remains, did Millard stumble onto the assailant who attacked Cassie and find himself in the wrong place at the wrong time? Or did he have incriminating information on Pettigrew? Then again, we can't rule out that *he* was embezzling money to cheat customers and got caught."

Jefferson had voiced the various possibilities chasing each other around Jack's head. "I wish I knew what the hell was going on. I want to force Pettigrew's hand if he's involved, but if I confront him, he might become more cautious. If he thinks I don't suspect him of wrongdoing he might make a careless mistake."

"What about the money Cassie had in her pocket?" Jefferson questioned.

"She requested my discretion. I'm keeping the information to myself," he said evasively.

Jefferson rolled his eyes then smirked. "I'm your brother. We've been through thick and thicker together. Doesn't that count for anything?"

"Yes, but she swore me to secrecy." He hitched his thumb over his shoulder. "Go fetch Suzannah and gather extra clothes for Cassie."

Jefferson appraised Jack a little too closely for his comfort. "Be careful, big brother."

"Be careful of what?"

Jefferson grinned slyly. "I think you already know, but if you don't, I predict you'll figure it out soon."

"Speak plain English," Jack said impatiently.

"All right. I think you're falling for that high-spirited firebrand. I also think you better tell her what's going on before things between you go too far and our deception spoils any chance you might have with her."

Jack flicked his wrist, shooing his meddling brother on his way. "Thanks for the free advice. I'll take it for what it's worth. Besides, you have your own problems."

"I do?"

Jack decided he'd let his brother figure it out for himself. Served him right for poking his nose into Jack's business.

Jack hiked off to interview the two people he knew had threatened Cassie the past week. One was Doreen Rowe and the other was Edgar Forrester. His first stop was the modest clapboard home Doreen shared with her widowed father.

Doreen met him at the door with a kiss, right smack-dab on his lips. "I'm so glad to see you," she gushed, then batted her baby blues at him the way she always did. "Isn't it just awful about Cassie killing poor Mr. Stewart?" She took his hand and led him into the spotless parlor then gestured for him to sit down.

Jack preferred to stand. The overzealous blonde might leap into his lap if he gave her the chance. "I need to know where you were about eight o'clock last night."

Doreen flashed a hurt, wounded expression that usually sent her male admirers scrambling to return to her good graces. Her expression didn't faze Jack one bit.

"Surely you aren't accusing *me* of involvement," Doreen gasped in offended dignity. "I brought your meal to you at the jail about six-thirty, as you recall. Then I came home to prepare a meal for Papa. I kept him company after he closed up shop."

"That's easy enough to check out," Jack replied. "I'll see if your father can verify the times."

She rushed over to throw herself in his arms. "Oh, Jack, don't let that barnstorming suffragist and murderer cause ill feelings between us," she insisted. "You know she's as guilty as original sin. The story circulating in town is that Cassie was upset about losing all her money in the robbery so she tried to convince poor Millard to skim some off for her. When he refused, she killed him."

Good God, he thought. Another incriminating rumor? "Listen, Doreen—"

She rushed on, refusing to let him get more than two words in edgewise. "Jack, you know how much I care about you. We can't let that troublemaker come between us."

"There is no *us*," Jack said bluntly.

She tilted her silver-blond head to a challenging angle.

"No? Try telling that to folks around town. People have seen us together often enough to think we might be a couple. That troublemaker is a walking disaster. I wish she'd never come here!"

"Whether Cassie is here or not doesn't change the fact that we are not a couple," Jack said firmly. "You need to make that clear to everyone who presumes otherwise."

Doreen's sticky-sweet smile evaporated and her arm shot toward the door. "You're upsetting me, Jack, so you need to leave. The very idea that *I* was involved in that deadly fiasco last night offends me deeply." She stared snidely at him then said, "When people start speculating about what you were doing in my house while my father is at work, I'm going to let them think what they will. Now get out!"

Jack scanned the room and the hall leading upstairs. He wished he had time to rummage through closets and dresser drawers to check for a sombrero, black hood and canvas duster. But the delay might invite more rumors. Doreen was exceptionally skilled at giving one performance after another to get her way. The woman had missed her true calling. She belonged on stage at the opera house. But surely Doreen wasn't spiteful enough to attack Cassie…though he wouldn't want to bet Cassie's life on it.

Touching his hat politely, Jack took his leave. He noticed several people on the residential street glance at him, then at Doreen, who was standing in the doorway, waving cheerfully at him. Well, hell, just what he needed. More damaging gossip whirling around town like a Texas tornado.

His next stop was the blacksmith's shop. He saw Edgar's bulky form hunched over the workbench. He was whaling away on the broken hitch of a plow.

When he saw Jack standing in the doorway, Edgar bit down on the cigar that constantly protruded from the corner of his mouth. "What can I do for you, Marshal?" He set aside his mallet, then wiped his grimy hands on his protective canvas apron.

"I need to know where you were about eight o'clock last night," Jack said without preamble.

Edgar's square chin jutted out. "I was workin' on this blasted plow," he insisted. "The hitch broke clean in two."

"Whose is it?" Jack asked as he ambled over to inspect the hitch, which was similar to the one he and his brothers used to work the fields before planting oats and hay for their herds.

"Henry Haskins. He brought it to me yesterday mornin'. He wants it repaired as soon as possible so he can till the ground for plantin'."

Jack glanced around the shop. "Can anyone corroborate your alibi?"

"*Alibi?*" Edgar nearly bit his cigar stub in two. "Why do I need an alibi?"

"Cassandra Bixby reported that you threatened her and blamed her for your wife's decision to spend time away from you."

Edgar's composure shattered like eggshells and he scowled sourly. "That woman's been puttin' crazed notions in Mildred's head. Now my wife's organizin' suffragists' meetin's and tryin' to hold 'em at *my* house when I'm not home!"

"It's your wife's home, too," Jack pointed out reasonably.

"No, it ain't," he protested. "It's *my* house. *I* built it with my own hands and *I* earned the money to pay for it. And she is *my* wife and I let her live there for free! At least

I did. If she comes to her senses and moves back in, I might ask her for rent."

Jack could imagine how that narrow-minded attitude went over these days with the "enlightened" women of Pepperville who had joined Cassie's ranks for reform. These women took offense at being considered chattels that were at the mercy of the men in their lives.

"You better watch out, Edgar," Jack advised with a wry smile. "If somebody clubs you over the head, like they did Cassie, or blasts you like they did Millard, your wife will inherit everything you have."

Edgar's deep-set eyes bulged and his mouth sagged open. The stub of a cigar plunged to the dirt floor.

"Did you club Cassie last night?" Jack asked bluntly.

"Hell, no. If I'd clobbered her she wouldn't have woke up. Ever."

Jack appraised Edgar's muscled arms. "Not unless you only wanted to teach her a lesson," he speculated. Then he asked, "What did you have against Millard Stewart?"

Edgar glared hot pokers at Jack. "You're really startin' to annoy me."

"I seem to have that effect on some people."

"So does that Bixby chit," Edgar muttered.

Unfortunately, that was true, thought Jack. But that blond-haired hellion had begun to grow on him and he took offense to folks hammering her on the head and accusing her of murder.

"Maybe you shouldn't stop seein' the butcher's daughter. You'd be better off spendin' time with your own kind. Ask me, you and that rabble-rouser are becomin' more trouble than you're worth." He squinted at Jack and said, "Maybe one of your brothers would make a better marshal."

Jack ignored the snide remark. "Mind if I take a look around?" He wandered off without waiting permission.

"Of course, I mind. Don't matter none, does it?" Edgar grumbled then went back to work on the damaged plow.

Jack checked in and around the stacks of metal, bundles of leather straps and other supplies that lined the shelves. He didn't find a canvas coat, black hood or sombrero, or anything else that tied Edgar to the assault.

Disgruntled, Jack exited the blacksmith's shop. He headed to the butcher shop to verify Doreen's story then he veered into the general store to question the owner about any recent purchases of canvas dusters.

Not knowing who had attacked Cassie and killed Millard left Jack with a growing sense of unease. If he didn't solve the case—quickly—Cassie might become a victim again. The thought of Cassie being hurt—or worse—filled him with a sense of fear and urgency and prompted him to quicken his step.

Chapter Ten

W**hile** Jack was searching for clues in town, Cassie sat at the dining-room table at his ranch. "I'm going crazy," she complained to Harrison when he joined her for lunch.

Harrison chuckled when she bounded to her feet to circumnavigate the spacious dining room.

"You have too much restless energy," he teased. "There are better ways to relieve it."

She cast him a withering glance when he waggled his dark brows roguishly. Then she plunked down to eat the meal Clara had prepared. "You might charm all your lady friends with that rakish grin, but it won't work on me."

"No, I'm sure it won't," he agreed before taking a bite of stew. "That's only because you're stuck on my big brother."

"I'm no such thing," she objected. He was right, but she'd shoot herself in the foot before she admitted it to Jack's rascally brothers.

"If you say so," he patronized her.

"How long does it take Jefferson to ride into town to

fetch clothing and writing tablets? Heavens, it's only a three-mile round trip."

"Jefferson had to pick up a few supplies, too," Harrison informed her, then grinned teasingly. "Besides that, there's no telling how long he'll be sidetracked when he starts rummaging through your unmentionables, under the pretense of packing your bag. Speak of the devil..."

Cassie glanced over her shoulder to see the middle Culpepper brother enter the room with a satchel under one arm and her notes and writing tablets clamped in his hand.

He set her belongings on the floor beside her. "Here you go. Everything you requested. Suz said to tell you hello and she hopes you're feeling better. Not to worry about your cat. She's taking good care of Maxwell."

"Suz?" Harrison goaded in wicked amusement. "You're using a shortened version of her first name already?"

"Leave him alone, Harrison." Cassie didn't want Harrison to make Jefferson self-conscious while she was practicing her matchmaking skills. "And thank you, Jefferson. I appreciate having extra clothing and tablets."

"Glad to be of help. I bought supplies and checked to see how Jack was coming along with the investigation. He's doing his best to get you off the hook."

The comment sent her spirits plunging again. "I hope he's having more luck with this case than he did with the bank robberies."

She watched the Culpepper brothers cast each other a discreet glance then look away.

Their odd expressions drew her curiosity. "Does Jack know more about the robberies than he's confided in me?"

"That's his professional business so I'm not at liberty to say," Jefferson replied. When Cassie sent him a perturbed glance he added, "It's just like when Jack told me that he wasn't at liberty to say how you came to have a pocketful of banknotes last night."

Cassie muttered under breath. He had her there. She also noticed that Harrison didn't seem surprised by the comment, which meant he'd been privy to the information. "Fine then. I'll discuss the issue with Jackson. I plan to work on my articles after lunch. Then I'm headed to the mineral spring for a good, long soaking."

"I don't know about that," Harrison said uneasily. "True, it's an insolated location, but that doesn't mean someone can't overtake you."

"Someone already pounced on me," she reminded them. "This time I'll be more cautious and I'll carry weapons."

"But—"

She made a slashing gesture with her hand to silence Jefferson's objection.

"Might I remind you that I am an independent woman who doesn't believe in that preposterous nonsense about needing a man to watch over me constantly. It's bad enough that I've been imprisoned—"

"You call this imprisonment?" Harrison hooted in interruption. "We're treating you like a queen."

"Queens are not ordered to remain anywhere indefinitely," she countered. "Furthermore, I feel perfectly fine—" that was a bit of a stretch "—and I'm returning to my home and my job tomorrow. If Jackson doesn't like it—"

"And I guarantee he won't," Jefferson didn't fail to interject.

"Too bad," she said stubbornly. "I'm leaving tomorrow."

Having that settled and out of the way, Cassie finished

her tasty meal then retired to her room to edit her newspaper articles for printing. Then she borrowed a horse and headed for the steamy spring and the homestead cabin where the Culpeppers weren't hovering over her constantly.

Jack entered the ranch house late that afternoon to find his brothers blocking his path through the foyer. "What's wrong?" he asked anxiously then glanced every which way to locate Cassie.

"We voted you out of the family," Jefferson declared.

Jack's brows shot up his forehead. "Why?"

"Because you've mishandled Cassie," Harrison explained.

"She's asking questions and demanding answers," Jefferson chimed in. "She's getting restless, too."

"It's time to tell her what's what," said Harrison.

Jack gave his brothers an emphatic, unequivocal "No."

Jefferson checked the doorways to make sure Clara wasn't there. "We need to return her money, at least."

"I told you that would only provoke more suspicious questions," Jack insisted. "You can't slip that kind of money under the door at the boardinghouse then dash into the night."

"Then *loan* her the money, as you suggested earlier," Harrison persisted.

"Incidentally, she informed us that she's returning to town tomorrow," said Jefferson. "Whether you like it or not."

"Which I don't," Jack scowled.

"That's what we told her. It didn't faze her one bit," Jefferson reported.

Jack blew out an agitated breath then veered into the family office to open the safe. "All right. I'll offer to loan her half of what we owe her. Maybe that will pacify her temporarily. Where is she?"

"At the springs," Harrison replied.

Jack rounded on his brothers. "Without a bodyguard?"

Jefferson grinned, undaunted by Jack's intimidating glare. "Cassie reminded us that she is her own woman and she doesn't want or need men hovering over her as if she's helpless. She took a pistol and knife with her for protection."

Grumbling, Jack turned back to cram the paper currency into his vest pocket. "Hard to believe you two pushovers used to be Texas Rangers," he sniped.

"You brought her here, *Marshal*," Harrison mocked as Jack exited the office. "You try to take care of her and see how much luck you have controlling her strong will."

"Forget that loan business," Jefferson called after him. "Just tell her what's going on. It will make all of our lives much easier."

Jack doubted it. He was sticking with the loan plan and would see how that worked.

Cassie thoroughly enjoyed her private bath in the steamy spring. The hollowed-out rock basin was like a gigantic bathtub where she could float and paddle around to her heart's content. For an hour, she mulled over the baffling incident that had left her unconscious beside a murder victim. And not, she reminded herself, in the same alley in which she'd been attacked.

How and why had that happened?

The thought prompted her to ease closer to the rim of the pool—to keep her pistol and dagger within arm's reach. Thus far, no one had tried to intrude, but she kept her guard up.

From out of nowhere, a long shadow spilled over the hill. Cassie reached instinctively for her pistol. When she recognized Jack, who was looking down on her, she yelped in embarrassment. Tossing aside the weapon, she sank neck deep in the steamy water.

"You should have announced yourself," she scolded.

"An outlaw or four-legged predator wouldn't have," he countered as he walked steadily toward her, his amber gaze boring down on her in blatant disapproval. "You shouldn't be here, and I should shoot my brothers for leaving you alone."

She covered herself as best she could, unsure how much of her body Jack could see through the mist of steam floating over the water. "I *insisted* strenuously."

"So I heard."

"Okay, you've made your point. Now you can go," she said, dismissively flicking her wrist to shoo him on his way.

He didn't leave, just parked himself on a boulder. "You are supposed to be resting at the house."

"I'll rest when I'm dead," she smarted off.

"If you keep up this sort of reckless activity, you'll be dead sooner than you think. I'm telling you this is a bad time to be taking unnecessary risks."

When he reached into his leather vest pocket then waved a stack of banknotes at her, excitement channeled through her. "You recovered my money? Where? Did you apprehend the bandits? Are they locked in jail? I want my turn at them—"

Jack flapped his arms to halt the barrage of questions. "This isn't your recovered money. I'm offering you a loan. It's only half of what you lost, but it will tide you over while you're in Fort Worth."

She furrowed her brows at him. "Fort Worth? I'm not going to Fort Worth."

"Yes, you are," he contradicted. "You're going to lie low until I solve this puzzling case."

Outraged, Cassie glowered at him. "I have had quite enough of your telling me where to go and what to do. You are not going to buy me off then shuffle me out of town indefinitely." She shook her finger at him. "You haven't solved the robbery that happened almost two months ago, much less the one that happened last week. You aren't sending me away from my job at your whim and I am not—I repeat *not*—a coward, so don't try to turn me into one!"

"It would make my life easier if you were," Jack muttered. "Next time your assailant might decide to use a pistol on you instead of a club. And although I questioned Doreen and Edgar, both of them claimed they had nothing to do with knocking you unconscious."

"And you believe them?" Cassie smirked. "Neither of them likes me and they both threatened me."

"Doreen's father claimed she was dining with him at the time of the incident. I spoke to Edgar's boss and he's fairly certain his assistant was working during that time."

Cassie muttered in frustration. "I didn't expect anyone to willingly to admit to assault and murder, but it would've been nice."

"In addition, the rain washed away all tracks near your body and Millard's," Jack continued. "Complications are playing hell with this case." He waved the money at her again. "Take this loan and leave town, Cassie. You've been knocked unconscious already. Rumors about your involvement in the murder are running rampant. It's time to cut your losses and clear out for a while."

Cassie bounded to her feet indignantly, then remembered she was naked. With a squawk, she plunked down in the water. But not before she unintentionally provided Jack with an eyeful of her nude body. Then she reminded herself that Jack had partially undressed her during their tryst in the cabin. And he'd disrobed her completely before he tucked her in Aunt Louise's bed after the attack. Nevertheless, she blushed profusely, but she didn't let that deter her for long.

"You will have to drag me kicking and screaming from town," she told him defiantly. "I came here to be near my aunt and to work in a profession I love. Plus, I intend to pursue my worthwhile causes."

"You'll have to put your project on the back burner until we find out who attacked you and why. Take the money I'm offering and leave town."

"Stop waving that loan money in my face," she demanded as she glided to the edge of the pool where she'd placed her clothing. "I want my stolen money returned or none at all."

He muttered something foul that she didn't ask him to repeat. Then he said, "Damnation, Cassie, you are the most stubborn, bullheaded female I have ever met."

"You would know stubborn and bullheaded, since you possess those infuriating traits yourself," she hurled back at him. "Now turn your back so I can climb from the spring and dress."

"No," he snapped. "I'm not turning my back unless you agree to take the money and leave town until I find out who else, *besides me,* wants to pound you over the head!"

Jack forced himself to drag in a calming breath.

"Honest to God, woman, you are driving me straight downhill to loco!"

"It's my life and *I* decide where I go and what I do!"

At wit's end, Jack stamped over to snatch up her garments before she could retrieve them. It took considerable self-restraint not to savor the sight of her lush body in the misty water, but he was a man on a mission. He untethered her horse and led it away before lust got the better of him, tempting him to strip off his clothes and dive in the steamy pool to join her.

"What the blazes do you think you're doing?" she railed as he stalked off.

"You can stay there and shrivel up like a prune for all I care," he flung over his shoulder spitefully. "I'll be in the cabin when you come to your senses and agree to take the money and leave. Then and only then can you have your clothes back."

"Damn you, Andrew Jackson Culpepper!" she spewed furiously. "I'd like to shoot you. Too bad I'd never get away with your murder because everyone thinks I disposed of Millard Stewart already."

He kept right on walking without looking back.

"Unbelievable!"

He flinched when he realized she had bounded from the pool and raced after him—stark bone naked. He really wanted to look back to survey every luscious inch of her body. He'd seen too much of Cassie's alluring curves and swells lately, but it wasn't enough. He wondered if his private cell in hell came with visions of this enticing but maddening female floating overhead night and day for eternity.

This is what you get for resorting to bank robbery to

expose a wily criminal like Floyd Pettigrew—or whoever really is behind this bank scam, he reminded himself. *Cassandra Bixby has become the curse of my life.*

"Give me my clothes," Cassie growled from so close behind him that he flinched again.

"Here you go, buttercup."

She snatched her garments from his grasp before he could open the cabin door. Then she slapped him upside the head with her clothes. Much as he wanted to, he didn't look back to visually devour the alluring female. But honestly, he didn't know why he bothered trying to be noble. He'd used up most of his self-control as it pertained to Cassie already.

To compound his torment, his brothers' demands kept ringing in his ears. *Tell her the truth,* they'd said. His involvement with the robbery scheme hounded him constantly. Not to mention the frustration he knew it caused Cassie. He hadn't been able to return her money, as he'd returned everyone else's. And that haunted him to no end, too.

Jack realized the time of reckoning had come—and he knew he was going to be on the wrong side of it.

"I have something else to say to you," Jack said, resigned. He strode into the cabin without looking back. "Get dressed, Cass."

He heard the rustling of clothing behind him as she dressed quickly. When she veered around him, Jack blinked in astonishment. He hadn't paid the slightest attention to the type or style of the garments he'd scooped up hurriedly beside the pool. But he was paying attention *now*. She was wearing fitted breeches that called attention to her curvaceous hips and the trim indentation of her waist. The blouse and midnight-blue bolero accentuated her breasts to their full advantage.

It suddenly dawned on him that Cassie's mount hadn't been equipped with a sidesaddle. She'd been riding astride, same as a man.

Now why didn't that surprise him?

She crossed her arms over her breasts and tapped her foot impatiently. Curly golden hair haloed her exquisite face, which showed signs of slight sunburn after her prolonged stay in the warm spring.

"What is the *something else,* Marshal?" she demanded.

"Have a seat."

She raised a rebellious brow at his terse command.

"Please," he muttered begrudgingly and thought, *Damn female, she refuses to give an inch.*

Eventually she sank into the chair beside the window. Jack sucked in a fortifying breath, gathered his thoughts then walked over to roll back the braided rug in front of the hearth. He watched Cassie's face register surprise when he opened the trap door in the floor.

"Because of the threat of renegade Indians, outlaws and dangerous storms, my family built a place to hide, as well as storage for our food supply."

"That's an interesting tidbit," she said caustically. "But what has that got to do with anything?"

"I'm getting to that."

Mentally preparing himself for the moment when all hell broke loose, Jack descended the steps. He reappeared a moment later to toss a sombrero, black hood, gloves, spurs and canvas duster at Cassie's feet.

"Have you seen these before, señorita?" he asked with a deeper voice and a heavy Spanish accent.

Her eyes rounded in disbelief and she stared at him with open-mouthed astonishment. In stunned silence, she inspected one garment after the other. Confusion, shock, understanding then furious outrage claimed her face.

"You?" she howled as she slammed the silver spurs to the floor then bolted to her feet. "How dare you! No wonder you were in no hurry to track the bandits. *You* were one of them. Who was the other? One of your brothers?"

"Both actually. We took turns," he told her calmly— one of them needed to remain calm. "Wilbur Knox, who's a former Texas Ranger, too, served as our lookout and signaled us when the coast was clear to enter and exit the bank."

"You sneaky scoundrel!" Her voice rose in seething fury. "No wonder I've sensed something eerily familiar about the way you tower over me occasionally. But I couldn't figure it out." She stormed toward him, bristling with indignation, her eyes flashing like green flames. "You've been laughing at me the entire time, haven't you?"

"No, I—"

"You went with me to hunt for tracks by the river," she raged at him. "But you knew full well that you and your bandit brothers had covered your tracks."

Breasts heaving, her face pulsing with color, she stabbed her forefinger into his chest. He was grateful she didn't have a knife in her hand.

"You, who have tracked outlaws with the Rangers, knew how to conceal your identity effectively. That explains the perfect disguise and thick accent. No one suspected the founding family of robbing the citizens you vowed to protect. Worse, you *encouraged* them to move here and now you've turned on them!"

"There's a good reason—"

Cassie was in a full-blown rage. She refused to let him speak until she had vented her anger. "You are beneath contempt," she said through clenched teeth. "I mistook you for an honest man. I even—"

She snapped her mouth shut before she blurted out that she was attracted to the handsome but cunningly corrupt lawman. She whirled toward the door, but Jack grabbed her elbow and yanked her back.

His scowling face was a few inches from hers. "I *am* an honest man who resorted to drastic measures to ferret out the shyster at the bank who's robbing our town."

Cassie's reply was a sardonic smirk. "What do you mean?"

"I'm fairly certain someone has been embezzling money from customer accounts," he explained.

"Someone like Floyd Pettigrew?"

Jack nodded somberly. "Or perhaps it was Millard Stewart. And Pettigrew, wanting revenge, found a way to dispose of him and frame you. I'm wondering if Millard and Floyd were working together. But I can't prove a damn thing," he grumbled in frustration. "Now the situation is even more complicated because you're embroiled in it and you were attacked.

"In addition, a mysterious stranger, somehow connected to the bank, appeared and then disappeared unexpectedly," he continued. "The bank teller is dead and the unidentified stranger might be, too, for all I know. Then there's your boss, Gerald, who might be conspiring with Floyd Pettigrew. I'm wondering if someone is killing off partners to retain a larger cut of the profit."

Cassie ceased struggling for freedom and listened

intently. Her feelings of outrage and betrayal subsided when she saw angry frustration in the expression on Jack's face and heard it in his voice.

"In the past, my brothers and I have returned the money and jewelry taken from each victim at the bank. One of us makes the rounds at night to leave a pouch at the door, along with monetary compensation for the inconvenience and a note requesting silence."

Cassie frowned pensively. "That explains why victims refused to offer details about the robberies for my newspaper articles."

"Most likely," Jack agreed. "We aren't Robin Hood and his Merry Men, but we *are* taking the authentic banknotes, printed in reputable banks, out of teller's drawer. We repay victims with legitimate currency, not the phony bills we believe Floyd and Gerald have printed and circulated in the town," Jack explained as he eased his grasp on her arm.

"You don't think the money in Pettigrew's bank is worth the paper it's printed on?" she asked anxiously.

"I've had my doubts for six months. The bank teller has limited the size of the withdrawals so he doesn't have to hand out too much legal tender that he's trying to keep for his own," Jack confided.

"I remember the limited withdrawals the day of the robbery," she said pensively. "Both cattle drovers were incensed when Millard told them they had to wait for the amount to be approved."

"That's what initially aroused my suspicion," Jack told her. "My friend, Nate Hudson, had the same problem. However, your numerous news articles and private pursuit of justice have increased public awareness and made it difficult for me to investigate discreetly."

"Well, it serves you right," she grumbled as she flashed him the evil eye. "I'm still annoyed at you for deceiving me so thoroughly and for letting me stew about the loss of my savings." She swatted him on the shoulder. "Damn it, Jack. You should have told me in the beginning!"

He released her arm then swooped down to gather up the evidence strewn on the planked floor. "If it makes you feel better, I've had a flaming case of the guilts and my conscience has been nagging the hell out of me."

"It doesn't make me feel better," she said, refusing to let him off the hook. "And good for your conscience for tormenting you."

When he descended the steps to stash the disguise from sight, she peered into the cellar. It was lined with shelves stacked with glass jars and extra supplies. There were a few chairs and a cot. The Culpeppers had tucked the items in the cellar for safekeeping but no fresh air circulated through it.

No wonder the clothes smelled musty, she mused. Unlike the garments worn by whoever had clubbed her over the head. Her assailant had used the bandit's disguise to throw her off track, just as Jack had insisted—and he ought to know, damn his sneaky hide!

Cassie's head was spinning with the realization the Culpeppers were bank robbers. But at least it was for a good cause and at least they were not killers. Unfortunately, there was one still running around loose and she didn't know who it was.

"I don't understand why you don't storm into the bank and look for evidence to prove what you suspect is going on." She kerplopped into the chair to massage her temples.

He said nothing until he had closed the trap door then

carefully replaced the braided rug. Jack rose to his full stature to stare grimly at her. "I'm waiting for confirmation that Floyd Pettigrew has a history of investment fraud. If he's swindling money from customers to use for his own greedy purposes, he isn't spending excessively enough to draw suspicion. I doubt the number of banknotes he printed up matches his actual assets.

"I don't know how many conspirators are involved. Maybe Stewart, Nash and the mysterious stranger. I don't want them to escape prematurely," Jack insisted. "I want to punish all conspirators involved."

"I still don't want to believe Gerald Nash is involved in this scheme," Cassie murmured, staring intently at Jack. "But why else would he have a stash of recently printed banknotes?"

Jack shrugged his shoulders. "If he told you that it wasn't his place to explain the situation, it indicates he's in cahoots with Pettigrew, but refuses to incriminate himself."

Torment and disappointment hung over Cassie like a black cloud. "Pettigrew and Nash are stealing real money and replacing it with counterfeit bills. Bank customers' accounts are probably sitting empty and they don't even know it."

Jack blew out an agitated breath. "I'd like to get a look at the bank ledgers, but Pettigrew will become suspicious and split town if I ask to see them. I wish I knew if Millard Stewart was involved in the fraud or if he accidentally stumbled onto the truth. Either way, he became dispensable, and the killer took the opportunity to throw suspicion on you."

Cassie thought it over for a moment and said, "I want to join forces with you."

Jake gaped at her. "You want to join the Culpepper Gang?"

"Yes, but I don't intend to hold up the bank. Since I've interviewed Pettigrew for news articles before, he won't be suspicious if I ask him a few questions about the deceased bank teller."

"No. Absolutely not," he said sharply.

If she heard him, she chose to ignore him. Whatever the case, she continued as if he hadn't spoken. "While I'm in the bank, I'll pay particular attention to where the ledgers and cash drawers are located. Then after dark—"

"I said *no* and I mean *no,*" he told her succinctly. "This isn't your fight. You didn't pledge to do whatever necessary to protect this town because your family bears its name."

She waved him off as if he were a pesky mosquito. "You know perfectly well that I am a champion of causes."

Jack threw her an exasperated glance and said, "Here we go."

"This is an important cause," she insisted. "You said so yourself. You're risking your reputation by resorting to unconventional means to lure out the culprits. And it's going to kill me to have Gerald Nash indicted if he's involved, but I want to see justice served."

Jack loomed over her, much the same way he'd done during the robbery. "I've told you the truth, but you have to promise to do nothing and to keep silent until I sort this out."

"You don't know me very well, do you, Jack?" She surged to her feet to stand toe to toe with him. "I might not be as capable of conducting an investigation as you are, but I have experience at digging for facts. Plus, my job at the newspaper office provides me with a perfect excuse to wedge my foot in the door at the bank so I can snoop around."

"No." He hooked his arm around her waist and drew her flush against him.

"Yes," she said defiantly.

He bent his raven head until his face was so close to hers that she felt his warm breath on her cheek. Wild tingles, which had no business whatsoever assailing her while she was in the middle of the heated debate, sizzled through her. Having Jack pressed familiarly against her increased her awareness of him tenfold. She stared at his lips and wanted to feel them moving expertly over hers. She felt his rock-hard chest beneath her hand and she wanted to explore him without the layer of fabric getting in her way.

"Repeat after me," he rasped, his golden eyes glowing like banked fires. "I will not become involved…"

She was already involved with this case and with him. Jack was heroic and courageous and he cared about this town to the point that he had risked everything he stood for to rout a criminal and his cohorts before they bled the prosperous community dry. She admired him for that. He was more of a crusader than she'd ever been and he didn't realize it.

"I'm involved already, Jack," she admitted as she looped her arms over his shoulders and arched instinctively against his masculine contours.

"Are you trying to seduce me into agreeing to your help?" he murmured as he ground his hips against hers, assuring her that she was having a dramatic effect on him, too.

"Yes." She skimmed her mouth over his sensuous lips, loving the taste of him, wanting more. "How is it working so far?"

He smiled with a mixture of devilry and sensuality that Cassie found irresistible, then he said, "I'll need more convincing, buttercup."

Chapter Eleven

The moment she kissed him, the world went out of focus. Desire pulsated through Jack's oversensitive body. He told himself to slow down and take his time savoring the delicious pleasure of having Cassie's alluring body pressed to his. But his brain couldn't control the hungry demands of his body.

Without breaking the heated kiss, he tugged at her bolero then tossed it carelessly across the room. He worked the buttons of her shirt impatiently, but the instant he got his hands on the full swells of her breasts he was in no rush to move on. Exploring her silky skin never failed to fascinate and distract him.

He could feel her trembling beneath his wandering caresses. He could hear her breathe raggedly. Knowing he aroused and excited Cassie gave him a unique kind of satisfaction. Yet touching her wasn't enough anymore. He wanted to taste every exquisite inch of her luscious flesh until he knew her body better than he knew his own. He wanted to feel her arching anxiously against him, hear her serenading him with her soft moans of pleasure.

"Jack?" she whispered when he broke the kiss and came up for air.

"You want me to stop?" he asked hoarsely. *Please say no.* "I will if that's what you want." *It will kill me, of course, but I would never force myself on you.*

Jack didn't want to overpower Cassie. There would be no satisfaction in that. He wanted her to meet him halfway in the throes of desire. He wanted her to be his equal partner in passion. It was all or nothing when it came to Cassie. He realized that he'd always known that it could be no other way.

"No, I don't want you to stop," she assured him as she worked the buttons on his shirt. "But you are overdressed and if I can't touch you I'll go crazy."

He lifted his head and grinned down at her. "Can't allow that to happen, now, can we?"

The glow of desire burning in her evergreen eyes bewitched him. He delighted in the way she pressed her hips eagerly against his arousal when he circled his fingertip around her taut nipples.

His thoughts scattered like buckshot when she peeled his shirt from his shoulders and sent it flying in the same direction as her blouse and bolero. Then she splayed her palm over his chest and flicked her tongue against his flesh. When her fingertips drifted to the band of his breeches, Jack forgot to breathe—couldn't remember why he needed to.

Hungry need clenched inside him as her hand grazed the fabric covering his erect flesh. "We need to be in bed," he growled as he angled his head to spread a row of kisses along the column of her throat.

"We also need to agree that I'm helping with this investigation," she murmured. "Don't tell me no, Jack."

He wondered if he'd ever be able to tell this enchanting siren no again. When she touched him familiarly and kissed him as if there was no tomorrow he was ready to give her the moon and every star in the sky. He, who prided himself in being a seasoned warrior, went down in flaming defeat when Cassie loosened the placket of his breaches and touched him intimately.

"You win," he wheezed, buffeted by the indescribable pleasure of her caresses.

She grinned impishly and said, "I haven't even declared war yet."

"No need. You can have whatever you want, buttercup. Starting with me." He scooped her up in his arms and carried her to bed.

"That's good because I want you, Jack." She glanced cautiously toward the open windows. "What about your brothers?"

"They can get their own women. I'm not sharing you."

She chortled as she traced the curve of his lips. "I'm not sharing you, either, but maybe we should close the curtains. Every time I get my hands on you, your brothers show up to interrupt us. I don't want another interruption."

He set her on the edge of the bed and said, "Don't leave." He hurried over to close the curtains, shutting out the golden rays of sunset.

"You couldn't get rid of me if you tried," she assured him as she turned back the quilts.

Jack groaned aloud when he spun around. Cassie had stretched out on the bed, wearing nothing but her trim-fitting breeches. Desire hit him with the force of a tidal wave and nearly knocked him to his knees.

Honest to God, he still didn't understand why he was so fiercely attracted to a woman who was absolutely nothing like the women he'd known in the past. Yet, this feisty, intelligent, challenging female was the one he desired.

Jack had one thing on his mind as he walked toward her. He wanted her to want him, for her desire to reach the same feverish pitch as his. To that dedicated end he stretched out beside her then kissed her as gently as he knew how. When she arched against him and he felt the erotic brush of her breasts against his bare chest need throbbed in rhythm with his accelerated heartbeat.

"You intrigue me, Cass," he admitted. His hands swirled over her breasts to tease her nipples to hard pebbles. "I keep wondering if I'll ever get enough of you."

"Mmm…" she moaned as his lips drifted down her shoulder to graze the tips of her breasts.

He grinned in masculine triumph. He'd left Cassie speechless. That was a first. The possibility of using the technique to keep her quiet on future occasions was an enticing thought. Almost as enticing as suckling her breasts and watching her arch helplessly toward him. When he plucked at her nipple with thumb and forefinger, another wobbly moan tumbled from her lips.

Jack worked his way down her body one kiss and caress at a time. When he reached the waistband of her breeches she stilled, unmoving, barely breathing. He felt her quiver, heard her sigh raggedly as he eased the garment down her hips and thighs to leave her gloriously naked beside him.

He'd satisfied one fantasy, but still it wasn't enough.

But then, he'd known he wouldn't be content until he'd explored all of her. He wanted to inhale the sweet scent of her body and feel her satiny flesh against his lips and fingertips. Then he wanted to seduce her all over again.

He glided his open mouth over the curve of her hip. When he caressed her inner thigh, her breath shattered. He could feel the moist heat of her desire against his hand, and aching need nearly overwhelmed him. When he stroked the sensitive bud between her legs, she clutched at his arm. Her nails bit into his skin, as if holding on to him for dear life. He smiled to himself, savoring the erotic effect his touch had on her.

Jack skimmed his lips over her abdomen then slid his fingertip inside her. He delighted in hearing the raspy sounds of pleasure that flowed from her lips as he caressed her and felt her burning around his fingertip. When he dipped his head to taste her very essence, she called out his name and moved restlessly beneath his intimate kisses and caresses.

He liked knowing that he satisfied her and that she ached for more. He'd discovered a new calling in life— watching this honey-haired beauty surrender to the heated passion he had aroused in her.

"Make the ache go away," she demanded, then writhed impatiently beneath his intimate caresses. "Now… please…"

Jack peeled off his breeches in fiendish haste. He came back to her, holding himself above her as he nudged her knees apart. Grinning, he murmured, "Nothing better than a woman who knows what she wants and doesn't hesitate to ask—"

His voice evaporated when her hand folded around his

arousal and she guided him to her. She caressed him provocatively with her thumb and forefinger. The sensual stroke of her hand caused need to explode inside him with killing force. Jack groaned as his body clenched and he tried desperately to control its urgent demands.

When she clamped her hand on his hip and drew him ever closer, Jack's self-discipline shattered. He closed his eyes and sank into the heated softness of her body then surged forward to bury himself to the hilt—

His eyes flew wide open when he discovered what he supposed he'd known all along—that he was Cassie's first experiment with passion. No matter what the consequences, he couldn't deny himself the exquisite pleasure of being with her. She fired his blood and he wanted her more than he wanted his next breath.

Cassie stared steadily at him while he tried nobly to hold himself perfectly still so she'd have time to adjust to the unfamiliar pressure of masculine penetration. Relief washed over him when she smiled and shifted beneath him.

"There's more, right?" she whispered.

"Only if you want there to be." He smiled down at her. "There's a whole lot more if you're up to the challenge."

His teasing remark provoked her to chuckle softly. "I want the best you've got. I've heard conflicting reports about whether passion is pleasure or womanly duty. Which is it?"

Jack withdrew with deliberate slowness then glided into her gently. When he looked into her lovely face, surrounded by a spray of silky hair, he vowed to himself that no matter what it cost in self-restraint he'd see to it that Cassie considered passion the most fulfilling enjoyment she'd ever experienced. Pride refused to let him offer her anything less than complete satisfaction.

He lowered his head to take her lips beneath his in a tender kiss as he moved rhythmically inside her. In less than a heartbeat, feverish need burned him alive. The control he valued so highly slipped its leash and he drove into her urgently. Need hammered at him as his masculine body sought to unite with hers. She met him—thrust for desperate thrust—until they were clinging to each other in breathless passion.

"Oh…my—" Cassie's voice fractured.

Her body screamed for release. Wild sensations expanded and radiated like the sun. She became hopelessly lost in her need for him. When Jack became the living, breathing flame inside her, it was impossible to tell where his swarthy body ended and hers began.

She held on frantically to Jack, stunned by the intensity of sensations that pelted her repeatedly, refusing to release her from their fierce grasp. Heat blazed through her, again and again, searing her from the inside out. Although Jack's powerful body enveloped hers, she swore she was floating in some mystical dimension of outer space where time ceased to exist.

So this was what ecstasy felt like, she thought, dazed and amazed. Inhibitions didn't exist, only incredible sensations. She arched against his muscled body, felt him throbbing deep inside her, filling her completely while they shared the same flesh, the same frantic heartbeat, and surrendered to the same ineffable pleasure.

When Jack buried his head against her shoulder, groaned hoarsely then shuddered above her, another wave of astonishing sensations flooded over her. She held on to him as tightly as he held her. In her wildest imagination, she had never expected passion to be so overwhelming and satisfying.

Feminine duty? Ha! she thought to herself. If a woman felt *obliged* to appease a man's needs then she was obviously intimate with the wrong man. Jack knew when, where and how to touch a woman, how to make her come undone in his arms.

"Are you okay?" he whispered as he eased away from her.

"Better than okay," she murmured. "You?"

"Same here, except I might not find the energy to climb from bed for a week."

"Really?" she propped herself up on her elbow to peer into his ruggedly handsome face. "I'm bursting with energy. I'm thinking of walking down to the springs. Want to join me?"

"We're expected for supper," Jack reminded her. "You do remember my wicked brothers, don't you? They might show up unannounced if we don't return after a reasonable amount of time."

Impulsively, she dropped a kiss to his sensuous lips. "You can go home if you want, but I'm going to soak to my heart's content. I'm supposed to be recuperating, after all. Those were *your* orders."

When she rolled off the bed to grab her discarded shirt she heard the bed creak. She glanced over her shoulder to see Jack rise to his feet. Sweet mercy! she thought as she admired every ridge and contour of muscular flesh on his masculine body. If there was a more perfect male specimen walking the face of the earth she couldn't imagine who it might be. Jack put Greek gods to shame.

Despite a few battle scars on his shoulder, thigh and ribs, he was the epitome of whipcord muscle, lean flesh and eye-catching virility.

Cassie blushed profusely when he caught her ogling him. He arched a thick black brow. "Something wrong?"

"Not that I can see."

He chuckled and raised an eyebrow rakishly as he donned his breeches. "Same goes for me, buttercup."

She exited the bedroom, wearing nothing but her long-tailed shirt. She halted on the porch to admire the twinkling stars that formed a glittering canopy over the rolling hills. Something about this place called to something deep inside her. She fully understood why Jack's family built their homestead cabin on the rise of ground. It *felt* like home.

Cassie trotted downhill to the springs then sighed appreciatively as she sank into the warm water. She glanced up in surprise when Jack appeared from the shadows.

"I thought you were headed home."

"I thought it over and decided I wanted to fulfill another of my fantasies about you. Just in case you come to your senses and decide this should never happen again."

"It probably shouldn't," she agreed, her smile fading.

"I figured you'd say that." He peeled off his breeches and walked straight toward her.

All eyes, she watched him walk naked into the mist-covered pool. She wondered how long it would be before the visual impact of Jack's muscled body no longer affected her. She guessed she'd have to be dead not to react so dramatically to him. No doubt about it, Andrew Jackson Culpepper would be difficult to replace as the starring role in her secret fantasies.

Willfully, she discarded her erotic thoughts and circled

back to Jack's initial comment. "I don't think you should risk being seen in public with me since I've become a murder suspect." She stared pointedly at him. "You're walking a fine line already. Your job might be in jeopardy."

"Then I suppose secret rendezvous will become the order of the day—or night, to be more accurate—until we get this mess figured out."

When he sank down in front of her in the steamy pool, Cassie yielded to the impulsive need to touch him as familiarly as he had touched her. She skimmed her hands over the broad expanse of his chest then explored the washboard muscles of his belly. When her hand dipped beneath the surface to stroke him intimately, Jack's breath hitched and he groaned huskily.

"Damn, woman, I don't have the slightest control when you touch me."

"Good to know," she teased impishly as she encircled his aroused flesh with her fingertip. "Now I can have my way with you anytime I please."

"Just don't tell my brothers that I'm putty in your hands," he said raggedly.

She flashed a wicked smile. "Putty is an inaccurate description. And don't try to sell yourself *short,* either."

A rumble of amusement rattled in his chest, but it evaporated when she caressed him intimately again.

"I want you," he whispered as he clamped hold of her legs then wrapped them around his waist. "Right here. Right now."

"No one is stopping you from having what you want," she assured him. "And just so you know, I want you, too, Jack."

Arousing him, touching him provocatively and hearing

him groan in pleasure, excited her to the extreme. She longed to feel those astonishing sensations pulsing inside her, just as they had in the cabin when she and Jack became one for an endless moment that defied time.

She looped her arms around his shoulders as he guided her hips against his and became the shimmering flame inside her. She gave herself up to the overwhelming need that only Jack had created and only he satisfied. Cassie kissed him hungrily as passion built inside her to a vibrating crescendo.

Sensual fire splintered the last of her control and spasms of pleasure radiated in every direction at once. She gasped when the same brand of indescribable ecstasy Jack had revealed to her earlier cascaded over her. She swore she was tumbling through the night sky like a flaming star. But Jack was there to catch her when he shuddered in release and cradled her tightly against his chest.

They clung together for the longest time, struggling to breathe normally. Cassie would have been content to cuddle up against him for several minutes, but Jack pulled away from her suddenly then shifted to place her protectively behind him.

A moment later, she realized why he'd planted himself in front of her like a shield. She looked around his broad shoulder to see the silhouettes of his brothers looming on the rise of ground. Cassie gasped and tried to make herself invisible.

"What are you doing here?" Jack demanded sharply.

"Making sure you and Cassie didn't kill each other," Jefferson replied.

"We gave up waiting supper on you," Harrison added. "Where is Cassie?"

"In the cabin," Jack lied convincingly while Cassie sank chin-deep in the pool. "Now go away. I'll fetch Cassie after my bath, then I'll bring her home for supper."

Although Cassie couldn't see the two men because she was cowering behind Jack, she heard their devilish snickers.

"We aren't as stupid as we look," Jefferson remarked.

"He is. I'm not," Harrison insisted.

"Could've fooled me." Jack thrust his arm out in the general direction of the ranch house. *"Leave."*

"You never let us have any fun," Jefferson complained.

"I told Cassie what's going on, just like you wanted," Jack said. "There. Happy now?"

"How did you convince her to keep a vow of silence?" Jefferson tormented him.

"Did you seal the pact with a kiss?" Harrison asked in wicked glee.

Jack scowled and said, "If you don't leave of your own accord I'm going to come up there and make you."

Jefferson flung up his hands. "Okay, big brother, you've scared us away. We're shaking in our boots."

When Jefferson wheeled around, Harrison called out, "See you later, Cassie." Then he followed his brother into the darkness.

"Good God," she whimpered, mortified. "I'll never be able to face those two ornery devils ever again."

Jack turned to gather her in his arms then nuzzled his chin against the crown of her head. "I'm really sorry. I deal with my evil little brothers constantly, but I never meant for you to suffer through their teasing."

"Why is it that every time we're together they catch us at something they can hold over my head for the rest of my life?" she grumbled.

"Because every time I'm with you, I can't keep my hands off you, so they're bound to catch us at something."

The admission made her feel better. Whatever he felt for her, however long it lasted, he seemed to be as drawn to her as she was to him. They had made no promises to each other. There were no strings, but it would break her heart if he turned to someone else—like Doreen—for sexual satisfaction.

"C'mon. We'd better dress and head home." He clutched her hand to lead her to the edge of the rock-lined pool. "Tomorrow we'll confront Gerald together and see if we can sort out the depth of his involvement in this case."

Cassie smile proudly when he said *we*. Although she regretted having to interrogate her boss, she was pleased Jack had accepted her offer of assistance. He was treating her as his equal and that made her adore him even more.

Jack mentally prepared himself to confront his brothers the moment he and Cassie returned to the ranch house. "Cassie, why don't you see if we have plates of food warming in the kitchen," he suggested. "I'll be there in a minute."

When Cassie strode off, Jack squared his shoulders and ambled into the parlor to meet his brothers' devilish grins and snickers. Jack gnashed his teeth. These yahoos weren't going to make this easy on him and he knew it. He planned to mount the first offense.

"If either of you say or do anything to make Cassie self-conscious or embarrassed, you'll deal with me and I'm not going to be brotherly about it," he said tersely. To emphasize his point he glared at them good and hard, and then added, "In fact, it might be the last conversation we have. Ever."

Jefferson and Harrison raised both hands, as if held at gunpoint. "Whatever you say, big brother," Jefferson patronized him, unable to keep a straight face.

"Right. Mum's the word," Harrison insisted, making no effort whatsoever to bite back a grin. "You won't hear me spreading gossip. I'll be as close-mouthed as the proverbial clam."

"So…tell us how Cassie reacted when you told her about the bandits," Jefferson insisted as he settled himself comfortably on the sofa then sipped his drink of whiskey.

"Once she got over being shocked and furious, she insisted on helping us resolve the case," he reported. "We compared notes—"

"So that's what you're calling it these days," Harrison teased as he saluted Jack with his glass.

Well, so much for bypassing their juvenile taunts. He glared at his brothers together and separately.

"I couldn't pass that one up," Harrison said. "Go on."

"We're going to confront Gerald about the recently printed banknotes and pressure him into admitting his part in the scheme."

Both men nodded pensively. "I hate to hear that Gerald let greed get the better of him," Jefferson murmured. "Just goes to show you that you never know what some folks are willing to do to pad their pockets."

"I'm disappointed myself, but all evidence suggests Gerald has conspired to defraud citizens of their money. However, I'm having trouble passing judgment on him after what we've done in an attempt to figure out what is going on at the bank. Now murder has been added to the mix and I want to know who is behind it. I hope Gerald has nothing to do with that part of the scheme."

Nodding grimly to his brothers, Jack spun on his heels to join Cassie in the kitchen for a late supper.

Chapter Twelve

"I'm greatly relieved that your brothers didn't harass me at breakfast," Cassie commented while she and Jack trotted their horses toward town the next morning. "Did you threaten them within an inch of their lives?"

"No," Jack replied. "I didn't bother with half threats. I told them I'd shoot them dead if they tormented you."

She chuckled at his comment. "Thank you for that. But you don't have to defend my honor. Crusading for women's rights and social reform has earned me dozens of rude, unflattering comments.... And, Jack?"

"Yes?" His golden-eyed gaze focused intently on her.

"I know what it's like to stand up for what you think is right," she assured him. "You did what you felt you had to do about the suspicious activity at the bank."

"I didn't want to have to take such drastic measures to force the culprit's hand. I don't want to have to interrogate Gerald about his involvement, either, but I will."

"I'll circle around to approach town from the west," she insisted as she reined away from Jack. "No sense spurring more gossip than necessary by arriving together."

Jack headed directly to town. "I'll stop by the jail then meet you at the newspaper office in a few minutes."

Resigned to an unpleasant encounter with her boss, Cassie trotted her horse down the street then dismounted in front of the newspaper office. Gerald glanced up from the printing press then wiped his hands when she entered.

"Feeling better?" he asked.

"Much better, thank you." When she saw Jack come through the door, she drew herself up in front of Gerald and said, "A few days ago, I asked you if there was something you needed to tell me and you said you weren't the one I should ask. I need you to explain that comment in detail."

Gerald swiped his hand over his receding hairline then shifted uneasily from one foot to the other. He darted Jack a quick glance when he came to stand beside Cassie. He fidgeted again. "First off, it wasn't my idea. You need to know that."

"Then whose was it?" Jack questioned.

Gerald stared pointedly at Cassie and said, "*You* know."

"Maybe she does, but you need to tell me, Gerald," Jack said sternly.

When Gerald stood there looking perplexed and befuddled, Cassie veered around him to enter the storage closet. She returned with several sheets of banknotes that had yet to be cut apart.

Gerald's jaw dropped open. "You weren't supposed to see those."

"But I did," Cassie replied, disappointed by Gerald's lack of shame over his involvement in the investment scheme.

"I need to know who's in this with you," Jack demanded gruffly. "We need to hear it from you. If you name names and cooperate with me, I'll make certain the judge grants you all the leniency the law allows."

Gerald's hazel eyes nearly popped from their sockets and he stared at them aghast. "What the blazes are you suggesting? That you're going to send Louise to jail?"

"Louise?" Cassie crowed in disbelief. "She's involved with you?"

"Who'd you think?" Gerald asked. "We've been involved since we met in Hillsdale over two years ago."

"You've been printing counterfeit money together and using it to establish your businesses in Pepperville?" Jack snapped in annoyance.

Gerald's gaze leaped from Cassie to Jack. "Of course not. But Louise wanted to keep it from Cassie. I thought you had figured it out after you tapped on the door to Louise's apartment last week and she sent you away. Isn't that why you asked me if there was something I wanted to tell you?"

Cassie finally understood what Gerald was referring to. The mental picture of the two of them enjoying the kind of intimate activity she had recently discovered with Jack assailed her. *"You and Aunt Louise?"* she bleated. "You're having a clandestine affair with my aunt?"

Gerald's round face flooded with embarrassment. "Er... Yes." He cleared his throat and tugged at the cravat around his neck as if it were a noose. "Isn't that what we're talking about?"

"No," Jack replied. "We are discussing your silent partner in this scheme to print counterfeit money."

"There is no counterfeit money," Gerald explained as he took the recently printed pages of currency from

Cassie. "And we are supposed to keep this under wraps so we don't incite panic and send customers storming the bank to demand money after the two robberies."

Gerald's explanation thoroughly confused Cassie. Apparently, she wasn't the only one. Jack looked as puzzled as she felt.

"You better start at the beginning, Gerald," Jack advised. "I'm not clear on what's going on."

"Floyd Pettigrew called me to a private meeting at the bank after the first robbery. He notified me that an auditor from the state was checking into the situation."

Cassie frowned warily. "Did you see the auditor's credentials?"

Gerald nodded his head. "He had all the necessary documents and he indicated that printing currency to match bank assets was a common practice to shore up the flow of currency in the area."

The light of realization dawned on Cassie. "Was this auditor a short, stocky man wearing a three-piece suit and bowler hat?"

"That's right," Gerald confirmed. "Jonathan Smythe. Texas Department of Treasury."

Cassie seriously doubted it. "Where did you conduct this meeting?"

"In Floyd's office." Gerald frowned at Cassie's skeptical tone. "As I said, I saw the proper documents that approved printing the money. In addition, Mr. Smythe explained that tight money policies and practices in Eastern banks have made money scarce in the West. The legislature authorized the printing of money, especially after the robberies. He said Kansas and Nebraska had relied on the practice a few years earlier and Texas was now implementing it. But there has been talk in Washington of a federal monopoly of coining currency."

"Which probably explains why the culprits wanted to print all the money they could before the federal government steps in," she mused aloud.

"According to Mr. Smythe's audit, the bank was sufficiently capitalized to redeem the new script on demand," Gerald added.

"Then why have cattle drovers, who previously made large deposits for safekeeping, been turned away when they try to withdraw money for supplies and wages?" Jack asked. "I've heard complaints about it for six months. Long before the robberies occurred."

Gerald shrugged. "All I know is what the state auditor told me when he authorized printing the new currency."

"Was Millard Stewart privy to this information?" Cassie questioned interestedly.

"I assume so, but I was told to keep the information to myself."

"Right," Jack said and smirked. "Squelch a panic before it begins."

"Exactly," Gerald said, despite Jack's caustic tone. "When did you happen on the newly printed banknotes?"

"The night I rooted around in the closet in search of more writing tablets," Cassie informed him. "The same night I was attacked and dragged to the alley where Jack found me lying beside Millard's body."

"Good God!" Gerald swallowed uneasily. "And you thought *I* was involved in *your* assault?"

"We think Floyd and the so-called auditor, who is probably carrying false credentials, are stealing money from customer accounts and replenishing it with worthless fake currency. They convinced you that it was legal and authorized. Somehow Millard ended up dead because he was dispensable or because he threatened to blow the whistle on Pettigrew and Smythe."

Gerald staggered back a step and his face paled noticeably. "*That* is what you thought I meant when I said that I wasn't the one you should ask about what was going on? You thought *I* was involved in defrauding the *public?*"

When Cassie nodded affirmatively, Gerald smacked himself on the forehead and groaned miserably. "If that isn't bad enough, Louise is going to kill me for blabbing our secret."

"I'm relieved to learn that you were an innocent victim in this scheme," Jack told Gerald. "I also request that you don't mention our conversation to anyone, especially Pettigrew. If he is the mastermind in this plot, I don't want to arouse suspicion while I'm investigating him. I need evidence to convict him and I don't have it yet."

"That conniving bastard," Gerald muttered angrily. "He used me like a pawn. I never realized what he was doing."

"Neither did anyone else. Except maybe Millard, and look what happened to him," Jack said. "The robberies and missing money forced Pettigrew's hand. But you have to give him the currency he asked you to print as if nothing has happened."

"I understand," Gerard replied. "But we need to move quickly so this next batch of counterfeit money isn't distributed to honest citizens."

"We are working as quickly as possible," Cassie assured him then pinned him with her gaze. "Now, about you and Aunt Louise. Why did you keep your affair from me as if I were a naive child?"

Gerald grimaced. "I've been teasing Louise about making an honest man out of me by marrying me, but she refuses."

Cassie nodded thoughtfully. "Because married women lose the privilege of having the final say in buying and selling their investments and businesses. I don't suppose she told you about Roland, the opportunist who dipped into her inheritance under false pretenses then fled with a wealthy woman, did she? Aunt Louise was humiliated and heartbroken. She swore off men for several years."

"No, she didn't tell me," Gerald murmured. "Clearly, it's a sensitive subject. She lost faith in men. Me included."

"But you would marry her and remain faithful to her if she agreed?" Cassie prodded.

"I've asked her three times," Gerald told her. "I thought the last time would be the charm, but I'm no closer to the altar than I was six months ago."

Jack glanced discreetly at Cassie, wondering if she shared her aunt's views on avoiding marriage to protect her independence and investments. Probably. She was the local leader of the women's rights activists, after all.

Cassie reversed direction to scoop up her notepad. "I'm going to interview Floyd about his departed bank teller."

"Be discreet," Jack cautioned. "Think of Millard Stewart."

She waved off his concerns, but he worried nonetheless. He'd found Cassie lying lifeless in the mud once this week. He didn't want to go through that mental anguish again.

"I feel like such a fool." Gerald plopped down in the chair at Cassie's desk. "I had no idea Floyd and that Smythe character were swindling our community. It will be difficult to act as if nothing is wrong when Pettigrew shows up to gather his new currency."

"Don't be so hard on yourself." Jack glanced away from Gerald to stare out the window, watching Cassie's progress across town circle. "Floyd and his cohorts have gone to considerable effort to deceive everyone in town. My brothers and I have spent six months trying to figure out how he's lined his own pockets without public knowledge."

"Nevertheless, I'm offering to do whatever necessary to help you put a stop to it," Gerald said emphatically. He gestured toward the scar above his left eyebrow and the broken bone in his nose. "I've taken on corrupt politicians and outlaws who retaliated against my editorial comments. I'm not afraid to stand up for what's right so don't hesitate to ask for my assistance, whether in person or in newspaper print, Marshal."

"Thanks, Gerald. I appreciate your support. Hopefully, I'll collect the evidence needed on the two men who appear to be responsible for this swindling scheme and murder case."

Jack stared out the pane-glass window to note that Cassie had arrived at the bank and struggled with the doorknob. "Pettigrew must have shut down after Millard's death."

"He did," Gerald confirmed as he came to stand beside Jack. "I thought he'd open his doors by now."

"Maybe he disposed of Millard as a reason to close the bank while he restructured and covered up his scheme," Jack mused aloud.

Gerald stared grimly at him. "Speaking of Millard's death, I don't like the ugly rumors spreading about Cassie's possible involvement in it."

"New ones?" Jack swore under his breath. "What gossip is circulating about her now?"

"Rumor is that she's playing up to you to make sure you don't bring charges against her for murder. So the story goes she insisted you house her at your ranch while she supposedly recovered from injury. She's working her wicked wiles on you."

"Hell and damnation!" Jack erupted.

"I doubt Louise believes the gossip, but she is perturbed at you." Gerald stared steadily at Jack. "She thinks you might be taking unfair advantage of Cassie's predicament… *Are you?*"

Hmm… How to answer that question? Gerald was behaving like an overprotective uncle and Jack didn't want to provoke his outrage. "Cassie and I have an understanding. Plus, we are uniting our efforts to stop Pettigrew and his cohort from robbing our town blind."

"Apparently, you didn't understand the question." Gerald's brows flattened and his gaze narrowed sharply on Jack. "I'm especially fond of Cassie myself. I don't intend to see her treated disrespectfully by anyone, not even the city marshal and a member of the town's founding family."

Jack scoffed. "You're having an affair with the woman who instilled ideas of independence and equal rights in Cassie's head. Do you honestly believe that any man can walk over either of those like-minded females and get away with it?"

A slow smile worked its way across Gerald's lips. "Now that you mention it, no…." He frowned as he stared across town circle. "Where did Cassie go? Hell! If she confronts Louise with her recent discoveries I'll be a dead man."

"You can hide out at my ranch," Jack offered.

He strode from the office and glanced this way and that, wondering which direction Cassie had taken while he was distracted by his conversation with Gerald. She might have gone to check on that demon cat she was so fond of. Either that or she'd sought out her aunt as Gerald predicted.

Jack took off at a jog when he noticed the man dressed like a hard-bitten cattle drover dismounting by the jail. No doubt another cattle herd had waylaid near Pepperville. Jack anticipated the arrival of boisterous cowboys by evening.

It would be another busy night, he thought, disgruntled. Patrolling town would deprive him of Cassie's intimate company.

No question, Louise Bixby would have his head—and other body parts—if she knew that he was doing more than protecting Cassie from possible harm. If Louise went on the warpath, Jack and Gerald would have to hightail it south of the border.

Cassie refused to be deterred from her assignment. Even though Floyd had bolted the front door of the bank, she veered around to the back. When she discovered the door was unlocked, she breezed inside as if she owned the place.

"Who's there?" Floyd called from his office. "I have a pistol and I'll use it. I'm not tolerating more robberies so get out before I blast away!"

"It's me, Cassandra Bixby," she called back. "I came by to say I'm sorry about Millard Stewart's untimely death."

"You should be since you probably had something to do with it," he said snidely. "Go away. I'm working shorthanded."

Cassie refused to let him dismiss her that easily. Moreover, look *who* was calling *whom* a murderer. Determinedly, she strode into Floyd's office. "I'm doing the obituary on Millard for the newspaper."

Floyd tilted back his reddish-blond head and appraised her in a disrespectful manner. "I can't help but wonder how many obituaries you've written that had your name listed as the cause of death."

Cassie gnashed her teeth as his dark eyes drifted over her once again. She'd pegged Floyd as a womanizer the first time she'd met him. Only, now she realized it was one of his lesser faults. It was tempting indeed to accuse Floyd outright of murder and thievery, but as Jack said, forewarning a suspect prompted him to cover his tracks.

Without invitation, Cassie walked over and sat down in front of Floyd's desk. His glare consigned her to a place where exceptionally hotter climates prevailed. She ignored it.

"Do you know where Millard hailed from?"

"Don't have a clue," he said crossly.

"Family?"

"Didn't ask. Wouldn't know."

She met his unreceptive frown, refusing to be deterred from her purpose. "What *did* you know about your loyal employee, who waited on your customers until the day he died at an unknown assailant's hands?"

Floyd's chin jutted out. "We did not socialize. Widow Lancaster rented him an upstairs room to help support her child. That is the extent of my knowledge about Millard's personal life. When I catch up on my bookkeeping I'll interview his replacement and open the door for business."

Cassie glanced discreetly at the blue ledger on Floyd's

desk. She would love to get her hands on it, but Floyd hunkered protectively over the open book and kept his left arm positioned atop the list of entries.

Pretending to ignore the ledger, she jotted more notes. "When do you anticipate opening the bank? I'm sure you can't delay too long without causing your customers a hardship."

"End of the week."

She met his hostile gaze and mustered a pleasant smile, difficult though it was. "Despite unfavorable gossip that states otherwise, I have no idea what happened to poor Millard. I'm as puzzled by this senseless killing as everyone else in town. I lament that his short obituary won't do him justice. He served our community and you for the past few years. I believe a man deserves to be remembered and honored for his contributions to society, don't you?"

Floyd mumbled reluctantly. "He worked here three years."

"Thank you for your time." Cassie rose to her feet, took another good look at the blue leather-bound ledger and forced another smile. "Good luck finding Millard's replacement."

He nodded mutely, still protecting his ledger as best he could without actually sprawling on top of it. Cassie was sure this was the ledger that no one but Floyd was allowed to touch. He kept track of debits and deposits in this book, but she suspected the one he showed to the *actual* state auditor was a book of another color—literally.

On impulse, Cassie veered toward the teller's desk rather than exiting through the back door.

"What are you doing?" Floyd demanded harshly.

She stared out of the barred window on the counter. "Checking for family photographs and trying to get a sense of what Millard's life was like for my article."

"You're going to be behind *jail* bars if you don't leave," Floyd growled at her. "You might have charmed our city marshal to prevent being charged with murder, but you don't fool me, Mizz Bixby. I predict a mob would've hanged you already, if not for their respect and affection for your aunt."

Cassie turned away from the teller's counter and paused beside the staircase leading to the second floor. Floyd practically stood on top of her, looking down his nose. "You should be nicer to me," she told him, undaunted.

He arched a thin reddish brow. "Oh? Why's that?"

"Because I'll likely be the one writing *your* obituary."

Then she walked out, smiling in spiteful satisfaction while he spat foul curses that didn't bother her in the least.

Cassie returned to the newspaper office to find Maxwell waiting for her to open the door. When she sat down to write the obituary, Maxwell hopped lightly onto her desk. She paused to rub him behind the ears. He purred in satisfaction as he leaned heavily against her shoulder.

"I'll bet you could tell Jack how I came to be in the alley, lying beside Millard," she murmured to Maxwell.

The oversize black cat yawned widely, walked across her desk and then hopped down to lounge in his favorite place on the windowsill. Cassie twisted in her chair to see Gerald hovering at the office door, staring anxiously at her.

"Something wrong?" she asked.

"You tell me. Did you speak to Louise since you couldn't get into the bank? How deep is the hot water I'm in?"

Cassie grinned impishly at her boss. "It amazes me that you had the courage to stand up to spiteful scoundrels and suffered physical abuse to print the truth in your newspaper, yet you're afraid of one petite woman."

"Not just any woman," he corrected. "She's the one whose opinion of me matters. She makes me happy. The prospect of losing her is driving me crazy."

His affection for Aunt Louise touched her deeply. Obviously, Gerald's intentions were sincere and long lasting. Cassie understood why Gerald was stewing in his own juice. She'd feel the same fierce impact if she lost Jack. When he tired of her and turned his attention to someone else, it would break her heart. She had to guard against that.

How had Jack come to mean so much to her so quickly? she asked herself. She was extremely passionate about her feelings for him—whether they were hotly debating issues or tumbling together in fiery desire. There was no room for indifference in her dealings with him.

"Don't keep me in suspense," Gerald said impatiently. "Did Louise tell you that she's never speaking to me again?"

"I didn't talk to her," Cassie said. "I circled to the back door of the bank and found Floyd laboring over his ledger—the one he keeps to himself, I suspect. I asked him some questions for Millard's obituary then he ran me out."

Gerald half collapsed against the doorjamb. "I've been granted a reprieve. I can have lunch with Louise without worrying about her going for my throat."

Cassie snickered. "I would be more concerned about her poisoning your food. But then, she does have access to several kitchen knives at the café."

"This is not funny," Gerald mumbled as he raked his fingers through his thinning hair. "She's important to me.

I don't expect you to make excuses for me or plead my case, but I hope I have your approval."

"I want my aunt to be happy," Cassie assured him. "You must know that I'm grateful for a job I enjoy. I have the utmost respect for you...." She grinned again. "Well, except for the past few days when I feared you were in cahoots with the crooked banker—"

She snapped her mouth shut when the door creaked open and Newton Rowe, Doreen's father, lumbered inside. The blond-haired butcher cast her a disgusted glance on his way to Gerald's office to discuss placing another ad for the paper.

No telling what twisted tale Doreen had told her father to turn him against her, too. Whatever it was, Newton made his distaste for her glaringly apparent.

After several minutes passed, the butcher exited Gerald's office then halted beside Cassie while she set type at the printing press. "You should watch your step, witch," he breathed down her neck. "I don't take kindly to anyone who makes my little girl unhappy. She doesn't want the man I picked out for her. She's set her cap for one of the Culpeppers. Jackson in particular. You are not to interfere."

"Is that a threat, Mr. Rowe? It must run in the family. Doreen tries to intimidate me every chance she gets. I must warn you that if you're receiving all your information from Doreen, you are hearing a slanted version. We in the newspaper business know how important it is to get the facts straight."

"You think that just because you have a way with words and a pretty face that people will flock to you? Think again," he said, and snorted derisively. "I'm waiting for the day Jackson comes to his senses and realizes you've caused him and everyone in this town too much trouble. It's a shame Millard Stewart didn't survive to point an accusing finger at you for shooting him."

He lurched around to stalk out. When Maxwell jumped down then crossed his path, Newton kicked him away— and none too gently—with the side of his foot.

"Damn cat," he muttered sourly. "The furry pest serves no useful purpose whatsoever. Like certain folks around here."

The cat put up its back, hissing.

"You're an excellent judge of character, Max," she said, petting the cat affectionately while Newton stalked down the street. "I don't like him, either."

Chapter Thirteen

Jack glanced up from the paperwork on his desk to see another cowhand with dusty clothes and leathery skin enter the jail. The drover had the look of a man who had spent weeks on horseback, herding cattle toward the Kansas railheads. He pulled off his hat and combed his long hair away from his face.

"The bank is locked up tight," the drover grumbled. "What am I supposed to do about withdrawing the money I put into the account so I can restock supplies and pay wages?"

Jack came to his feet to offer the disgruntled drover his hand. "I'm sorry about the inconvenience. I'm Marshal Culpepper."

The cowboy reluctantly shook hands. "Robert Patterson. Sorry won't pay the bills, Marshal. I deposited that money last fall on my way home from Dodge City so I wouldn't have to fret about getting robbed by my own men or those damn outlaws who try to rustle my cattle."

"I understand your concern because my brothers and I

have moved our livestock up the trail in the past," Jack commiserated. "The bank teller was shot and killed a couple of days ago and the owner closed the door for a few days."

"Was he shot by a drover who couldn't get hold of his own hard-earned money?" Patterson asked sardonically.

"I'm still trying to figure that out. In the meantime I've made arrangements with the owner of the general store to extend credit to you and the other drover who came by earlier this morning."

The tall, lanky cowboy nodded begrudgingly. "Thanks. But I still have a problem because I can't pay wages and my men have been on the trail for a long time. They anticipate venturing into town to enjoy the saloons and dance halls."

"How long do you plan to lay over?" Jack questioned.

"Two days, unless bad weather sets in," Patterson replied. "I plan to turn loose half my men tonight while the others stand watch over the herd. Tomorrow night they'll switch off."

"I'll try to square it with the banker so you can have your money today," Jack offered. "If not, I'll tell the saloonkeepers to set up tabs, too."

"Much obliged, Marshal." Patterson plunked his widebrimmed hat on his head then turned on his high-heeled boots. "I'll tell my men to mind their manners while they're in your town. Not that they always listen."

"If they don't they'll be stuck in jail. I intend to keep this town in one piece. No exceptions."

Jack followed the drover outside. When Patterson rode away, Jack glanced down at Wilbur Knox who divided his time between the warm spring and the wooden bench outside the jail.

"Keep an eye on things, will you? I'll be at the bank."

"Nobody to keep an eye on yet," Wilbur reminded him as he draped his trusty rifle over his lap. "Expecting rowdy cowboys tonight?"

"Afraid so."

"Still, this is easier than patrolling thousands of acres on the frontier," Wilbur remarked. "I'm damn glad that old, used-up Rangers like me have a place in your bunkhouse to lay my head. Nice to have a use, too." He grinned slyly. "Like being the lookout in the park during bank robberies."

Jack bit back a grin. "I didn't hear you say that."

"That's because I didn't say nothin', didn't see nothin', didn't hear nothin' and don't know nothin'."

"You're a good man. Couldn't get along without you," Jack murmured before he walked off to alert saloon-keepers and dance hall owners that cowboys were due in town at dark.

Cassie glanced up from typesetting and noted the time. She wondered what had become of her cat. She'd let Maxwell out earlier and he had yet to return. Although he had the run of the town during the day, he usually wandered back to the office to take several naps on the windowsill.

An uneasy sensation skittered through her, as she remembered how Newton Rowe had kicked aside Maxwell. Surely he wouldn't take out his dislike of her on her cat…would he? Heavens! The man owned a butcher shop. Cassie cringed at the prospect of Maxwell ending up like one of Newton's cuts of meat.

Shivering, Cassie wiped off her hands on a towel then poked her head around the corner in Gerald's office.

"Maxwell is missing. I'm going to look for him."

Gerald nodded. "After you find him, go by to talk to your aunt," he requested. "I want to know if I'll be welcome at the café for supper or if I'll have to find somewhere else to dine for the rest of my life."

Cassie buzzed off, wishing she had checked on Maxwell much sooner. "Here, kitty, kitty!" she called as she hiked along the boardwalks of town circle.

Her repeated summons brought three cats that didn't belong to her. Unfortunately, there was no sign of Maxwell.

When Cassie reached the side alley by the bakery and butcher shop, she heard a cat meow in the near distance. She called out to Maxwell as she stepped into the alley where an unknown assailant, wearing the bandit disguise, had attacked her. The unpleasant thought prompted her to glance every which way to make certain no one was lurking nearby, using her cat to lure her into a trap.

"Here, kitty, kitty," she called softly.

"Meow…"

Cassie checked behind stacks of discarded crates to make doubly certain someone wasn't waiting to pounce on her as she scuttled toward the muffled sound of the cat.

"Maxwell, where are you?" she called.

The cat meowed again.

Cassie cast another cautious glance at her surroundings then reached over to lift the lid of a garbage can. She nearly leaped out of her skin when Maxwell jumped out.

"Scare me half to death, why don't you," she fussed as the cat curled himself around her legs. "How did you get stuck in there?"

Cassie was about to replace the lid when she noticed a rolled up garment that looked suspiciously like a canvas duster lying among crumpled paper. Without bothering to inspect the clothing, she hastily replaced the lid then dashed around the corner to the boardwalk.

Lickety-split, she scurried past the warm springs to reach the marshal's office. To her disappointment, she found Wilbur Knox sitting in Jack's chair with his scuffed boots propped on the edge of the desk.

"Where's Jack?" she asked, out of breath.

"Busy." Wilbur squinted his eyes at her. "Why do you need to know?"

"I think I just now discovered the disguise my attacker wore in the alley a few days ago. I'd like Jack to examine the evidence."

Wilbur hitched his thumb north. "He's down at the saloons, making arrangements for cowhands to sign tabs for their drinks, if he can't pry loose the money from the bank."

Too anxious to wait until Jack returned, Cassie whirled around and dashed off. She was halfway down the street that she referred to as Sinners Row when Jack appeared from one of the billiard halls. She glanced up to the second floor where soiled doves engaged in activities that had nothing whatsoever to do with card games and billiards.

Despite what Wilbur had told her, she glanced down the street of sin again, then stared suspiciously at Jack. Although they had made no promises to each other after they had become intimate, possessive jealousy nipped at her. If Jack had been with another woman this afternoon, she had a good mind to strangle the handsome rascal.

"Have you been seeking out a diversion, Marshal?" she heard herself ask and then mentally kicked herself for it.

"No, buttercup. You're diversion aplenty," he said.

Relief washed over her as she clutched his hand and tugged him along with her. "Maxwell went missing—"

"I'm not wasting time looking for that damn cat," Jack interrupted. "You know I'm not fond of your pet."

"You should be," she insisted. "He found what looks to be the disguise used by my assailant."

"Your cat found evidence?" he hooted, incredulous.

"He managed to get himself stuck in the garbage can located in the alley where I was knocked unconscious. Someone replaced the lid and trapped him inside."

Jack quickened his step, forcing Cassie to jog to keep up with his long, swift strides. "I checked the alley and every garbage can in sight the day I found you," Jack reported.

"Someone obviously waited until later to discard the disguise."

Cutting across the park near the warm springs, they hurried to the side alley by the bakery and butcher shop. Jack reached into the garbage can to lift out the garment. A shiver went through Cassie when he unrolled the duster that was covered with bloodstains. A crushed sombrero was inside it.

"Dear God," she wheezed. "Do you suppose the killer used the duster to conceal Millard Stewart's body until he dumped it in the alley beside the opera house and general store?"

Jack stared at her grimly. "Do you suppose Millard was the one who attacked you then someone else shot him and discarded him, too?"

Cassie frowned ponderously. "I don't think so. Millard wasn't much taller than I am. I think whoever grabbed me was stronger and bulkier…." Her voice trailed off as she glanced speculatively toward the back door of the butcher shop. "Someone like Newton Rowe. He came by the newspaper office earlier and issued a warning that I should keep my distance from you because Doreen has set her cap for you."

Jack clutched the filthy disguise in one hand and latched onto Cassie's elbow with the other. "Let's see what Newton has to say for himself, shall we? I asked him to verify Doreen's alibi the night you were attacked, but *she* might have been covering for her *father.*"

"I wouldn't be surprised to hear that Doreen manipulated Newton into coming after me," she replied.

Jack halted by the back door of the shop then swooped down to deliver an impulsive, lip-blistering kiss. He'd found himself doing that a lot lately—stealing a kiss here and there like a schoolboy swiping candy to satisfy his sweet tooth.

"Let me do the talking," he instructed.

"Okay, Marshal, but what was that kiss about?"

"*About* one minute shorter than I would have preferred," he teased. "It's also a reminder of what I said earlier. You are all the diversion I need. Besides, I don't make a habit of visiting bordellos."

"Probably don't have to with Doreen waiting to pounce on you every time you happen by," Cassie remarked.

That was true, but Jack let the comment slide. He glanced down at the bloody duster in his hand, then opened the back door. Cassie was a step behind him as he walked directly toward Newton Rowe, who was wrapping cuts of meat in butcher paper. It looked exactly like the paper Jack had seen crumpled around the discarded disguise that had been wadded up and crammed in the garbage can.

"This belongs to you, Newton." It wasn't a question. It was a gruff statement of fact.

He watched Newton's pale blue eyes fly wide-open and his whiskered jaw scrape his chest. It took a moment for Newton to recover from his surprise, but his telling reaction was as good as a signed confession in Jack's book.

Jack bore down on the butcher like the flapping angel of doom. "You almost killed her, you son of a bitch!" he growled ferociously. Then he thrust the stained duster at Newton's broad chest. "You knocked Cassie out then dragged her off so she wouldn't be found so close to your place of business."

"When did you toss out the duster and sombrero?" Cassie demanded as she stepped in front of Jack to stare down the butcher.

Although Newton outweighed her by at least a hundred pounds, she showed no fear. But then, Jack knew she was a scrappy fighter because he'd tangled with her during the bank robbery. Plus, she had Jack to back her up—which he'd do with great relish if Newton dared to strike out at her.

"I don't have the slightest idea what you're talking about," Newton snapped defensively.

"Of course you do," Cassie contradicted. "You grabbed me in the alley and told me to stop causing trouble. You were referring to your daughter's intention of dragging Jack to the altar, weren't you? You told me as much when you visited the newspaper office earlier and said Doreen had her heart set on Jack. You kicked my cat and you tried to scare me off!"

Newton glared hot pokers at Cassie then looked up at Jack. "She is plumb loco. You better shake yourself loose before this witch drags you completely under her spell."

Jack ignored the snide remark. "So Doreen maneuvered you into clubbing Cassie," he presumed. "After you carted her away from the alley where the attack took place, you left her by the opera house and general store. Then you killed Millard and wrapped him in this blood-stained duster."

"I did no such thing!" Newton protested hotly. "He wasn't there when I—" His voice evaporated and he looked away.

"He wasn't where you dumped me in the dirt?" Cassie finished for him. "So *then* you shot Millard and dragged him to the spot where you left me."

"I didn't shoot Millard," he muttered. "I don't know how he got there. For all I know he found you and you shot him before you passed out again."

Jack frowned pensively. They'd only solved half the case. He still had no idea how Millard came to be in the same alley where Newton left Cassie unconscious in the dirt.

"I'm closing your shop," Jack announced abruptly. "You're coming to my office to give your confession. Cassie is going to file charges against you for assault. Then I'm going to bring in Doreen and listen to her side of the story."

"No!" Newton shouted. "You leave her out of this." He glowered at Cassie. "This is all your fault. You're trying to steal Jack from her."

"I'll tell you the same thing I told Doreen," Jack inserted as he strode over to lock the front door. "The gossip, which I suspect Doreen circulated herself, couldn't be further from the truth. Your daughter has turned out to be jealous, vicious and spiteful. If you can't see her for what she is, that isn't my problem. It isn't Cassie's, either. Now let's go."

Reluctantly, Newton removed his stained apron then lumbered toward the back door. "Okay, but you need to know those aren't human bloodstains on the duster. That came from the rags I used while butchering a pig, so don't try to blame murder on me."

When they reached the street, Cassie hung back. "I told Gerald that I would speak to Aunt Louise," she explained to Jack. "I'll be at your office by the time you bring in Doreen."

When she reversed direction and strode off, Jack nudged Newton down the street. Five minutes later Jack locked up Newton in a cell—and considered throwing away the key.

"How long are you going to keep me here?" Newton demanded. "I have a business to run, you know."

"You can send in Doreen, unless I decide to stuff her in there with you for conspiring to commit a crime."

Newton's fair complexion turned as white as salt. "You can't expect a woman to run my business and you can't lock up a woman, either."

"Of course I can." Jack smiled caustically. "Wake up, Newton. It's a new age. Before we know it, women will control the world. You better adjust to the fact."

His reply was a disgusted snort. Clearly, Newton wasn't going to join the women's movement anytime soon.

Jack bit back a grin while Newton grumbled about women being incapable of taking charge. Jack certainly had no complaints about that. Cassie had taken charge of him the previous night in the heat of passion. He had surrendered without a fight—and he'd loved every delicious moment of it.

* * *

Cassie was thankful she arrived at Bixby Café during the afternoon lull. Aunt Louise was lounging at a table, sipping coffee and chatting with Suzannah.

"Is everything all right?" Aunt Louise questioned when she saw Cassie approach.

"Everything is fine," she assured the two women. "But I need to have a private word with Aunt Louise before I keep an appointment in a few minutes. Can we go upstairs?"

Aunt Louise popped up to lead the way. "Are you sure there is nothing wrong?" she persisted worriedly.

"I'm positive," she said as she scaled the steps. "In fact, Jack and I are making progress with my assault case."

"Good. I can't wait to find out who is responsible for that fiasco. I'm going to club the culprit over the head and see how he likes it."

Cassie reminded herself that she was short on time and she needed quick results. Jack and his brothers had resorted to drastic measures to force the banker's hand so she decided to use the tactic on her aunt.

Cassie inhaled a quick breath and said for shock value, "Gerald is under suspicion for attacking me. He claims he has no alibi for the night of my assault and Jack is going to arrest him."

Aunt Louise gasped for breath and kerplopped in her chair. *"Gerald?"* she squeaked.

"Yes, Jack is furious with him and he's going to make an example of him by hanging him."

"Hanging him?" her aunt parroted, wide-eyed.

"Why not?" Cassie countered, determined to test her aunt's affection for Gerald. "If Gerald won't tell us where he was or who he was with at the time of the attack then he is going to suffer lethal consequences."

"You can't hang Gerald," she erupted frantically.

"Why not?" Cassie challenged, biting back a wry smile.

"Because…" Aunt Louise swallowed hard then glanced out the window.

"Because why?" Cassie prodded relentlessly.

She was going to be hugely disappointed if her aunt didn't hold Gerald in the same high regard. It was evident that Gerald was in love with Aunt Louise and he'd made all sorts of concessions just to be with her whenever possible.

Finally, Aunt Louise slumped in her chair. "You can't hang him because he was with me all night," she admitted.

"He was also with you in this apartment the night I tapped on the door and you claimed you couldn't visit with me because you had a headache."

Her aunt's face blossomed with color. "Yes."

"Gerald has been with you since Hillsdale where you two first met and you came here together, isn't that right?"

Aunt Louise sat up straight in her chair and stared intently at Cassie. "Did he tell you that?"

"I figured out most of it by myself," she hedged. "But I want you to know that I like Gerald as a boss and a friend. You have my blessing and approval, not that you need it, of course."

"I love him," she burst out. "But after Roland's betrayal I swore I'd never allow a man to have any power over me."

"I seriously doubt Gerald is anything like Roland, and you shouldn't judge him by Roland's unscrupulous standards," Cassie replied. "Yet, if Gerald wanted to marry you—" and Cassie knew for a fact that he did "—there is such a thing as a prenuptial agreement that has been in effect for about ten years. You can retain control of your business ventures and the five thousand dollars I plan to pay you when this robbery case is solved."

Aunt Louise nodded pensively. "I suppose that would relieve my fears."

"Gerald strikes me as the kind of man who recognizes and accepts your strength of personality and character. He isn't intimidated by your independent nature and he advocates women's rights," Cassie reminded her. "But I'm willing to bet that he won't be offended if you ask him to sign an agreement that allows you complete control over the café while he retains control of his newspaper business."

Aunt Louise sighed in relief. "Thank God you aren't going to hang Gerald for a crime he didn't commit. Shame on you for scaring me like that, Cass!"

Cassie grinned impishly. "I might have exaggerated a bit to force you to make your feelings known. In addition, I'm going to send Gerald over to have supper with you. I'll be excessively disappointed if I don't get to call him Uncle Gerald sometime in the near future."

Aunt Louise studied her contemplatively for a long moment. "I don't think I've given you full credit for the assertive woman you are... And don't scare me like that again!"

"Sorry, but I was short on time. I have an urgent errand to tend. Plus, I've gone into the matchmaking business. Besides you and Gerald, I'm doing my best to place Suz and Jefferson together whenever possible." She leaned down to brush a fond kiss over her aunt's cheek. "I hope to hear good news from you and Gerald this evening. For now, I have someplace I need to be."

* * *

"You can't possibly be serious about holding my father in jail! Our family will be publicly humiliated!" Doreen railed.

Then she wept a few crocodile tears for Jack's benefit. She wasted water because her tears didn't bother him a bit.

"He never touched that awful, troublemaking suffragist. Papa was with me, having supper. I already told you that!"

Jack watched the performance for another few seconds then waved his arms and said, "Newton confessed to assaulting Cassie because *you* convinced him that she was the reason you and I weren't seeing each other socially."

Amazingly, Doreen's tears dried up in two seconds flat. "What are you suggesting?" she said cautiously.

"I'm saying you purposely poisoned him with lies. You conspired to have Cassie assaulted. That makes you as guilty as your father."

When Cassie entered the office, Jack glanced past Doreen. "I was just telling the gossipmonger that she and her father will be serving jail time for assaulting you."

"I vote to hang them both," Cassie declared.

Doreen's face turned milky-white and she pretended to swoon. Cassie shoved a chair beneath her. She circled the chair to prop her hands on the arms so she could confront her nemesis at close range. "If you give me your solemn promise that you'll never start rumors about me or Jack again, I might be persuaded to drop the charges against you and Newton."

"That's exceptionally kind of you, Cassie, considering the assault left you lying in the mud and set you up for Stewart's murder," Jack inserted. "I recommend that we file the report then tuck it away for safekeeping, just in case Doreen forgets our agreement."

Cassie smiled at him. "Excellent idea, Marshal."

"That's blackmail." Doreen pouted.

Cassie lifted a perfectly arched brow. "So you are admitting that you plan to continue passing malicious gossip? If that's the case, I'll file formal charges right now and you can read about the details of the assault in the newspaper. I, of course, will keep the public updated on the progress of your trial." She grinned impishly. "I promise you'll receive front page headlines for several weeks, Doreen."

"Oh, all right," Doreen muttered begrudgingly. "I promise not to let your name pass my lips."

"Thank you for your cooperation." Jack retrieved the proper forms from his desk to write the report. "Your complete confession, alongside your father's will set you free."

Jack wrote the boiled-down version of the assault and noted Doreen's tactic of using her father as her weapon of retaliation against Cassie. "Sign this and you can leave."

Doreen's pretty face puckered in irritation, but she signed her name then bolted to her feet. She cast him and Cassie a sour glance before flinging her nose in the air and flouncing off, her blond curls bouncing around her face like coiled springs.

"One down and one to go," Jack said to Cassie before he entered the back room where Newton waited behind bars.

When Newton glared at Cassie as if she were the source of all his woes, Jack clucked his tongue. "Be nice to her. She agreed not to press charges if you promise to keep your distance and ensure your scheming daughter does the same."

Newton's brows shot up his forehead as he stared at Cassie in surprise. "You're going to let me go back to work?"

"Bygones will be bygones. Your role in the attack will not become public knowledge," she informed him. "But as I told Doreen last week, if I go missing, the two of you will head up the suspect list and Jack will file the formal charges for this assault and the next one. Do you agree to the terms?"

Newton bobbed his head then stepped back when Jack unlocked the cell. "The truth is I hadn't planned to hurt you, only to scare you. I just tried to defend myself and hide my identity when you fought back. I didn't know what else to do but run. I never dreamed you'd end up beside Millard. I'll be delivering fresh meat to your aunt's café, free of charge," he mumbled.

"How very considerate, Newton," Cassie replied. "I'm sure she will appreciate the neighborly gesture."

When Newton exited, Cassie pushed up on tiptoe to press a kiss to Jack's lips. "Thank you for resolving my conflict with the Rowes."

He hooked his arm around her waist to hold her close when she tried to step away. "There are *two* Rowes. *Two* kisses is the going rate."

She gave him a smacking kiss on the lips. "There, Marshal. You've been thanked properly twice."

"You're welcome." He grinned rakishly. "You know I'm always at your service, buttercup. Whatever you need, whenever you need it."

"You sound like your ladies' man of a brother," she teased. "Do you say that to all the needy females in town?"

"No, only you," he whispered huskily. "You're my greatest distraction."

"Jack, I—" She stopped short then wiggled from his grasp long before he was ready to let her go.

"You what?" he prompted.

She shrugged noncommittally then smiled. "Nothing."

Damn, he'd really like to know what impulsive thought almost found its way to her tongue.

"I confronted Aunt Louise and convinced her to admit that she's as devoted to Gerald as he is to her. I'm hoping that my aunt will accept Gerald's fourth proposal." She chortled triumphantly. "Then I can focus my efforts on Suz and Jefferson."

"That will have to wait until we figure out who disposed of Millard. I'm on my way to see Pettigrew right now. There are two drovers in town who need the money they deposited to restock supplies and pay wages," he reported. "If Pettigrew doesn't hand over what he owes, he might find himself robbed again…"

His voice trailed off when a pensive frown settled into Cassie's bewitching features. She tried to turn away quickly, but he clutched her arm before she swept off.

"I want to know what you're thinking," he insisted as he stared into those deep green eyes that could mesmerize and hypnotize him if he wasn't careful. *"Tell me."*

"My, but you are a suspicious soul," she teased as she wormed from his grasp.

"I'm a lawman. I deal in suspicious."

She tossed him a radiant smile. "I was thinking I need to return to the newspaper office to inform Gerald that Aunt Louise has agreed to meet him for supper to discuss their future. Then I need to finish the articles for the paper and set the rest of the type."

He let her go, but instinct warned him that she had

something else on her mind, though she refused to share it with him. Whatever the hell it was, he hoped it wouldn't get her into trouble. The gorgeous firebrand seemed to attract trouble without trying.

Jack exited his office and asked the old Texas Ranger to take charge again.

"You're sure spending a lot of time with that woman," Wilbur noted disapprovingly. "Hope you know what you're doing. That's a lot of spirited woman for a man to handle."

"Mind your own business, Wilbur."

"I'm telling you, son, that fighting outlaws and renegades is child's play compared to dealing with females. They're like an ambush. By the time you hear gunshots you're already hit. Especially one like Mizz Bixby."

Jack smiled to himself as he walked away. He'd definitely seen Cassandra Bixby coming, but there had been nothing he could do to stop the kaleidoscope of emotions she stirred inside him.

The arousing image of Cassie—lying naked and eager in his arms the previous night—bombarded him while he strode across town circle. He wondered how she'd react if he sneaked into her ground floor window at the boardinghouse after he made his evening rounds.

The tantalizing prospect made him grow hard in one second flat.

Jack forcefully cast aside the erotic thoughts and focused his attention and his gaze on the bank. He was looking forward to speaking with Floyd Pettigrew. He might not be able to pin any crimes on the banker yet, but he was going to recover the drovers' money from their accounts.

Chapter Fourteen

Jack pounded on the back door of the bank. When no one answered, he hammered on it again.

Above him, a window on the second floor opened and Pettigrew stuck out his head. "What do you want, Marshal? The bank is closed out of respect for Millard Stewart."

Jack didn't think the red-haired banker looked the least bit aggrieved about the loss of his teller.

"I'm coming up," Jack called to him. "We have a situation that needs to be resolved immediately."

Pettigrew's fair features puckered in annoyance. "I'll be down in a minute. Wait in the hall by my office."

Jack defied the instructions and went in the unlocked back door directly into Pettigrew's office, hoping to find incriminating evidence lying around. There was none, of course.

He really hadn't expected to be that lucky.

When he heard Pettigrew clattering hurriedly down the steps, Jack stepped away from the desk to lean negligently against the doorjamb.

"Now what is this about?" Pettigrew asked peevishly as he stepped inside and closed the office door behind them.

Jack thought it was odd to close the door since they were supposedly the only two people in the bank. Pettigrew's actions suggested that he'd been upstairs with a woman who was trying to make a discreet exit out the back door. Either that or he'd been meeting with his partners in crime.

"As you can imagine, *I'm* very busy." Pettigrew went to stand behind his desk. "I have a lot of business to tend to and I'm without any help."

"And as you can imagine, I'm busy protecting business owners and a town full of citizens," Jack shot back. "Also, two drovers have their herds camped outside of town and they are waiting to withdraw the money they deposited to pay for needed supplies and wages. Storeowners and saloonkeepers have agreed to accommodate the incoming cowboys who need to make purchases by extending credit until you do your part to reimburse the drovers."

Pettigrew rolled his eyes. "I don't know why I should accommodate those heathens who ride in to shoot up the town."

"Because they buy food, supplies and beverages from our shopkeepers and they have deposited money in *your* bank," Jack replied. Then he looked at the desk, as if he hadn't given it the once-over already. "Where's your ledger? You are going to empty the accounts for Robert Patterson and Fred Ingram so they can pay their expenses for their cattle drives."

Pettigrew flung his nose in the air. "I will deal directly with them. That's my policy."

Jack took an intimidating step forward and tried very

hard not to drop into his former role as a bandit. No need to tip off this red-haired sidewinder, he reminded himself.

"They appointed me as their agent while they settle their herds near the river," he said in his most authoritative voice. "It isn't their fault that Millard turned up dead and you locked the bank."

"No, it's that rabble-rouser's fault," Pettigrew muttered sourly. "I've heard that she's playing up to you so you won't charge her with the crime of shooting poor Millard when he refused to embezzle money from the bank to compensate for her losses during the robbery."

"Well, you heard wrong," Jack contradicted. "The evidence didn't add up. Plus, I have a confession from the assailant who knocked Cassandra unconscious."

Jack watched Pettigrew's thin brows rocket up his forehead. "Who did it? Who shot Millard?"

As if you don't know, Jack thought in disgust. "I'm not at liberty to say until all the paperwork is in order and I request a trial date." He hoped Pettigrew got sloppy while thinking someone else had been arraigned for the crime....

"What was that?" Jack asked when he heard what sounded like the creak of the back door.

Pettigrew waved his arm dismissively. "This building creaks and groans when the wind blows. Nothing to worry about."

When Jack whirled around, as if to check on the door, Pettigrew grumbled then said, "All right, I'll fetch the money from the till. But I have to check my ledger first to see how much to withdraw from the drovers' accounts."

Jack thought he heard the door creak a minute later, but Pettigrew was making as much racket as possible to override any unexplained sounds. He kicked his chair out of the way, causing it to scrape across the floor. He rattled open the middle desk drawer, mumbled something to himself, then pulled out the bottom drawer. He plopped down in his chair and dropped the black, leather-bound ledger noisily on his desk.

"Now what did you say their names were?" Pettigrew demanded impatiently.

"Ingram and Patterson." Jack came around to stand behind Pettigrew so he could look over his shoulder at the ledger.

"Do you mind?" Pettigrew said sarcastically. "The tallies in this book are privileged information."

"Not today," Jack disagreed. "I'm making certain those drovers receive every penny they have coming so I don't have to return to look you up again."

Pettigrew jerked up his rounded chin and his dark eyes flashed. "If you are suggesting—"

"I'm not suggesting a damn thing," Jack cut in abruptly. "I'm here to follow the letter of the law that states a customer is entitled to withdraw all his money from his account at his request. Now hurry up, Pettigrew. Like you, I have dozens of tasks to attend before the cowboys, fresh off lonely trail drives, hit town. They'll be looking to buy new clothing, get shaves and haircuts. Then they'll frequent our local watering holes for drinks and female companionship."

Pettigrew trailed his forefinger down the pages until he located the information for Ingram and Patterson. "Here we go." He took a piece of paper to jot down both amounts. "I'll fetch the currency from the teller's drawer."

"I'll go with you," Jack insisted.

Pettigrew flashed him a disgruntled glance then

opened the office door slowly. He craned his neck around the corner—to make sure the coast was clear, no doubt. Then he sauntered down the hall to open the teller's drawer.

Jack glanced toward the safe on the back wall then studied the wooden steps leading upstairs. Damn, he'd love to know who had exited the bank while Pettigrew strategically shut him inside the office. He'd also like to look around upstairs to see if he could find incriminating evidence.

"Here you go, Marshal." Pettigrew thrust the banknotes at Jack.

Jack shook his head when he noticed the counterfeit currency. Obviously, Pettigrew had visited the newspaper office this afternoon to retrieve the money Gerald had printed. "Give me banknotes issued from somewhere else," he insisted. "Patterson and Ingram are aggravated with you because you closed up when they needed you most. Currency with Pettigrew Bank stamped on it won't be well received."

Pettigrew muttered under his breath then lurched around to count out other banknotes. "Those drovers are a rough, independent lot."

"They are faced with a difficult job," Jack defended. "My brothers and I have done it several times ourselves. Herding contrary cattle, controlling rowdy cowboys and fending off thieves and rustlers for months at a time isn't easy. Have you ever done it for a living?"

"No, I haven't the slightest interest in cattle unless I'm looking at a prime cut of beef on my dinner plate."

I was talking about being a thief or rustler, Jack mused resentfully. Although he still hadn't been able to pin down Pettigrew's past criminal activities, he was sure the man excelled in shady dealings. Which was why the cunning bastard was still running loose.

After Pettigrew counted out currency that Jack knew was worth the paper it was printed on, he rolled up the notes separately for each drover then tucked them in his vest pockets.

"The drovers and local business owners thank you. I've heard citizens voice concern about withdrawing their money to cover expenses," Jack didn't hesitate to inform the banker. "I advise you to reopen soon, unless you want to incite panic." He smiled faintly. "You know how folks are when you try to separate them from their money."

"Right, like that Bixby chit who tried to take on a bandit during the robbery." Pettigrew expelled a snort. "That woman has too much spunk and daring for her own good. It's a wonder she wasn't shot during the holdup."

Jack agreed that Cassie was bursting at the seams with spunk and daring, but he wouldn't have shot her. He wasn't so sure about Pettigrew being that lenient, however.

"That is the last kind of woman I'd be interested in," Pettigrew went on to say.

Jack, on the other hand, had developed a fascination for assertive, high-spirited, courageous women who challenged him.

After Pettigrew walked Jack to the back door to make sure he left the building, he heard the key turn in the lock. Jack glanced around, wondering what had become of Pettigrew's mysterious guest.

When the sound of gunfire erupted in the distance, Jack scowled. The cowboys from the two cattle herds had hit town earlier than expected. Jack needed to find the drovers and let them dole out money while he tried to keep a lid on the town.

His erotic fantasy of slipping into Cassie's window at the boardinghouse shattered like fragile crystal. He had the unshakable feeling that it was going to be a long, eventful night in Pepperville.

"Wilbur!" Jack called as he strode briskly toward the jail. "Do me a favor and fetch my brothers from the ranch. I might need reinforcements to control all these boisterous wranglers from two separate trail herds."

"Sure thing, Jack." Wilbur hobbled off to fetch his horse. "I'll hold down the fort when I return. I doubt your lazy deputy will find the energy to show up. Damn rascal drinks too much."

"Amen to that," Jack mumbled as he headed off to find the drovers who were likely visiting the string of saloons and brothels on the northwest side of town.

Although Cassie was sure Jack would read her every line and paragraph of the riot act if he knew she'd lurked in the alley, she had watched him enter the back door of the bank for his conference with Pettigrew. A minute later, the mysterious Mr. Smythe scurried out. Cassie was most interested to note that he was back in town. She was also curious to know which one of them had killed Millard. Unfortunately, without the damning evidence in that blue, leather-bound ledger, she doubted she and Jack could convict those conniving thieves of any crime.

Taking advantage of opportunity, Cassie had sneaked in the back way the moment Mr. Smythe scurried around the corner. She'd heard Jack and Pettigrew's muffled conversation through the closed office door as she tiptoed down the hall. Removing her shoes, she scaled the steps quietly. From her hiding place upstairs in the storage area

adjacent to a small bedroom, she'd heard Jack and Pettigrew's conversation while they milled around the teller's
counter. She silently commended Jack for refusing to
take the freshly printed banknotes to pay the disgruntled
cattle drovers.

When Jack exited the building, Cassie heard the sound
of rapid gunfire announcing the arrival of the trail hands.
Half of them—according to Jack—were on their way to
town to celebrate. She knew Jack would have his hands
full this evening so it was up to her to gather the evidence
needed to accuse Pettigrew and Smythe of embezzling,
fraud, murder—and who knew what else!

The thought stiffened Cassie's resolve. She was going
to locate that secret blue ledger if it was the last thing she
ever did. With that in mind, she fashioned makeshift
breeches from her cumbersome skirts by drawing the back
hem between her legs and securing it around her waist
with a string she'd removed from a canvas money pouch.
Now she could climb up the storage shelves or sprawl
under the bed while searching for damning evidence.

She snapped to attention when she heard Pettigrew's
footfalls in the hallway. She hoped he'd make himself
scarce so she wouldn't have to be so cautious about being
discovered.

No such luck.

She inched forward to peer over the railing to see the
fashionably dressed banker striding over to double-check
the dead bolt on the front door. Then he tucked the key
into his pocket. Cassie inwardly winced. She hadn't
thought far enough ahead to figure out how she was going
to exit the bank if Pettigrew used his master key to lock
all the doors.

She glanced speculatively at the pane-glass windows downstairs. Metal bars protected them. "Damn," she mumbled under her breath. She'd need to sprout wings to fly out the second-story window.

"Is someone there?" Pettigrew called out from below.

Double damn, thought Cassie. Her soft utterance must have echoed through the quiet bank.

"Is that you, Sam?" Pettigrew demanded.

Sam? Who the devil is Sam? she wondered as she shrank into the shadows, hoping to make herself invisible.

Panic assailed her when she heard the click of Pettigrew's boots on the steps. Curse it! He was coming to investigate. Cassie snatched up her shoes then darted from the storage area into the small room that contained a double bed, dresser and washstand. She glanced around frantically, but she had no option but to slither under the bed and hope Pettigrew didn't make a thorough search.

Her heart pounded like stampeding buffalos while she scrunched down so she could wiggle under the bed. Hardly daring to breathe, she plastered herself against the back wall. She tugged at the bedspread, hoping the dangling hem would conceal her.

"Sam?" Pettigrew called out again.

Cassie didn't dare move while Pettigrew strode through the storage area. She heard him shut the window he'd left open when Jack dropped in on him earlier. Then he entered the bedroom. Cassie prayed for all she was worth that the banker made a quick search then returned downstairs.

Fortunately for her, he did exactly that. He walked around the room, but he didn't check under the bed. When he left the room, Cassie breathed an inward sigh of relief. She was grateful he hadn't spotted her.

When the footfalls receded, Cassie wormed from her hiding place then tiptoed toward the storage area. She stared through the window, watching as Pettigrew exited the back door. She plastered herself against the wall when he glanced up at the window he had closed earlier.

Carefully, she peeked at him while he surveyed the area behind the bank that butted up to the freight office and lumberyard. She presumed that he was reasonably satisfied that no one was sneaking around his bank.

With Pettigrew gone, Cassie hunted for the blue, leather-bound ledger in earnest. She decided to scour his desk and the teller's counter first. If he returned unexpectedly, she could dash upstairs to hide again.

In her stocking feet, she bounded downstairs and headed straight for Pettigrew's office. She checked every drawer, but she only found the black ledger. According to the black book, there were monetary deposits in every account. She noticed the withdrawals Pettigrew had dated for the two drovers Jack had represented.

A few minutes later, when her extensive search turned up nothing productive, Cassie returned every item to its proper place then exited the office. She moved swiftly to the teller's counter to check the money drawer. When she spied the recently printed currency, she silently cursed Pettigrew for deceiving Gerald into thinking the state government approved printing new banknotes.

The thought aggravated her to the point that she decided to clean out every legitimate banknote left in the drawer. Pettigrew was welcome to the counterfeit bills. However, he was not going to walk away with the money that belonged to unsuspecting citizens of Pepperville…

Her vindictive thoughts trailed off when she realized

she had resorted to the same desperate tactic of bank robbery that the Culpeppers employed. She had become the Bandit Queen of Pepperville. Cassie grimaced. She didn't want to see those front-page headlines staring back at her in her own private jail cell. She better not get caught!

The rattle of a key inserted into the lock of the back door sent Cassie darting up the steps as fast as her legs would carry her. She frantically stuffed the money into her bodice, her waistline, her pockets and the folds of her makeshift breeches. She glanced down the steps to make sure she hadn't dropped any currency and left an incriminating trail in her haste to flee upstairs.

When she saw nothing to give her away, she backed into the shadows. Two sets of footfalls echoed in the hall.

"What did the marshal want?"

Cassie didn't recognize the voice. She suspected it might be Sam—whoever Sam was. She didn't have a clue.

"He strong-armed me into withdrawing money for two cattle drovers who complained to him," Pettigrew explained.

"I hope you gave him the counterfeit bills."

"Couldn't. He insisted on taking the other banknotes."

"Why? Do you think he's figured out what we're doing?"

Cassie wanted to answer that question with a resounding *yes!* but she didn't want to get caught eavesdropping and risk being shot before she located the blue, leatherbound book that likely held damning evidence.

"I'm not sure, but I think the marshal might be getting suspicious," Pettigrew replied. "It's definitely time to put the rest of our plan into motion and skip town. Did you make the arrangements with our investors while you were in Fort Worth?"

"Yes, the real-estate arrangements are in place."

Pettigrew chuckled devilishly. "I'd like to be here to see the look on the sellers' faces when they realize they sold their property."

"I'd rather be long gone," his cohort muttered.

Cassie frowned. She wasn't sure what scheme they referred to, but she intended to find out.

"Let's take the rest of the money and clear out," Pettigrew said as he approached the teller's counter. "This will be the perfect evening for our grand finale."

"It better be," his companion grumbled. "We'd be on our way already, if not for the two robberies that forced us to stay longer than originally planned and the meddling of your weasely bank teller." He gave a snort and added, "Did he honestly believe he could blackmail us when he figured out what we were up to?"

Pettigrew chuckled devilishly. "It was a stroke of luck that we found that troublesome suffragist unconscious in the alley when we dumped off Millard. The bastard threatened to tell his story to her if we didn't cut him in."

"The fool," his cohort scowled. "All he received for his efforts was cutting himself *out*. Permanently."

A few moments passed then he asked, "Is that female journalist in jail for shooting Millard, like we hoped?"

"No. I think she's trying to seduce the marshal into believing her story," Pettigrew muttered sourly. "The marshal claims he has a confession from the man who pounded that feisty hellion over the head and dumped her in the dirt."

"Who's taking the blame for that?"

"I don't know and I don't care, as long as it isn't us."

Cassie couldn't wait to tell Jack that it was Pettigrew or Sam who had shot Millard when he tried to blackmail these two thieves into giving him a share of the embez-zled money. Obviously, one of these scoundrels was the killer and the other was the accomplice.

She wondered where Millard's body might have ended up if Pettigrew and his cohort hadn't stumbled onto her.

"What the hell…?" Pettigrew erupted a moment later.

Cassie predicted the men had opened the drawer to find the money gone—except for the counterfeit bills.

"Damn it, Floyd, don't try to pull a fast one on me," his companion snarled hatefully. "Half of that money be-longs to me. That was our deal. If you think you can dis-pose of me as easily as you discarded your bank teller then think again!"

So it was *Pettigrew who pulled the trigger,* she mused.

Her thoughts scattered when she heard a yelp, fol-lowed by an angry snarl. She inched toward the railing to see the banker attacking the man she recognized as Jonathan Smythe. No doubt, Smythe was an alias for Sam Whoever-He-Was. No matter his name, Pettigrew was pounding him repeatedly with doubled fists. Sam fought back viciously and resorted to biting and kicking whenever he couldn't land a blow.

Cassie wasn't sure who to cheer for because both men were swindlers and thieves. However, since Pettigrew had killed his employee she decided to side with Sam. Unfortunately, he didn't possess Pettigrew's natural agility and strength. Sam went down with a thud and a groan and Cassie leaped away from the railing before he could look past Pettigrew to see her lurking upstairs.

Both men cursed each other viciously as they landed punishing blows on each other. Cassie didn't risk peering over the railing to see if one man got the better of the other. But she could hear wild thrashing and the sound of fists pummeling flesh. Furniture toppled and muttered oaths turned the air black-and-blue. Then one of the men commenced pelting the other with a stick of furniture. Cassie predicted someone would end up as unconscious as she'd been after she was attacked on the street.

Cautiously, she inched forward to peer down. Pettigrew was still on his feet. He cast aside the broken leg of the chair that he'd used to hammer Sam in the head. Sam lay bleeding and unconscious amid the broken furniture and counterfeit money. She watched with disgust while Pettigrew dug into Sam's pockets to retrieve his money. He also confiscated what looked to be some sort of legal document or contract. Cassie wondered if it was the real-estate deed Sam had mentioned earlier.

While Sam lay unmoving on the floor, bleeding all over himself, Pettigrew crammed the money and document into the pockets of his jacket then whirled toward his office. Cassie glanced anxiously toward the steps. She needed to escape—and quickly. If Pettigrew spotted her while he was in a murderous rage, she could become his next victim.

Pettigrew stormed from his office, muttering and swearing. When the back door slammed shut and the key rattled in the lock, Cassie half collapsed in relief. As much as she wanted to flee for her own safety, she had to locate that incriminating blue, leather-bound ledger before Pettigrew hightailed it from town.

Casting one last glance over the railing, Cassie noticed that Sam still lay sprawled among the broken furniture. His face and head were bloody and puffy. He hadn't moved since the last time she checked on him.

Assured that Sam wouldn't hear her rummaging around upstairs, Cassie whirled around to resume her hurried search.

After a hasty once-over of the shelves stocked with bank supplies, Cassie came up empty-handed. Then she scurried into the bedroom to check in—and under—the dresser drawers. When she lifted the corner of the mattress, she hit pay dirt.

"Voilà," she whispered triumphantly.

She retrieved the blue ledger that lay atop the wooden bed slats. She took a quick look at the ledger, noting Pettigrew had emptied several accounts—her aunt's included. Dear Lord! Only a minimal amount of money remained in most local accounts. Those cunning bastards had practically bled the town dry!

Cassie was still cursing Pettigrew to hell and back when she heard the back door open and shut. Panic set in when she heard footfalls approaching. Clasping the ledger protectively to her chest, she slid under the bed, concealing herself between the overhanging bedspread and the wall.

And not a moment too soon. She heard Pettigrew pelting up the steps. Her breath stalled in her chest and her heart hammered furiously against her ribs when the murdering banker stalked into the bedroom. She nearly suffered apoplexy when Pettigrew jarred the far side of the bed—looking for the ledger she'd swiped, no doubt.

"That son of a bitch!" Pettigrew roared viciously. "Damn you to hell, Sam! Where'd you put it?"

Cassie froze in place when Pettigrew jerked off the sheets, quilts and bedspread then levered up the corner of the mattress higher this time. He pounded on the bed and swore ripely. Cassie knew it was only a matter of time before he spotted her lying against the wall. Pettigrew was in a fit of rage and any minute now, he was going to take his murderous fury out on her.

And confound it, here she was without a weapon to defend herself!

Chapter Fifteen

Pettigrew swore savagely then hurled the sheets and quilt against the wall. Cassie didn't move a muscle when the rest of the bedding tumbled into a pile on top of the bedspread that concealed her. Pettigrew spat curses to Sam's name as he dumped the dresser drawers upside down then slammed them against the floor, shattering them in several pieces.

To Cassie's everlasting relief, the outraged banker stalked from the room. She had escaped execution at Pettigrew's hands—for the moment. As long as she was locked in the bank with him, he was still a lethal threat and she had best beware.

She scooted from her hiding place when she heard Pettigrew bounding down the steps. She waited anxiously, hoping the bastard would leave the bank so she could escape with the evidence of his fraudulent activities.

"Where did you put it, you son of a bitch?" Pettigrew railed at Sam.

Sam didn't reply. That was not a good sign—unless

Sam was injured and playing possum, hoping Pettigrew would leave so he could slither away to lick his wounds.

When Cassie heard Pettigrew dragging furniture across the wood floor she frowned, bemused. Alarm sizzled through her when she heard glass shattering. The smell of kerosene rose in the air. Sweet mercy! Had Pettigrew decided to burn down the bank since he couldn't locate the ledger? Or had that been his plan all along?

The more she thought about it—and she had plenty of time to think about it while she was trapped upstairs—the more convinced she became that the banker wanted to turn all possible evidence to ashes and burn every bridge behind him.

Panic set in when he dragged more broken furniture to the teller's counter. He was building a bonfire of broken chairs, deposit slips—and whatever else he could get his hands on—to torch the bank.

Cassie had to give him credit. It was the perfect solution to exit the banking business with the money he had swindled from his customers and investors. He intended to leave the building in smoldering ashes, fry his partner to a crisp and claim all the money he could get his greedy hands on. In addition, Floyd Pettigrew was going to walk away with cash and the funds from whatever real-estate scheme he had mentioned.

Cassie glanced at the ledger she had clutched tightly to her chest and wondered how she could salvage the evidence, even if she burst into flames doing so.

Escalating panic threatened to overwhelm her while smoke rose from the fire Pettigrew had started downstairs. While the kindling crackled and popped, she dashed toward the storage area. She cursed Pettigrew a half dozen times when she noticed that he'd set another fire at the base of the staircase. It was clear that he intended to burn the upstairs, just in case the ledger was still hidden up here.

Cassie bit back a gasp of fear when heat, flames and smoke rolled toward her. She rushed back to the storage shelves to grab two canvas money pouches. She pulled one over her head so her hair wouldn't catch fire. Then she tied another one around her nose and mouth. In afterthought, she dashed back to the bedroom to dump the contents of the pitcher of water over her entire body.

With the ledger crammed down the front of her dress, she headed for the steps, hoping she could leap over the flames and roll onto the floor below. To her dismay, she realized Pettigrew had slopped kerosene up the staircase, setting it ablaze before he raced out the back door. There was no way to make a flying leap without landing in one fire or the other.

For a moment Cassie stood there, watching the dancing flames and billowing smoke with fanatic fatalism. Fire leaped at her like a dragon breathing flames.

She was going to die. She was never going to see Jack or Aunt Louise again. She would never know if Aunt Louise agreed to marry Gerald. She'd never know if the match she'd tried to make for Suzannah and Jefferson worked out, either.

Worst of all, Jack would never know that she had fallen in love with him. Furthermore, she had gathered the evidence he needed to convict Pettigrew of murder, arson and fraud. Unfortunately, it was going to burn right alongside her.

As if mesmerized by the gloom and doom of her situation, Cassie stood there, staring into the golden flames, watching her life flash before her eyes. The only proof of her existence was her past. She wasn't going to have a future and she hadn't achieved her goals of equal rights and social reform.

When heat radiated around her, she instinctively backed away. She glanced hopelessly toward the window, noticing darkness had settled over the town.

Jack! Help me! she cried silently.

She swallowed a yelp when she tripped over the broken drawers Pettigrew had strewn across the bedroom floor. She held her breath as the fire-breathing monster loomed in the doorway, waiting to devour her.

Jack muttered irritably when more gunfire and boisterous laughter erupted from one of the six saloons that abutted each other on the northwest side of town. Thankfully, Wilbur had returned with Jefferson and Harrison, who provided the necessary reinforcements. It seemed Jack and his brothers barely had time to quell one disturbance before another one broke out between rival trail herders in another saloon.

"Cassie is right," Jack said as he and his brothers jogged across the street. "We should outlaw whiskey and send these yahoos to some other hapless town to feud with each other while they are drinking to excess."

"Only problem is that business owners will lose profit," Jefferson reminded him.

The Culpepper brothers burst into the Horseshoe Saloon to see six men pounding on each other and tumbling over broken chairs and tables. Cards and coins littered the floor like casualties of war. Onlookers hung back to ensure they weren't dragged into the fracas.

"That's enough!" Jack bellowed at the top of his lungs.

The commanding shout earned him a glance or two, but the drunken wranglers ignored him and resumed their brawl.

"I'll grab a makeshift club and pound some sense into a few hard heads," Harrison volunteered as he swooped down to retrieve a broken table leg.

Jack and Jefferson followed suit. Within a few minutes, all six brawlers were rolling around on the floor, holding their bruised heads.

Jack grabbed two men by the nape of their shirts and hauled them to their feet. They swayed slightly so he propped their shoulders together to support each other.

"Your trail boss paid you an hour ago and here you are, wasting your hard-earned wages. You're going to pay for the furniture you've destroyed."

"We was just havin' fun," the burly wrangler slurred out.

"You lost all privileges in our town," Jefferson snapped as he jerked two more brawlers to their feet.

"The good news is that you've won a free trip to jail," Harrison told them.

Jack and his brothers quick-marched the brawlers through the door and down the street. They were halfway to the jail when Jack noticed a cloud of smoke hovering over town circle.

"The bank's on fire!" someone shouted in the distance.

Jack swore colorfully as he quickened his step, bustling the drunken men alongside him. When he reached his office, Wilbur was standing on the boardwalk, staring grimly at the flames glowing in the first-floor windows of the bank.

"I sent a bucket brigade to the warm springs," he told Jack. "The men are placing barrels on wagons to haul to the fire. Unfortunately, the place went up like dry kindling. It's just a guess, but it's burning so hot already that I'm betting it was set on purpose."

Jack shoved the drunken cowboys toward the office door. "Put these six hooligans in separate cells," he told Wilbur hurriedly.

"We could use 'em to carry water," Wilbur suggested.

Jack shook his head. "They're stumbling drunk and their bellies are sloshing like barrels of whiskey. They'll probably explode if they get too near the fire. Besides, I don't trust them not to pick another fight with each other."

"Fine, I'll lock 'em up," Wilbur assured him.

"They have exhausted my patience. If they give you the slightest trouble, shoot them," Jack said sharply.

The men blinked like owls and Wilbur winked conspiratorially. "Good idea. I haven't taken target practice today."

Wilbur marched the men into jail to lock them in the cells while Jack and his brothers raced off to help douse the fire. It only took an instant to realize the bank was a lost cause. The volunteer firemen hurled water that turned to steam immediately, but did nothing to contain the billowing flames.

"Oh, God!" Louise Bixby groaned in dismay when she and Gerald came to stand beside Jack and his brothers. "There is no saving the building or its contents. What are we going to do about all these people who have their savings stored in the bank?"

Jack didn't know the answer to that question. He wasn't sure how much money was left now that Pettigrew and his partner had gotten their greedy hands on it.

"Where's Cassie?" Gerald asked as he glanced every which way at once. "We were on our way to find her so we could tell her that we're getting married."

"Congratulations," Jack inserted.

"Thank you." His smile faded. "Cassie didn't return to the newspaper office or the café. She wasn't at the boardinghouse, either. I can't imagine where she is."

Growing unease skittered down Jack's spine. It was uncharacteristic for Cassie not to be on hand when news was in the making and there was a story to tell. In fact, she was usually right smack dab in the middle of...

"Oh, hell!" Jack howled as he mentally backtracked to the last time he'd seen Cassie.

"What's wrong?" Louise asked anxiously.

Jack didn't reply. He was rehashing his last conversation with Cassie. He'd told her that he was on his way to the bank to withdraw the money from the drovers' accounts. She'd become pensive and no amount of cajoling had prompted her to confide what she was thinking or planning to do while he was confronting the banker.

It only took a moment of putting himself in that daredevil female's frame of mind to predict what she'd done. She had mentioned the blue, leather-bound ledger that she was sure held valuable evidence. Jack would bet the ranch that *she* was the one he'd heard entering the bank after Pettigrew's accomplice sneaked out. The back door had opened and closed twice while Pettigrew tried to make plenty of racket.

"Damn it to hell!" Jack roared in unholy torment. "I think Cassie might be trapped in the bank!"

"What!" Jefferson stared goggle-eyed at him then focused his horrified gaze on the rolling smoke and leaping flames.

Louise fainted dead away. If Gerald hadn't grabbed her arm, she would have fallen into a crumpled heap at his feet.

Jack wished he'd kept his grim speculations to himself for Louise's sake. Cursing himself up one side and down the other, he took off like a shot, dashing toward the bank in fiendish haste.

He'd endured dozens of hair-raising ordeals while riding with the Rangers and serving as city marshal. He'd learned to respond with intellect, not fear, in tense situations. But honest to God, the thought of that green-eyed beauty burning like Joan of Arc scared the living daylights out of him.

He couldn't seem to breathe. His heart thudded so frantically inside his chest that he was sure it cracked a few ribs. His brain froze up and he simply stood there, thinking the worst, incapable of figuring out what to do next.

Cassie needs you, damn it. Move! Jack gave himself a mental shake then raced toward the front door of the bank.

"No, Jack!" Jefferson yelled at him when he tried to kick down the door.

Jack tried to shake off his brothers who grabbed his arms and dragged him away from the inferno that had once been the bank. The appalling thought of Cassie burning alive provoked him to battle his brothers for release.

"You can't go in there!" Harrison growled at him. "It's too late. Killing yourself won't save her."

"Hell! She might not even be there," Jefferson snapped as he and Harrison tackled Jack and held him to the ground.

"At least let me check the windows," Jack snarled as he elbowed his brothers out of his way so he could bound to his feet.

When Harrison and Jefferson backed off, Jack charged around the corner of the building. His heart ceased beating when he saw someone—and he was pretty certain who it was—wearing one canvas money bag on her head and another one over her face. Cassie was hanging upside down like a bat beneath the second-story window. She was barefoot and she had a death grip on the improvised rope she'd made from bedding.

"Cassie! Jump! I'll catch you!" Jack yelled at her.

She twisted sideways to stare at him while smoke rolled around her. "I can't. I'm hung up."

He skidded to a halt beneath her to see that she'd fashioned her skirt into breeches that had snagged on the splintered edge of the windowsill. To make matters worse, the sheet she'd secured inside the upstairs room had begun to smolder. When the fabric burned through, she would be dangling by her snagged breeches. If her clothing caught flame, she'd be on fire and she'd plunge headfirst to the ground.

Jack grimaced. If that wasn't bad enough, she might crack her head open on impact. Her chances of survival weren't worth mentioning.

"There's Pettigrew!" Cassie shouted down at Jack, while she held on to the smoldering sheet with one hand and tried to unsnag her makeshift breeches with the other. "He killed his partner in crime and he's trying to burn the evidence of murder and fraud."

Difficult though it was to drag his anxious gaze off Cassie, he noticed the shadowed figure slithering around the back of the building to take cover among the loaded-down freight wagons.

"Go after him," Jack shouted at his brothers.

Jefferson and Harrison raced off to seize Pettigrew before he slipped away in the darkness.

When Cassie yelped in alarm, Jack glanced up. "Hang

on, sweetheart. I'm coming to get you," he promised her. He just wasn't sure he could reach her in time. The grim thought turned him wrong side out.

"Better make it snappy," she muttered. "I've been basted on both sides already. This fire is *hot!*"

Jack latched on to the first horse he could find, then stood up on the saddle as he guided the mount near the building. But Cassie was still too far above him to reach her.

And she was right, he noted. The bricks on the building radiated heat. He could feel the fire pulsing inside the building like a volcano ready to erupt. Any moment it could collapse, raining sparks and flames and debris everywhere. He and Cassie would be knocked loose and they'd plunge to the ground to be covered by an avalanche of flaming rubble.

"Gerald!" Jack yelled. "Get someone to help you gather up anything that can be used as padding. If I get Cassie loose we may have to jump!"

Gerald and Louise—who had regained consciousness and nearly collapsed again when she saw her niece hanging from the burning building—dashed to the café to retrieve towels and tablecloths. Other onlookers raced to the hotel to grab spare bedding.

Although the horse stamped uneasily beneath him, Jack grabbed hold of the drainpipe secured near the corner of the building. The metal was hot so he used his shirtsleeves to protect his hands while he shimmied upward to reach Cassie.

He leaned away from the drainpipe, stretching himself sideways until he could tug at the fabric of her makeshift breeches. The fabric ripped. She shrieked in terror and dropped several inches.

"Don't panic, Cass. You'll be okay."

"I'd feel better if I could have that in writing," she wheezed. "I've got the ledger stuffed inside my dress. If anything happens to me, make sure—"

"You're going to be fine." He hoped. "Grab my hand and hold on tight."

"What? No! I can't reach you…ack!"

The sheet she was clinging to burned in two. Now that Jack had freed her makeshift breeches, there was nothing to secure her to the side of the building. Growling in fierce determination, Jack strained sideways and managed—just barely—to grab her wrist a split second before she plunged headfirst to the ground.

Relief washed over him as he watched the smoldering sheet drift to the ground. Jack swung Cassie toward him and hugged her possessively against him. He nuzzled his head on the smoky money pouch that protected her hair.

"Jump!" Gerald called up to Jack, who clutched the drainpipe with one hand and held Cassie in one arm. "The pallet is ready and waiting—"

Crack…Creak…

The additional weight of Cassie clinging to Jack for dear life—while he anchored himself to the drainpipe—caused too much pressure. The pipe came loose from its shoring and broke apart as it toppled down. With a growl of defiance, Jack used his legs to push away from the building, hoping to project his downward flight toward the waiting pallet.

He and Cassie landed on their feet on the pallet and he cradled her body against his as he rolled sideways—away from the building that might crumble any moment.

"Get up!" Louise yelled frantically. "All of us have to get away from the building. It isn't going to hold up much longer."

No sooner were the words out of her mouth than the wall caved in on itself. Jack clutched Cassie's hand as he bounded to his feet to dash to safety. They barely escaped the falling bricks. Flames burst overhead like fireworks on the Fourth of July. Wild screams filled the air. People scrambled like ants from a contaminated colony to escape the shower of sparks. They grabbed the waiting buckets and barrels of water to soak down the hotel next door, hoping to prevent the fire from spreading.

"Are you okay?" Jack asked as he nuzzled his chin against the smoky money bag that covered Cassie's blond head.

"I…can't…breathe…."

He leaned back to survey the ledger she had shoved into the bodice of her gown. He predicted the book had slammed into her chest during their bone-jarring landing, knocking the breath clean out of her. When he turned her away from the crowd to preserve her modesty, he reached into her bodice to remove the ledger. That's when Jack noticed that her breasts had increased two sizes since the last time he'd seen her.

He dipped his hand into her bodice again to grab several banknotes. "You're losing your stuffing, buttercup," he teased.

Then he laughed uproariously because emotion was bubbling out of him like a geyser. He was thankful she was alive and smiling like an idiot—until she sent him a dour glance.

"It isn't that funny," she grumbled. "I'm a walking tinderbox, stuffed full of the money I managed to recover before the bank went up in flames."

"So you turned to crime, too, did you?"

He dropped a playful kiss to her smudged cheek. After the tormenting ordeal, he couldn't seem to stop touching her, couldn't stop kissing her and couldn't stop thanking his lucky stars that she hadn't perished.

"I knew you'd understand about stealing money," she said, tossing him an impish grin. "And Jack—?"

"Arrest her!" Pettigrew yelled in interruption. He tried to break Jefferson and Harrison's stranglehold on him— but to no avail. "She set the bank on fire when I refused to loan her money for what she lost in the robbery!"

Suddenly all eyes circled back to Cassie. Despite her exhaustion and the throbbing pain in her twisted knee— compliments of the hard fall to the ground—she took a defiant step toward Pettigrew.

"Arrest *him,* Marshal!" she demanded. "He killed Millard because the teller discovered his fraudulent scheme to steal money from everyone's accounts!"

A collective gasp erupted from the crowd. Everyone's accusing stare shifted from Cassie to Pettigrew.

"She's lying!" he insisted loudly. "*She* tried to rob the bank and steal your money tonight."

Cassie commenced digging the rest of the banknotes from her bodice, her pockets and her improvised breeches. She made a big production of handing it over to Jack. "I saved all the legal tender I could gather up and carry away after Pettigrew murdered his accomplice, who used the alias of Jonathan Smythe. Pettigrew and Smythe were fleecing bank customers and working a real-estate scheme at the same time."

She glanced at Jefferson. "Check Pettigrew's coat pockets. I saw him retrieve a legal document from his cohort after he beat him unconscious. Pettigrew tucked it away, along with the money Smythe carried. Then Pettigrew started the fire by tossing kerosene on the furniture. This murderer left Smythe to fry!"

"That's another of her vicious lies!" Pettigrew contested furiously. "She came to our town with her suffragist propaganda and turned women against men. Then she killed my bank teller because he wouldn't embezzle money to replace her losses. Tonight she tried to rob me then she set the building aflame for spite—"

Pettigrew slammed his mouth shut when Jefferson dug the contract from his pocket. The document was right where Cassie said it would be.

"You bastard!" Jefferson roared after he read the contract, illuminated by the flaming building. "You forged the Culpepper name to sell the other warm spring site on Culpepper Avenue."

Harrison leaned over to peruse the contract. Then he snarled viciously. "You conniving scoundrel! You fooled a Fort Worth investment company into thinking they had gained the right to build bathhouses and spas on our property!"

Another collective gasp rose from the astounded crowd.

Jefferson waved dozens of banknotes under Pettigrew's nose. "And here's the money Cassie claims *you* stole from your partner after *you* knocked him out and left him to die."

Gerald turned to face the gathering crowd. "Pettigrew deceived me into printing new currency. He and his cohort produced forged documents that granted permission from the state government to print new bills after the two robberies."

"And here is the evidence of how much money Pettigrew stole from each customer's account," Cassie said as she held up the ledger.

The onlookers glowered vindictively at Pettigrew.

"Let's toss him in the fire!" the bakery owner yelled spitefully.

"Let's hang him and *then* fry him!" said the hotel owner who'd come dangerously close to losing his business in the fire.

When five would-be vigilantes headed straight toward Pettigrew, Jack waved his arm to demand attention. "The first thing we're going to do is toss Pettigrew in jail," he said authoritatively. "We are going to follow the letter of the law because I do not intend for this murdering thief to be declared innocent because of some technicality during his trial. He's going to face charges of double murder, attempted murder, fraud, counterfeiting and whatever else we can pin on him."

"What about our money?" someone called from the back of the crowd. "We're all broke."

"No, you aren't," Cassie insisted. "Although Pettigrew torched the counterfeit money that he deceived Gerald into printing, I have several thousand dollars in currency right here. I suspect Pettigrew has collected the money from the safe and has money stashed in his house, ready and waiting for him to gather it up and make his getaway."

Jack singled out several storeowners then sent them to Pettigrew's house to search for the stolen money.

"Let's do our best to contain this fire," Jack shouted. "Gather all the barrels and buckets you can lay your hands on."

Citizens darted hither and yon to splash more water on the hotel and soak the wagons at the freight company. Everyone worked tirelessly. It was hours later before the fire was no more than a trickle of black smoke curling into the night sky.

"Oh, hon, I'm so relieved you survived," Aunt Louise gushed as she hugged the stuffing out of Cassie during a letup in the activities.

Cassie clung to her aunt for a long, grateful moment. "I have to admit that I wasn't sure I would make it out alive."

"When you're fully recovered from your ordeal, I'd like for you to be my maid of honor," her aunt requested.

Cassie leaned back to grin excitedly at her aunt. "So you finally said yes to Gerald? That's wonderful news."

When Gerald strode up to drape his arm possessively around Aunt Louise's waist, Cassie noted the proud smile on her boss's face. For the first time in two years, he could display his affection for the woman he loved.

Cassie wondered what it would be like to have Jack staring at *her* with the same depth of emotion she witnessed in her aunt's and Gerald's eyes.

"I'm glad you're all right," Gerald said to Cassie. "Louise and I nearly suffered heart seizure when we saw you hanging upside down on the burning building. Do not scare us like that again." He grinned wryly. "I didn't realize you'd go to such extremes to scoop a story. But you did solve two murder cases before Jack saved you from disaster. Now you and I can testify against Pettigrew."

Louise touched her cheek fondly. "You look exhausted. I'll have Suz escort you to the boardinghouse so you can get some well-deserved rest."

"When I'm feeling better, can I help you with the arrangements for your wedding?" she asked eagerly.

"Count on it," Gerald and Aunt Louise said in unison.

Cassie was so weary from the physical and emotional ordeal that she wondered if she had the strength to walk to the boardinghouse, even with Suzannah beside her for additional support. The anticipation of soaking in a cool bath and crawling into bed was the motivation Cassie needed to keep placing one foot in front of the other.

Of course, she'd prefer to snuggle up in Jack's arms to sleep the night away, but she'd have to settle for a relaxing bath and some rest.

At the moment, Jack was corralling the cowboys—who had taken time out from their wild night on the town to help douse the fire. They had returned to the saloons and bordellos to celebrate in a raucous fashion. No telling when Jack would be off duty.

"I thought you and Jack were goners," Suzannah said as she and Cassie ambled down the hall to her room.

"I was thinking the same thing while I was hanging upside down," Cassie murmured, then yawned widely. "I don't even want to consider what condition I'd be in if Jack hadn't grabbed hold of me when he did."

Suz shuddered. "You were extremely lucky." She clutched Cassie's shoulders then turned her toward the door to her room. "Now go inside and sit down. I'll have the landlord and a few tenants help me fill your tub then you can peel off those smoky clothes and soak to your heart's content."

Cassie nodded gratefully then entered her room to plunk into a chair. Absently she massaged her aching knee. When she glanced in the mirror, she burst out laughing at her reflection. She looked a fright with the money pouch on her head and her face smudged with soot. Her amusement fizzled out when she remembered the unconscious man who had been incapable of fleeing from the fire Pettigrew set.

She might look hideous, but she was alive.

Knowing she'd come within a hairbreadth of dying was another sobering thought. Although Cassie had snapped to her senses in time to braid the bedding and use it as a rope to escape from the second-story window, any number of things could have gone wrong and she might have perished.

She owed her life to Jack. He had placed his own life at risk to rescue her when she became entangled on the splintered windowsill and dangled upside down until she nearly passed out from blood rushing to her head. Jack had materialized from the smoke and flames to grab hold of her before her lifeline burned in two. He had cushioned her body with his own during the fall, taking the brunt of the jarring impact when they hit the ground.

She smiled and mentally organized the rave review she planned to write, giving Jack full credit and high praise for his selfless heroics. She would like to thank him personally—and privately, as well.

The whimsical thought prompted her to glance toward the window—she'd left it open so Maxwell could enter when he tired of tomcatting around. She'd prefer to see Jack, but it was the black cat that hopped onto the windowsill a few minutes later. Max bounded to the floor then trotted over to curl himself around her legs.

"Your bath is ready and waiting," Suzannah announced, breaking into Cassie's thoughts. "Get plenty of rest, dear friend. Your aunt and your boss gave me strict orders to inform you that you are not to show up for work tomorrow. Apparently, when you *save* the day, you earn a day off."

Nodding graciously, Cassie locked the door then sank into her bath. After very nearly frying—like the souls of the newly damned in the fiery pits of hell—the lukewarm bath water was pure heaven.

Chapter Sixteen

In the middle of the night, Cassie stirred drowsily and squirmed to gain more space. "Move over, Max," she mumbled. "You're crowding me."

"I'm not Max."

The sound of Jack's husky voice and his light caress filled her with pleasure. A welcoming smile played on her lips as she rolled onto her back to see his shadowy form poised above her.

"No, you definitely aren't Max." She traced the curve of his sensuous lips. "You're much better."

"Glad to know I'm more important to you than that cussed cat," Jack whispered as his head came steadily toward hers. "I've been aching with the want of you all night."

"I haven't thanked you properly for saving my life." Cassie skimmed her lips over his full mouth, savoring the addictive taste of him.

"You're welcome."

Her hand drifted down his bare chest. She was delighted to discover that he was completely and gloriously naked. Good. It saved her time disposing of any clothing that stood in her way.

"Do you know what happens to bandits who steal into my room by the light of the moon?"

"No, buttercup, tell me—" His breath caught when her hand skimmed over his abdomen.

She was pleased to note this brawny, wildly desirable man surrendered to her without a fight. That was good because Cassie didn't want to waste a single moment when she had Jack all to herself. After her near-death experience this evening, she had vowed to live in the present and let the future take care of itself. She wanted to rediscover every whipcord muscle and masculine contour of Jack's powerful body. She wanted to pleasure him to the same breathless extremes that he'd pleasured her—before they soared off into ecstasy as one.

When she glided her hand over his hip, he moaned softly. When she wrapped her hand around his hard shaft, he growled her name. And when she lowered her head to flick at the tip of his erection with her tongue he gasped for breath then shuddered in helpless response.

"Mmm…this is much more interesting than stroking my cat," she purred as her hand swept up and down his hair-roughened chest.

Jack managed a chuckle—barely. The erotic pleasure of her caresses nearly sent his pulse through the roof. He tried to reach for Cassie, but she pushed his hand away to continue her sweet, maddening assault on his body and his senses. He dragged in a shaky breath as she measured him from base to tip then cupped him in her hand. He groaned in exquisite torment when her moist breath whispered over his rigid flesh.

He swore the top of his head was about to blow off when her silky hair drifted over his abdomen like an erotic caress. When her warm lips and velvety fingertips grazed his swollen manhood again—and again—desire hammered at his sensitive body.

"Cassie…" he rasped as inexpressible pleasure spilled over him like molten lava.

"I'm right here," she whispered impishly. "I'm not going anywhere, Jack. I'm having too much fun making a feast of you."

Jack struggled to draw breath when she suckled him intimately, repeatedly, driving him to the crumbling edge of self-control. Her hands and lips felt as gentle as a summer breeze. Yet, each place they touched burned with fiery pleasure. Jack sighed raggedly as her alluring scent saturated his senses and fogged his brain. She kissed him intimately once again and he trembled in helpless response.

He hadn't realized it was possible to be so utterly and completely lost in a woman, to crave her kisses and caresses like an addiction, to want her like a maddening obsession. But this bewitching siren, with sun-kissed hair and fathomless green eyes, had become his hopeless downfall.

Jack was long past caring that Cassie had taught him the meaning of willing defeat. She had satisfied his every need and showered him with the most incredible pleasure imaginable. She left him shaking with ravenous hunger and he ached to consume her as completely as the desire he felt for her consumed him. Yet, when he reached for her again, she flitted away to arouse him with more of her tantalizing caresses and kisses.

"Cassie, stop…." he rasped when erotic sensations converged like a beam of heat burning into his very core. "I can't take much more…"

"I don't want to stop touching you," she whispered as she stroked him tenderly. "I almost died tonight—"

"Don't remind me," he groaned in interruption. "But I'm about to die *right now.*"

"I would have missed being with you like this," she murmured. "My new motto is to make the most of every moment. Most especially when it comes to being alone with you. I've also decided to embrace passion to its fullest so don't distract me while I'm learning all the ways to please you."

He chuckled hoarsely. "Buttercup, if you please me more than you have already, you'll have to explain to my brothers how and why I expired in your bed."

When Cassie lifted her head, her curly hair glowed like a halo in the moonlight. Jack lost what was left of his heart when she flashed him an elfin grin and caressed him intimately, repeatedly. His breath wobbled when sweet, tormenting sensations vibrated through every part of his being.

"I'm about to kill you with pleasure? Fascinating. I wonder how much more you can endure, big, strong, utterly masculine man that you are."

"I already told you that I—"

A moan gushed from his lips when she kissed her way back down his chest and belly. She took his throbbing manhood into her mouth and suckled him in such an erotic way that Jack swore he was on the verge of passing out from an overload of sensual pleasure.

"Stop!" he gasped. "I really mean it this time."

"I thought you meant it last time." She tormented him

with another round of sizzling kisses that caused desire to strike with the force of a lightning bolt.

She worked her way up and down his passion-racked body one kiss and caress at a time, driving him to the brink. He tasted his own desire for her when her lips settled over his in an exquisitely tender kiss. Jack knew he couldn't hold out a moment longer. He had to be inside her. He had to be surrounded by her silken warmth. He had to hold on to her while the world spun furiously around him. He was about to shatter in a million pieces and scatter like the embers of a fire filling the night sky.

"I want you as I've wanted nothing else…and I want you *now*," he growled impatiently.

Cassie found herself flat on her back, staring up at the handsome bandit who had crept into her room like a thief to steal her heart and capture her soul. His golden eyes glowed with the passion she had aroused in him. She felt empowered by the knowledge that she had learned to pleasure him as thoroughly as he pleasured her.

He wanted her and he'd said as much. But Cassie wished he could love her as deeply as she had come to love him….

Her thoughts flittered away as he braced his hands on either side of her shoulders. He lowered his ruffled raven head to take her lips at the same moment that he glided inside her. He rocked gently above her, penetrating and withdrawing until she was arching toward each delicious and deliberate thrust. Her breath broke when intense pleasure coiled inside her then expanded to consume her body, mind and soul.

Desperation overwhelmed her as she hooked her legs around his lean hips, urging him to plunge deeply inside her, over and over again. When he gathered her in his arms and held her tightly while he pumped into her with the same frantic urgency that clamored through her, she savored the immeasurable pleasure building like a crescendo.

Cassie chanted his name as spasms of ecstasy rippled through her. There were no adequate words to describe all the incredible feelings and sensations of rapture that poured through her while she soared in motionless flight and drifted weightlessly through space.

When Jack shuddered above her then buried his head against her shoulder in the aftermath of wild, sweet splendor, Cassie smiled contentedly. "I'm glad you saved my life tonight. I surely wouldn't have wanted to miss *this*."

He raised his head and grinned rakishly. "Let's strike a deal, buttercup. Just name the times and places and I'll gladly save you every time you need saving…as long as we always end up like this…together."

She giggled contentedly as she ruffled the thick strands of raven hair that tumbled over his forehead. "Deal."

"Just for the sake of curiosity, you won't go *looking* for trouble and make my job more difficult, will you, imp?"

She arched a challenging brow. "So now there are limitations? You won't come to my rescue if I *invite* trouble? Only when it *finds* me?"

"I'm a busy man, buttercup," he insisted as he dropped a kiss to her flushed cheek. "I have a whole town of citizens to watch over, too, you know."

She shrugged negligently. "Then I'll have to call upon your brothers. They seem very capable—"

He kissed her into silence. When he raised his head, laughter no longer glistened in his amber eyes. "Leave my little brothers out of this. I'm not sharing you. It's just you and me, Cassie."

"Mmm...I like the sound of that." She glided her arms over his broad shoulders then cupped the back of his head to bring his lips to hers. "You don't have to flit off into the night just yet, do you, Mr. Bandit?"

"No." He kissed her again—and again. "Why?" he asked eventually.

"I'm not finished thanking you for rescuing me tonight."

He chuckled scampishly. "I was hoping you'd say that, buttercup. For you, I'm always happy to oblige."

With a groan and hoarse cough, Cassie pried open one eye to see the sun glaring through the window of her apartment. She glanced sideways to note that Maxwell, not Jack, lounged beside her on the bed. She scraped her fingers through the wild tangle of hair that tumbled over her face then frowned pensively.

She didn't dream that Jack sneaked into her room to make love to her repeatedly, passionately...did she? No, she assured herself as she levered onto her elbow. It was every fantasy come true. He *had* been there with her, hadn't he? They'd had their way with each other so many times she lost count. That couldn't have been an arousing dream, right?

When she rolled to the edge of the bed, muscles she didn't realize she had objected. Hanging upside down from the windowsill of a burning building had taken its toll on her body. She smiled wryly when she remembered that passion—Culpepper-style—had taken a different kind of toll on her body.

Not that she was complaining.

Despite Gerald and her aunt's insistence that she take the day off to recuperate, Cassie freshened up. With Max trotting alongside her, she headed to the café for breakfast. Afterward she planned to write her firsthand account of the destructive fire and murder that landed the scheming banker in jail where he belonged.

To Cassie's amazement, she looked across town circle to see a crowd gathered outside the café. When she noticed the members of the recently formed Women's Club standing on the boardwalk, Cassie frowned, bemused. Mildred Forrester, the assistant blacksmith's estranged wife, waved to her enthusiastically.

"What's going on?" Cassie asked as she stepped onto the boardwalk beside the stout, middle-aged woman.

"We are here to honor your heroism," Mildred declared as she turned to face the crowd. "This is a public appreciation ceremony."

When the crowd applauded, Cassie smiled graciously then glanced sideways at Mildred. "How did you know I'd be here this morning?"

Mildred grinned as she gestured toward the back of the crowd where Jack and his brothers stood, surrounded by other men who had gathered behind the women who were standing twenty deep near the boardwalk.

"The marshal said you wouldn't let a little thing like a dramatic escape and solving several crimes in one fell swoop slow you down, even if you were told to take the day off," Mildred reported. "Louise and Gerald agreed this would be the perfect time to show our appreciation."

Mildred gestured in Cassie's direction as she faced the crowd. "I present to you Pepperville's woman of the hour!"

Another round of applause filled the air. The Women's Club members were exceptionally enthusiastic. The men joined in—in a more reserved manner, but they joined in, nonetheless.

Even Edgar Forrester clapped his hands. Cassie suspected he'd shown up hoping to convince his estranged wife that he'd changed his narrow-minded ways and was ready to make amends.

The jury was still out on that, Cassie mused.

"Thank you for this honor," Cassie said humbly. "But the truth is your city marshal and his brothers are the unsung heroes who saved this town. Although they suspected fraudulent activities at the bank, they were hesitant to conduct a public investigation for fear Pettigrew would become cautious and cover his tracks so that it would be difficult for Jack to recover the money and bring charges against him."

The crowd glanced appreciatively at the members of the town's founding family.

"The Culpeppers made a vow to protect this town from criminal elements and see to it that residents are safe and prosperous. They have kept that promise to you again."

The Culpepper brothers shifted self-consciously and smiled humbly while all eyes remained focused on them.

"They asked the help of former Texas Rangers, that heroic band of brothers with whom they served, to pose as bandits to rob the bank," Cassie continued, twisting the truth to protect their secret. "These brave men recovered as much legitimate currency as possible during the holdups so Pettigrew couldn't embezzle all of it."

The onlookers, looking like wide-eyed owls, glanced back and forth between Cassie and the Culpeppers for confirmation. The brothers nodded humbly and shifted from one foot to the other.

"Those of you who were victims of robbery know that Pepperville's version of Robin Hood and his men returned your money and jewelry, along with monetary compensation for your inconveniences. You also received a request to keep silent about the return of your valuables. Pettigrew remained unaware that the noose was slowly but surely closing around his neck."

Several former victims nodded, including Edgar Forrester and the other men on hand with Cassie during the robbery.

"Each of you played an important role in forcing Pettigrew's hand. You helped by keeping silent," she insisted.

"That's why Pettigrew and Smythe had to approach me with their fake documents," Gerald said as he came to stand beside Cassie. "They needed to print counterfeit money to pass out to customers so they could hoard the legitimate currency for themselves."

Jack circled the crowd to join Cassie on the boardwalk outside the café. "After a thorough search of Pettigrew's house I'm pleased to report that we have recovered all the money he stole from our bank accounts and from the would-be investors from Fort Worth."

The crowd cheered. When the noise died down Jack added, "Since Cassie recovered the ledger that Pettigrew tried to burn to ashes in the fire, we know how much money each of us is entitled to receive."

When the applause died down, Jack added, "My brothers and I, along with the city council, are searching for a replacement bank that has authentic credentials and a solid reputation to serve our community. In the meantime, shopkeepers have agreed to extend credit, as they did when this town first came into existence."

The crowd burst into another round of applause.

"Also," Jack went on to say, "the property Pettigrew tried illegally to sell to investors, who wanted to build spas and bathhouses at the warm springs on Culpepper Avenue, has been donated to the Women's Club to establish an orphanage. My family wants to support worthwhile causes that will bring recognition to our community as progressive leaders in our state."

Cassie's jaw dropped to her chest while the crowd cheered. "Oh, Jack, that is so generous and thoughtful. I'm forever indebted," she said, her voice cracking with emotion.

He smiled as he leaned down to say confidentially, "I'll be around later this evening, in case you want to thank me as properly as you did last night."

Cassie battled a blush when the vivid memory of their intimacy and passion flooded her mind and body.

"I want to thank you properly in return, too," Jack murmured. "You sure know how to put a spin on a story to make my brothers and me look admirable and heroic."

"You *are* admirable and heroic," she confirmed, smiling.

Gerald raised his arms, requesting silence. Then he motioned for Louise to join him on the boardwalk. "One last thing—Louise is doing me the honor of marrying me next week," he announced.

The crowd applauded excitedly.

"Everyone is invited to our celebration, catered by Bixby Café. We'll use town circle to host the city-wide event."

A moment later Cassie found herself surrounded by members of the Women's Club, who offered to help her serve food and beverages for the upcoming wedding. They also praised her efforts to single out the fraudulent banker.

A sense of pride and accomplishment filled her heart. Since her arrival in Pepperville, she had become a social pariah to the men who disapproved of her campaign for equal rights and progressive social reform. Now the townspeople had accepted her because she had risked her life to expose Pettigrew's devious scheme.

Cassie glanced over the dispersing crowd, noting Jack and his brothers had walked off. Aunt Louise clutched her arm and bustled her inside to discuss her ideas for the wedding.

All was right in her corner of the world, Cassie mused. In addition, Jack had promised to return to her apartment tonight to take up where they had left off the previous evening. She wondered if she and Jack would spend the next year or two engaged in a secretive affair like Gerald and Aunt Louise. Or would Jack tire of her sooner rather than later and leave her nursing a broken heart?

"Cassie?" Aunt Louise prompted.

She snapped to attention and smiled sheepishly. "Sorry. My mind was wandering. What did you say?"

"I'm trying to decide what to serve for the wedding reception," Aunt Louise repeated. "What do you suggest?"

"Beef," Cassie replied with a wry grin. "This town thrives on surrounding cattle ranches and the trail drovers headed north with their herds. Serving chicken might get you arrested for heresy."

Louise chortled and her emerald-green eyes glistened with amusement and happiness. "You're right. What could I have been thinking? This *is* the beef capital of the county."

"I have to hand it to Cassie," Jefferson remarked as he, Jack and Harrison ambled across town circle toward the jail. "She managed to artfully twist the truth and make our robberies sound like noble endeavors to serve justice."

"Which they were," Jack interjected.

"Yep," Harrison agreed. "She's intelligent and she has

a way with words. Not to mention that she's incredibly attractive." He looked over at Jack. "When are you going to follow Gerald's lead and marry that woman?"

Jack opened his mouth to reply, but Jefferson beat him to the punch and said, "You can't sneak into her boardinghouse apartment every night without someone seeing you eventually. You'll ruin her reputation…and yours."

"It will reflect badly on us, too," Harrison teased.

"Yeah, we'll have to live with the shame and scandal," Jefferson added.

Jack nearly tripped over his own feet. "How—?" he bleated.

"We are ex-Texas Rangers." Jefferson smirked playfully. "You should know that nothing gets past us."

"Besides, we followed you last night," Harrison informed him unrepentantly.

"I don't want to rush into anything," Jack mumbled.

Not to mention that he didn't know if Cassie truly cared about him or if the newness of passion was all that tied her to him.

Jack was accustomed to women in town pursuing him because of his name and his influential position in a community named after his family. But damn it, he wanted Cassie to want him for all the right reasons, and he didn't know for certain if she did. She had never been with another man, he reminded himself. Maybe she *thought* she should feel something special toward him because she had yielded to temptation. Her guilty conscience might have controlled her actions.

How was he supposed to know how she really felt? He wasn't a leading authority on women.

"What do you mean you don't want to rush into

anything?" Jefferson snorted sarcastically. "What would you call these steamy trysts that little brother and I keep catching you at?"

Jack wondered if his brothers could see the blush that heated his cheeks. He could only hope his suntanned complexion disguised it.

"I'm not sure Cassie is interested in me other than…"

His voice trailed off and heat suffused his face again. Even though he'd been to hell and back, fighting beside his brothers, he felt excruciatingly self-conscious about discussing his uncertainty about Cassie's affection for him.

"Oh, come now, big brother," Harrison said, grinning broadly. "You think a woman like Cassandra Bixby doesn't know her own mind? She wouldn't be with you if she didn't care."

"If you had any brains left in your head, after too many years of hard riding and hard living with the Rangers, you would know why you've delayed taking a wife and settling down to raise a new generation of Culpeppers," Jefferson remarked.

Jack frowned, befuddled. "What are you talking about?"

"I'm talking about wandering around for years with women who never really suited you," Jefferson explained.

"Calm and complacent women," Harrison scoffed. "Women who give in to your whims and cater to you. No, no, big brother, you've been looking for the wrong kind of woman."

"You thrive on challenge," Jefferson insisted. "You need a woman who stands up to you. Someone who stands up for you the way Cassie just did. You need someone who can match you step for step." He grinned roguishly. "Someone who provides stimulating conversation in the parlor as well as the bedroom and gives you a reason to wake up every morning."

Jack stared somberly at his brothers as he halted to watch the warm springs gurgling from the rocks in town circle. "You think I should ask her to marry me?"

"Or you could *tell* her to marry you," Harrison teased. "That should go over well. Or maybe you could tempt her by promising to live together in the homestead cabin until we can help you build a proper home on the ranch. I know she loves that cabin by the heated springs."

"You could return her stolen money, under the stipulation that she has to marry you if she wants it back," Jefferson supplied helpfully, his blue eyes glinting with teasing amusement.

"All good selling points, I'm sure," Jack said. "But I was sort of hoping the woman I married would want me just for *me.*"

Harrison and Jefferson rolled their eyes at him—as if they were leading authorities on how to deal with women, which they most definitely were *not!*

Jack smirked at his know-it-all brothers then zeroed in on Jefferson. "You have your own problems and you don't even know it yet."

He shifted his stern gaze to Harrison. "And you have developed a reputation as a ladies' man so you'll have a devil of a time convincing the woman you eventually take as a wife that you are sincere about her."

"Granted, we have our own problems," Harrison contended, "but if you let a woman like Cassie slip through your fingers then you are the biggest fool of all."

"Thank you so much for the insult," Jack snapped.

"You're welcome." Jefferson wheeled around to walk

off. "We'll be back to help you keep a lid on this town when the other half of the cowboys show up to drink and carouse tonight. In the meantime, we have cattle and horses to check."

"You're free this evening," Harrison said with a wink and a grin. "If you're too much of a *coward* to pop the question, you can send me to do it for you."

"No thanks," Jack said darkly. "I wouldn't trust you with any woman I'm interested in—"

Jefferson spun around and he and Harrison snickered at Jack's unintended confession.

"Maybe you should tell *her* that and see what happens," Jefferson suggested.

Jack watched his brothers walk away. He was offended because they had labeled him a coward. Well...they were right, damn it. Wild renegades and ruthless outlaws firing rifles, hurling knives and shooting arrows at him he could face unafraid. He'd been shot and stabbed a few times, but he had recovered.

This was completely different.

If Cassie rejected him, she would break his heart.

Jack wasn't sure there was a cure for that.

That night, Cassie lay awake for two hours, expecting Jack to show up via the window. He didn't. Maxwell arrived, smelling as if he'd visited every garbage can in town. She put him outside and closed the window, despite his offended caterwauling, but she didn't lock it...just in case Jack showed up.

Finally, Cassie fell asleep. She knew Jack had his hands full corralling the riotous cowboys, but she was still disappointed.

A few hours later, she felt warm kisses skimming her neck. She smiled drowsily then shifted from her side to her back to see Jack's shadowy face a hairbreadth above hers. When she reached up to pull his head to hers for a welcoming kiss, he grabbed her hand and held it in his own.

"I need to ask you something," he said anxiously.

"What's wrong?" she asked, alarmed by his serious tone.

"I don't know yet. I was hoping you could tell me."

Bumfuzzled, Cassie leaned out to light the lantern on the nightstand. She gaped in astonishment when she noticed six bouquets of wildflowers on the dresser, end table and the commode. Bewildered, she glanced at Jack who looked ill at ease. Sort of like he did before he admitted he was a bandit, back when his conscience hounded him constantly about it.

"Are you okay? What can I do to help you?" she asked as she levered herself into a sitting position on the edge of the bed.

"You can say yes," Jack replied. "That will help tremendously."

"Yes," she said without hesitation. Anything to erase that uneasy expression in his golden eyes.

A broad grin spread across his lips. "Whew, that was a lot easier than I thought it might be."

Exasperated, Cassie stared him down. "What the devil are you babbling about?"

He pulled a gold band from his pocket and held it up to her. Her mouth fell open and her eyes nearly bugged out.

"I adore leaving you speechless," he murmured. "I would like for you to wear this…but only if you want to. I won't arrest you and throw away the key if you reject my offer."

"Whuh?" Cassie couldn't form an intelligible word to

save her life. She gaped at him then tried again. "You… me?" she finally managed to get out.

He bobbed his head. "Jefferson says I need a woman who challenges and stimulates me. Harrison says I should offer to bribe you by suggesting we live at the homestead cabin until we can build a suitable house at the ranch. I said you had to love me first or you wouldn't get a single bonus or perk."

"Yes!"

Jack watched Cassie astutely, lost in the entrancing sparkle in her evergreen eyes, the radiance of her smile. "Yes to what?" he asked specifically.

"Yes, I'm in love with you," she admitted, "but no, I can't marry you yet."

He blinked, stunned. "Why not? When can you?" he demanded.

She tossed him another endearing smile that melted his heart. "When you tell me you love me, too. And not just because I publicly proclaimed you to be the hero you are. You are still the bandit I first met. You stole my heart and I know I'll never be able to get it back."

He grinned, so damn happy that he was about to burst wide-open. He retrieved the banknotes he'd held in safe-keeping and waved them in front of her. "Then I don't have to sweeten the deal by returning your stolen money to get you to agree to marriage?"

She shook her head and spun-gold curls bounced around her beguiling features. "I'm giving the money to Aunt Louise, but you don't have to bribe me to marry you. You're all I need to make my life complete," she told him sincerely. "I have my noble causes, my aunt and my uncle-to-be as family and I have a job I love. But when I fell in love with you, I knew the other parts of my life weren't going to be enough to satisfy me anymore."

She trailed her forefinger over his cheek then sketched his lips. "I need you, Jack. Not just the incredible passion we share, but because I like being with you. I love who you are and what you stand for."

He angled his head to savor the dewy taste of her lips. "I'm in love with you, too, buttercup. Last night—when I thought I was going to lose you—I knew if I couldn't save you that I would lose myself. You are my heart, Cassie. You're the better half of my soul—"

Jack's voice came out in a whoosh when Cassie leaped on him, forcing him to his back on the bed. She hovered over him with that glorious mane of frothy hair tumbling over her shoulders and a mesmerizing smile on her face.

"When are we moving into the cabin?" she asked before she showered him with steamy kisses.

"Name the day," he insisted.

"Is next weekend too soon? A double wedding, alongside Gerald and Aunt Louise, in their town-wide celebration would suit me fine. If they agree to let us share their limelight, of course."

"I'll be there with bells on—"

"You probably should wear more than that for the ceremony," she cut in, her eyes sparkling with impish amusement. "Save the bells for our honeymoon."

"Done," Jack promised.

"What about Maxwell?" she negotiated.

He huffed out his breath and said, "You know how I feel about that spit wad of a cat."

"He comes with the package," Cassie insisted as she unbuttoned his shirt on her way to remove his breeches.

The moment her warm lips and featherlight kisses drifted over his aroused flesh, Jack groaned in pleasure…and defeat. "Then by all means bring the cat. Just as long as I always have you by my side, buttercup."

"You will have me for always and ever," she promised faithfully. "You are the love of my life, for all the days of my life, Andrew Jackson Culpepper."

Jack wrapped Cassie in his arms and gave himself up to the blazing passion she always ignited inside him.

She would always have his heart.

He would support her noble causes.

But he was never going to like that pesky black cat.

* * * * *

COMING NEXT MONTH FROM

HARLEQUIN®
HISTORICAL

Available June 29, 2010

- **ALASKA BRIDE ON THE RUN**
  by **Kate Bridges**
  (Western)

- **PAYING THE VIRGIN'S PRICE**
  by **Christine Merrill**
  (Regency)
  Book 2 in the *Silk & Scandal* miniseries

- **UNTAMED ROGUE, SCANDALOUS MISTRESS**
  by **Bronwyn Scott**
  (1830s)

- **THE MERCENARY'S BRIDE**
  by **Terri Brisbin**
  (Medieval)
  Book 2 in the *Knights of Brittany* trilogy

HHCNM0610